Kiss Me in Kotor

a novel

KACIE FOOS

This is a work of fiction. The characters, the town of Woodard,
Alabama, organizations, and events portrayed in this novel are either
products of the author's imagination or used fictitiously.

Kiss Me in Kotor
Copyright © 2025 by Kacie Foos

Library of Congress Cataloging- in Publication Data Title:
Kiss Me In Kotor / Kacie Foos

First American Edition: 2025

Cover Design: Caterina Baldi
Interior Book Design: Taryn Nergaard
Artwork by Victoria on Adobe Stock

Hardcover ISBN: 979-8-9900997-8-4
Paperback ISBN: 979-8-9900997-7-7

1

phelia Carpenter woke on her wedding day to a racket that sounded like someone had decided to knock down the kitchen walls with a cast iron skillet. "Rise and shine, Phee!" her grandmother hollered down the hall, punctuating the words with the clang of pans. "You can't keep a groom waiting while you snore like a sawmill!"

Ophelia rolled over, groaning into her pillow. She didn't think she'd been snoring but given the nerves that had rattled through her body all night, it was possible she'd made noises she wasn't aware of. She had half a mind to pull the quilt back over her head and pretend the day hadn't come. If she didn't get up, she thought dizzily, maybe nothing could start. No makeup, no guests, no whispered judgments, no vows that would make her officially belong to someone else. But then the smell of bacon—smoky, greasy, perfect—slipped under the bedroom door and tangled itself around her empty stomach. Her resolve cracked. Even on her wedding day, bacon still had authority.

Barefoot, she padded down the hall and into the grandmother's kitchen, where the morning light slanted across the faded linoleum floor. There sat Tilda, her best friend since they were three, perched on a stool with her knees drawn up like a child, shoving a biscuit into her mouth so quickly that melted butter glistened on her lips. "You're supposed to wait until the bride sits down," Ophelia said, tugging her robe tighter.

Tilda licked her fingers, utterly unbothered. "You're supposed to stop looking like you're about to bolt out the back door. Eat a biscuit. It's Alabama law."

Her grandmother, standing at the stove with her back stooped but hands still quick, gave a short laugh. "Law of Alabama is don't marry a man who can't split firewood or skin a deer. Lucky for you, Charles Morrison can do both."

At the sound of Charles's name, Ophelia's heart did its usual leap. Even with the knot in her stomach and the fatigue in her bones, her pulse answered for her: yes, she wanted this man. Yes, she loved him. Still, she sat heavily at the table, reaching for a biscuit, and pulling it open to let the steam rise.

Her grandmother swatted Tilda's hand away from the butter dish. "Let the bride eat first, for heaven's sake."

Tilda stuck her tongue out. "Bride privilege," she muttered. "Fine. But only because she looks like she might pass out."

Ophelia tore off a piece of biscuit and let the buttery warmth melt on her tongue. Somehow, even on this trembling morning, the taste grounded her. She thought of the first time she'd baked biscuits for Charles—the way he'd closed his eyes after that first bite and said, "Darlin', if you marry me, I'll never ask for anything else again."

Her cheeks flushed at the memory. That had been two years ago, on the rickety porch swing outside her grandmother's house. He had half a mind to propose then and there with a ring made from a twist tie. But Charles Morrison had been patient, and careful, and serious about forever. He saved up for a real ring and just a few months prior, slipped it on her finger.

"Thank you again for letting Charles and I stay with you until the house is finished up granny."

"Absolutely darlin, you two can stay here if as long as you need to. Tonight though, he's taken you somewhere special for your wedding night."

"Where is Charles taking you too Phee?" Tilda asked.

"To the lake." Ophelia grinned.

"Well if they aren't here tonight can I stay one more night Granny? I love your cooking." Tilda begged.

"Sorry dear, you are just too loud for my little old ears." Ophelia and her grandmother giggled together at Tilda.

The rest of the morning blurred into a storm of tasks. After breakfast, her mother arrived in a flutter of perfume and disapproval, clucking at the state of Ophelia's hair, fussing with the dress bag, barking orders at cousins who were supposed to fetch flowers but instead had been caught sneaking cokes.

The church basement, normally reserved for bible study and committee meetings, had been transformed into a makeshift beauty salon. Curling irons hissed. Perfume clogged the air. Bridesmaids darted around with armfuls of hairspray and half-open compacts. Somewhere above, the organist tested chords that groaned like the floorboards of an old ship.

Ophelia sat in front of the cracked mirror, barely recognizing herself. Someone had pinned her hair into glossy curls. Someone else had painted her lips rose. Her veil cascaded like spun sugar. She looked like a girl on top of a wedding cake, not the Ophelia she knew—the one who usually wore flour on her jeans and ChapStick on her lips.

Tilda leaned over her shoulder, squinting. "Well, hell. You look like a Hallmark bride."

"Is that good?"

"Depends on if you want people expecting a snowstorm and a small-town Christmas tree lighting before the reception."

Her Father walked into the room coughing through the spray. "How's my baby girl doing? Oh darlin, you look beautiful."

"Thank you." Ophelia shyly grinned.

"It's almost time!"

Ophelia tried to laugh, but her throat was too tight. "I think I'm going to faint."

"Don't you dare." Tilda stuck another bobby pin between her teeth, anchoring a curl in place. "If you faint, I'll faint out of solidarity, and then we'll both ruin the pictures."

Ophelia's grandmother shuffled in, cane tapping against the floor, eyes watering the second she laid them on her granddaughter. "Lord have mercy," she whispered, pressing a hand to her chest. "You look just like your mama on her wedding day. Only prettier."

"Don't tell her that," Ophelia muttered.

Her grandmother leaned down, brushing her cheek with a hand as soft as worn linen. "Gentle hands, baby. Always gentle hands."

The words brought her back to childhood: standing on a stool, flour up to her elbows, being taught not to fight the dough. Gentle hands. A lesson about biscuits, but also about life, and now about love.

By late morning, the chaos reached a fever pitch. Someone lost the bouquet. Someone else lost the flower girl—eventually found hiding under a folding table, cheeks puffed with Jordan almonds. Her mother nearly burst a blood vessel when she noticed one of the groomsmen had a visible tattoo, as if ink alone might curse the marriage.

Through it all, Tilda kept a steady stream of sass, like a comedian hired to ease the bride's nerves. "If Charles doesn't show up, don't worry—I've got a getaway car and a cooler of margaritas."

"I don't need a getaway car," Ophelia whispered back, biting her lip. "I need to not throw up in front of half of Woodard, Alabama."

"Then chew a mint and smile. Nobody will notice."

Easy for Tilda to say. Ophelia's hands were already trembling. She kept staring at her reflection, wondering how she had arrived at this exact moment: a small-town girl in a big white dress, about to promise forever.

And forever—well, it was a word that scared her as much as it thrilled her.

By noon, the basement air had turned swampy with hairspray, perfume, and nerves. Ophelia's mother fluttered about in a lavender suit like a general preparing for combat, issuing orders and corrections in rapid-fire bursts. "Straighten those candles. Is that boutonniere pinned or stapled? No, no, not that ribbon, the ivory one! Lord help me, why does nobody listen?"

The bridesmaids lined up in the narrow hallway, dresses the color of buttercream, fanning themselves with programs as if it might save them from the August heat. The flower girl held her basket like a weapon, pouting because someone had told her she couldn't throw all the petals at once like confetti at a parade. And Ophelia—Ophelia stood just outside the sanctuary doors, gripping her bouquet as though it were a life raft. The murmur of the crowd swelled on the other side, every cough and shuffle echoing through her ribcage. Tilda leaned in, her perfume sharp and citrusy. "You look like you're about to walk into a firing squad."

"Half of the town is in there," Ophelia whispered, throat tight.

"Good," Tilda said. "Now they'll have to say you look like a goddess."

Ophelia tried to laugh, but it came out shaky.

The organist hit a discordant chord upstairs, then another, as if testing the limits of the pipes. The preacher's voice carried faintly from inside, welcoming everyone, saying words like "union" and "holy covenant."

Her grandmother reached for her hand, eyes glinting. "Gentle hands," she murmured again.

The double doors creaked open. Sunlight spilled down the aisle like a flood. It was time.

2

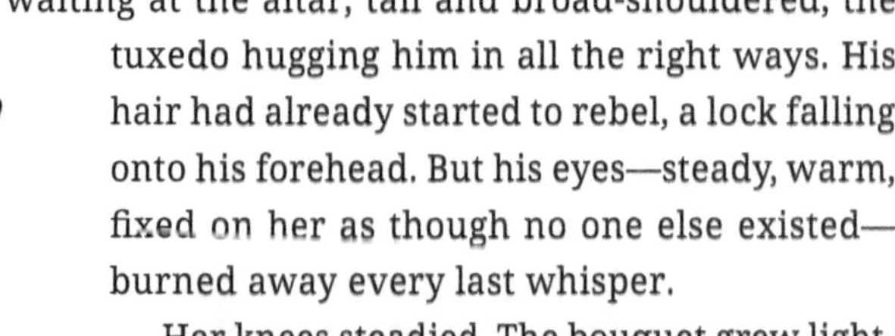

The bridesmaids stepped forward one by one, heels click-ing, petals scattered. Then it was her turn. Ophelia's Father offered his arm and she inhaled shakily, adjusted her bouquet, and took her first step down the aisle.

The sanctuary was full to bursting. Every pew packed. Mrs. Yates adjusting her feathered hat like a peacock. Mr. Jenkins wrestling with his suspenders as though they'd betrayed him. Children climbing on their knees to see better. The whispering started as soon as she appeared—hushed voices darting across the pews, as inevitable as crickets at dusk.

"She looks just like her mama."

"Dress is a little plain, don't you think?"

"Hush, she looks beautiful."

Ophelia tried not to hear them, but it was impossible. Her cheeks burned. Her stomach flipped.

And then—Charles.

He was waiting at the altar, tall and broad-shouldered, the tuxedo hugging him in all the right ways. His hair had already started to rebel, a lock falling onto his forehead. But his eyes—steady, warm, fixed on her as though no one else existed— burned away every last whisper.

Her knees steadied. The bouquet grew light-er in her hands. With each step, the world nar-rowed to just him. By the time she reached him, her breath came easy again. He took her hand, his palm warm, his thumb brushing across her knuckles like he was reminding her: *We're here. We're together. Breathe.*

"Who gives this woman to be married to this man."

Her father grinned, "Her mother and I."

The preacher launched into scripture, his voice booming with the zeal of a man who'd seen too many weddings and was determined to make this one stick. He spoke of covenant, of faith, of two souls becoming one flesh. He also reminded them, in a tangent nobody had asked for, that divorce was a scourge upon the land and that television was full of immoral programming. Ophelia heard none of it. Her heart thundered so loudly it drowned out everything but the sight of Charles's crooked smile.

When it came time for vows, Charles went first. He cleared his throat, voice roughened with nerves but strong. "Ophelia, I promise you laughter. Even when life tries to steal it. I promise to take care of you when you're sick, and I promise not to complain too much when you hog the covers. I promise to never eat the last biscuit unless you say I can—and even then, I'll probably save you half. I promise to love you when you're cranky, when you're tired, when you're doubting yourself, and when you're unstoppable. And I promise to spend every day proving I deserve the gift of you."

The congregation chuckled at the biscuit line, then sighed audibly at the ending. Someone blew their nose like a trumpet. Ophelia's hands shook. Her voice quivered but did not break. "Charles, I promise to love you with everything I have. I promise to dance with you, even if I can't find the beat. I promise to argue with you, but to always make up before bed. I promise to cook too much food, so you'll never go hungry, and to always make biscuits in batches big enough for both of us. I promise to stand beside you, even when life scares me, even when it's hard, even when it feels impossible. You're my home. And I promise to never forget that."

The preacher nodded in approval. The congregation murmured. Rings were exchanged, warm metal sliding onto trembling fingers. The preacher raised his hands and declared, "By the power vested in me, I now pronounce you husband and wife. Charles, you may kiss your bride."

Charles leaned in, kissed her soft and sure, and the crowd erupted in applause. Feet stomped, babies cried, someone whistled so loudly it startled the organist into hitting another sour chord. Ophelia felt light as air. For one suspended moment, she thought: *This is forever. This is mine.*

The recessional was chaos. Children darted into the aisle, nearly tripping the bridesmaids. Tilda winked at her as she passed, mouthing, "Nailed it." Birdseed was already being handed out in fistfuls despite the reception not yet begun. The air smelled of lilies and sweat and too many bodies crammed into one sanctuary.

When they finally made it back to the church doors, Charles squeezed her hand, eyes glinting with joy. "Mrs. Morrison," he whispered, as though trying the name on his tongue.

She laughed, half giddy, half dazed. "That's me."

They stepped into the sunshine together, a shower of birdseed already being prepared by the eager mob. The day was hot, bright, and unbearably alive.

For the first time, Ophelia thought maybe forever wouldn't be as terrifying as it sounded. The fellowship hall of First Baptist Woodard had seen its fair share of celebrations and food to go with it. On Ophelia's wedding day, the long folding tables practically sagged under the weight of the food her cousin's catering company had provided. Aluminum pans steamed, Deviled eggs marched down one platter in neat rows, paprika dusting their tops like confetti. Fried chicken towers leaned dangerously close to collapsing. Crockpots hummed quietly, each with a passive-aggressive note taped to it: "Don't touch until serving time" or "Use the ladle, not your hands." The desert table covered in cupcakes surrounding the wedding cake.

Against both Ophelia and her cousin's wishes Aunt Marlene's insisted on contributing to her daughters catering service her infamous seven-layer salad. It glowed under the fluorescent lights like a radioactive specimen—peas, lettuce, mayonnaise, shredded cheese, and enough bacon bits to choke a horse. No one wanted to be the first to take a scoop, but everyone knew they'd have to, or else Marlene would never let them forget it.

"Oh, good Lord Charles, Aunt Marlene snuck her seven layer-salad in here."

"Smile, darlin'," Charles murmured, his hand finding Ophelia's as they entered. "They're all staring."

"Not at me," she whispered back. "At the food."

They barely made it two steps before the gauntlet began. Mrs. Yates intercepted them first, adjusting her hat as though preparing to bless the Pope. "Well, if it isn't the happy couple! Ophelia, you look just like an angel. Charles, you clean up nice—though I do hope you'll trim that hair once you're married. Men should look respectable."

"Thank you, ma'am," Charles said smoothly, already tugging her along before Mrs. Yates could launch into her sermon on the decline of modern barbershops.

Then came Mr. Jenkins, red-faced from the heat, sweat dripping down his suspenders. "Knew you two would tie the knot eventually. I won twenty bucks off Harold Simmons on it. Don't let me down now."

Ophelia choked on a laugh, and Charles muttered, "Glad our love life is fueling the local economy."

By the time they reached the head table, Ophelia's cheeks ached from smiling. She collapsed into her chair, fanning herself with a program, while Charles grinned like he'd just won a county fair pie-eating contest.

The first toast came from Charles's best man, a lanky fellow named Paul who cleared his throat so dramatically it rattled the punch bowl. "Well," he began, "when Charles told me he was getting married, I said, 'Son, does she know what she's in for?' And he said, 'She makes biscuits from scratch.' And I said, 'Good enough for me.'"

The hall erupted with laughter, clapping, and several people shouting, "That's right!"

Ophelia hid her face in her hands while Charles raised his glass with a grin.

Next came Tilda. She seized the microphone with the confidence of a woman who'd been waiting for this moment since kindergarten. "Now, listen. I've known Ophelia since she was three years old, which means I've seen her through bangs, braces, and the ill-fated cut offs. And Charles? Well, buddy, you may think you married a sweet Southern angel, but don't be fooled. This woman once stole the last honey bun out of my lunchbox and swore blind it wasn't her. So, you'd better keep your snacks locked up. But also... she's the kindest, most stubborn, most loving person I know. And if you ever hurt her, I'll haunt you until the day you die. And then longer because ghosts don't need sleep."

The crowd howled. Even the preacher chuckled, though he tried to disguise it with a cough. Charles leaned over to Ophelia and whispered, "Remind me not to cross her."

"You're only just now realizing?"

The food line opened, and the chaos began. Plates clattered, forks scraped, people jockeyed for position like cattle at feeding time. Children piled their plates so high that macaroni and cheese slid in slow motion onto the floor. The jello salad tipped over with a gelatinous splat. "Careful now," Charles murmured, guiding Ophelia along the buffet. "Don't let Aunt Marlene see you skip her salad."

Ophelia forced herself to scoop a quivering mound onto her plate, smiling painfully as Marlene hovered nearby like a hawk. The second Marlene turned her back, Tilda swooped in and dumped half of it onto her own plate. "Taking one for the team," she whispered.

At the dessert table, a child had already taken three of the cupcakes and was covered cheeks to chin in frosting. Their mother shrieked, horrified, while half the hall collapsed into helpless laughter. "Lord help me," Ophelia muttered.

"You wanted forever," Charles teased. "This is forever."

After plates were scraped clean and stomachs stretched to capacity, the dancing began. The first song was Patsy Cline's *Crazy*, crooning over the clumsy shuffle of guests. Charles led Ophelia to the center, his hand firm at her back, her steps uncertain but safe in his rhythm. "You're terrible at this," he teased as she stumbled.

"Shut up," she whispered, laughing breathlessly.

"Don't worry. I'll always catch you."

The words landed heavier than he knew, sinking into her chest like a promise etched in stone. Around them, children twirled wildly, elders clapped along off-beat, and Tilda tried to teach Cousin Tyler how to two-step with such aggression he nearly tripped over his own shoes.

The cake cutting followed. A massive three-tier confection stood waiting, its buttercream roses already starting to melt in the heat. Charles fed her a polite bite—then smeared frosting on her nose. The crowd erupted. Ophelia shrieked, grabbed a fistful of cake, and smashed it gently against his cheek. Cameras flashed. Aunts gasped. Children cheered like it was a wrestling match.

"You're done for Charles," Tilda cackled from the sidelines.

"Worth it," Charles whispered, licking frosting from his lips before kissing her again.

By late afternoon, the fellowship hall had transformed into something between a carnival and a battlefield. Empty pans stacked precariously, punch stains dotted the floor, and all the children running around the room high on sugar from the cupcakes.

Ophelia sank into her chair, breathless and overwhelmed, watching Charles laugh with his cousins, his whole face lit with joy. Her chest ached with the enormity of it—this man, this love, this crowd of people rooting for them in casseroles and applause. Tilda plopped down beside her, fanning herself with a paper plate. "How're you holding up, Mrs. Morrison?"

The new name still startled her. She smiled faintly. "Like I'm floating."

"Well, don't float too high. You've still got cans to drag behind that truck tonight."

Ophelia laughed, though tears burned behind her eyes. She blinked them away, unwilling to dampen the brightness of this day. Across the hall, Charles caught her gaze. His smile softened, and for a moment, the whole room blurred. This, she thought, was what forever felt like.

By the time the last crumb of cake was eaten, and the final casserole lid snapped shut, the sun was already sliding low in the sky, painting the parking lot gold. Guests swarmed the church steps, handfuls of birdseed ready, tin cans already tied to the back of Charles's old Ford truck.

Ophelia clutched Charles's hand as they made their way through the gauntlet. Birdseed rained down like hail, stinging her arms and hair, bouncing off Charles's tuxedo jacket. Children shrieked, adults clapped, someone whooped loud enough to rattle the stained-glass windows. Charles laughed, shielding her head with his arm. "Run for it!"

They bolted together, skirts and tux flapping, tripping over the gravel as the crowd roared. The truck gleamed in the evening light, "JUST MARRIED" scrawled across the back window in shaving cream, tin cans clattering like a parade behind it. Charles opened her door with exaggerated gallantry. "Your carriage awaits, Mrs. Morrison."

Her heart fluttered at the sound of it again—Mrs. Morrison—as she climbed in, gathering her dress around her knees. With one hand on the wheel and the other locked firmly around hers, Charles drove out of town, honking back at every neighbor waving from their porch. Birdseed clung to her veil. The air smelled like honeysuckle and summer asphalt. "You ready?" he asked softly, glancing over at her.

"I've been ready since the biscuits," she whispered, eyes damp but shining.

He chuckled, squeezing her fingers. "One day, those biscuits are going to be the death of me."

"Don't joke like that." She meant to scold, but her smile betrayed her.

They drove in companionable silence for a while, listening to the rhythm of the cans clattering behind them, echoing down the country roads like wedding bells. The last of the light caught in the fields, fireflies beginning their nightly dance.

The inn by the lake appeared at the end of a winding drive. It wasn't fancy, but to Ophelia, it looked like heaven. Inside, the wallpaper was floral, the bed squeaked if you breathed too hard, and the jacuzzi style tub in the corner looked like it hadn't been filled since the Biden Administration. But Charles carried her across the threshold anyway, both laughing when he nearly tripped on the rug. She kicked off her heels with a groan. "If I never see pantyhose again, it'll be too soon."

"You looked beautiful," he said, tugging off his tie.

"I looked sweaty."

"Beautiful and sweaty."

She threw a pillow at him. He caught it, tossed it aside, and pulled her into a kiss that was softer, slower, more real than any they'd shared that day. For a moment, forever felt close enough to touch.

It started small. A flicker across his face. A hand pressed suddenly to his temple. "Headache," he muttered, wincing. "Out of nowhere. Bad."

Ophelia froze. "Do you need water?"

He staggered, knees buckling, and collapsed onto the bed. His body jerked once, violently, then went still. "Charles!" Her scream tore through the quiet cabin. She shook him, her voice breaking. "Charlie, wake up! Please, please—this isn't funny!"

His lips moved faintly, like he was trying to shape her name, but the sound never came.

Her hands scrambled for her phone, slick with sweat. She dialed 911 with trembling fingers, words tumbling out in a sobbing rush: "My husband—he just collapsed—he's not waking up—please, you have to come—" The dispatcher's voice tried to cut through the hysteria, asking questions she could barely hear. She pressed her hand to Charles's chest, begging. "Stay with me, please, stay with me."

The minutes stretched like hours. The sirens came at last, wailing through the night, lights splashing red and blue across the peeling wallpaper roses. Paramedics swarmed the room, voices brisk and sharp. "Massive rupture. Likely aneurysm. No response. Nothing we can do." Ophelia clung to his hand, cold already, refusing to release it even when they gently tried to pull her back. Her dress was wrinkled, her veil half torn, her heart splintering in her chest.

The world had shifted without warning—from bride to widow in a single night. By dawn, the tin cans still tied to the back of the truck outside clattered in the wind, a cruel reminder of a joy that had vanished before it even began

3

The morning after her wedding, Ophelia woke not to birdsong or the gentle warmth of Charles beside her, but to the hollow silence of her grandmother's house and the dull ache of mascara crusted against her skin. She hadn't even bothered to change out of her dress after the hospital. The gown lay crumpled on the floor, veil tangled like seaweed, silk wrinkled and stained with the salt of her tears.

She stared at the ceiling, unable to move. Her body felt both too heavy and too light, as though gravity had stopped obeying the rules. The quiet pressed in on her, broken only by the occasional honk of a car outside, ordinary life carrying on as though hers hadn't just imploded.

It wasn't until the doorbell rang that she sat up, her muscles screaming in protest. She stumbled down the hallway barefoot, still in her slip, hair a rat's nest of pins and tangles. When she opened the door, she was met with the beaming face of Mrs. Yates, holding a casserole dish the size of a newborn calf.

"Bless your heart," Mrs. Yates said, forcing her way inside before Ophelia could respond. "I heard the terrible news. Just terrible. But don't you worry, we've got enough food coming to last you until the Rapture."

Ophelia blinked at her, unable to speak. Mrs. Yates marched straight into the kitchen, muttering about oven temperatures and foil, while Ophelia stood at the door, stunned. Her grandmother appeared and swept her out the door as quickly as possible.

19

"Ophelia, go lay back down and rest. I'll handle this."

But how could she. Five minutes later, the doorbell rang again. And again. And again. By noon, the kitchen counters were buried in an avalanche of casseroles. Green bean, tuna noodle, chicken divan, lasagna, shepherd's pie. Each one came with a note: *Thinking of you, Praying for you, He's in a better place.* Ophelia wanted to scream. What better place? He'd been right here, laughing, holding her hand, teasing her about biscuits. What place could possibly be better than here with her?

She closed the refrigerator after trying to fit in casserole number eleven. It wheezed ominously, stuffed to the gills. She turned to find Tilda leaning against the doorway, arms crossed, surveying the carnage with raised eyebrows.

"Well," Tilda said, "if grief doesn't kill you, sodium will."

Ophelia let out a strangled laugh that broke halfway through into a sob. She sank onto a stool, burying her face in her hands. "I can't do this, Tilda. I can't—he was just here, and now..."

Tilda crouched beside her, wrapping an arm around her shoulders, crying with her. "I know, honey. I know. It's not fair. It's the opposite of fair. But we're going to get through it. One casserole at a time."

Ophelia hiccupped through tears. "I don't even like tuna noodle."

"Good thing grief diets are all the rage," Tilda said dryly. "We'll use it as ammunition if people get too pushy.

The pushiness arrived swiftly. By late afternoon, Ophelia's living room had transformed into a revolving door of sympathy. Neighbors in their Sunday best sat awkwardly on the floral couch, sipping sweet tea like they were at a wake already. They patted her hand. They patted her knee. They patted her back so aggressively she thought she might develop bruises.

Everyone had something to say.

"He's with the angels now."

"You're so young, Ophelia, you'll find love again."

"God doesn't give us more than we can handle."

"At least it was quick."

She wanted to scream *Stop talking. Just stop talking.*

But she nodded, murmured thank you, and kept pouring sweet tea, as though hosting a grief-stricken tea party were part of the bride-to-widow transition. Every so often, Tilda intercepted like a linebacker. "Well, isn't it kind of early to suggest remarriage, Mrs. Jenkins?" Or, "Actually, God absolutely gives us more than we can handle, that's why Xanax exists."

Ophelia loved her for it, even as she wilted deeper into the couch, drained by the endless parade of pity. By evening, the house was so full of casserole dishes and platitudes that she felt like she was suffocating. Her grandmother finally snapped, clapping her hands together like a drill sergeant. "All right, y'all have said your piece. Time to let the girl breathe."

There were murmurs of disapproval, but eventually the neighbors trickled out, leaving behind their condolences in foil-wrapped mountains. The silence that followed was worse.

Ophelia stood in the kitchen, staring at the wall of casseroles, her body swaying with exhaustion. "What are we supposed to do with all this?" she whispered.

Tilda popped open a lid, wrinkling her nose at the pungent tuna. "We could open a restaurant. 'Grief & Cheese: All You Can Eat.'"

Ophelia barked out a laugh before clapping a hand over her mouth, horrified at the sound of it in the middle of her misery. But Tilda only squeezed her arm. "If you can laugh today, you'll survive tomorrow." Ophelia wasn't sure she believed her. But she let Tilda's words settle anyway, small, and stubborn as seeds.

When her parents arrived later that day, they sat her down and calmly explained that they had met with Charles' parents and had made all the funeral arrangements. Both families had agreed it would be best for her to just rest. Ophelia was both appalled and relieved. Such conflicting emotions that she ended up running to the nearest bathroom to throw up.

~

The funeral fell on a Wednesday, because according to Pastor Elmer, "Midweek keeps folks from getting too rowdy at the visitation." As if anyone was going to use Charles's wake as an excuse for debauchery. Still, the sanctuary of First Baptist Woodard was overflowing again, this time with black dresses, muted ties, and enough floral arrangements to make the place look like a greenhouse in mourning.

Ophelia stood in the foyer, her black dress clinging in the humid August air, feeling as though her bones had been replaced with lead. Her hands trembled around the folded tissue she hadn't actually used, afraid if she dabbed her eyes even once, she wouldn't stop. Beside her, Tilda adjusted her dress with all the subtlety of a peacock. She was wearing leopard print heels that squeaked against the polished floor, and a fascinator so large it looked like it might take flight.

"This is a funeral, Tilda," Ophelia whispered hoarsely.

"And I dressed for battle," Tilda shot back, eyes scanning the crowd like she was ready to shoo away any well-meaning busybody who tried to corner Ophelia.

The open casket at the front was almost too much to bear. Charles lay still, his face smoothed into a peace that mocked her. His hands folded neatly; a Bible perched there like some cruel prop. She wanted to throw herself onto the casket, shake him awake, tell him to quit pretending. But she stayed rooted, her father's arm anchoring her in place.

The preacher began with solemn words about God's will and heaven's gain. Ophelia's ears rang. Every word passed through her like static, meaningless and relentless. "He was a good man," the preacher intoned. "A man who knew how to love, how to laugh, and how to fix a car."

A ripple of chuckles passed through the pews. Only in Woodard would someone's mechanical skills be considered gospel worthy.

Ophelia's throat closed. She remembered the grease under his nails, the way he'd wipe his hands on his jeans when she would visit him at his father's auto shop. The memory carved into her chest like glass.

The choir sang "Amazing Grace," voices wobbling under the weight of grief. A baby wailed halfway through the second verse, and its mother shushed it frantically. Tilda muttered under her breath, "Finally, someone's honest about how this feels."

When it came time for testimonies, people stood one by one to share.

"Charles helped fix my late husband's car."

"Charles fixed my mower for free."

"Charles always gave the shirt off his back."

Ophelia wanted to scream: *He gave me his whole heart, and it was mine for less than a day.* Instead, she sat in silence, nails digging crescents into her palms.

At the graveside, the sun beat down mercilessly, cicadas buzzing like electric wires. The casket gleamed an unnatural bronze, lowered into a hole that looked far too small to contain something so enormous as her love. Pastor Elmer droned about dust to dust, earth to earth. People dabbed their foreheads with tissues that had seen more sweat than tears. Someone fainted, whether from grief or heatstroke, no one was sure.

Ophelia barely heard any of it. Her whole body was tuned to the sound of dirt hitting the casket—each thud a hammer against her chest. Her Father put his arm around her. When it was over, she turned mechanically to thank people she barely registered.

"Such a fine service."

"He looks at peace."

"You're so strong, Ophelia."

Strong? She felt like a porcelain doll that had already shattered, her pieces taped together for display. One woman even whispered, "You're lucky you didn't have children yet. Imagine if you had little ones to raise alone."

Ophelia's vision went white with rage. Tilda grabbed her

elbow, steering her away before she could lunge. "Don't you dare waste your grief on idiots," Tilda muttered.

~

The reception afterward was, of course, another parade of casseroles. They had colonized not just the kitchen now, but the dining room table, the counters, the tops of the washer and dryer. Every surface gleamed with foil. Ophelia stood in the doorway, watching people pile plates as though this were a church potluck instead of a funeral feast. She half expected someone to shout "Bingo!"

Her grandmother fussed with serving spoons, muttering, "Well, at least no one will starve."

Tilda stood guard near the sweet tea, intercepting each person who tried to corner Ophelia with platitudes. "Nope," she said to Mrs. Yates, who was winding up a monologue about heaven. "Not today. Go admire the deviled eggs."

Ophelia tried to eat, but every bite turned to dust in her mouth. She pushed noodles around her plate, staring blankly. Charles should have been here. He should have been making jokes, piling food, licking frosting from his thumb. Instead, the room roared with voices that blurred together into one endless drone of pity. Finally, she excused herself, stumbling out onto the porch. The air was hot, but at least it was quiet. She pressed her back against the railing, sucking in shallow breaths. The door creaked, and Tilda stepped out, holding two glasses of sweet tea. She handed one over. "Hydration, darling. It's the Southern cure for everything."

Ophelia took it, the ice clinking, condensation dripping down her palm. She whispered, "It feels like the world just... went on without him. Like he was here, then gone, and now everyone's back to casserole duty."

Tilda leaned against the railing beside her, sipping. "That's small towns for you. They don't know what to do with grief, so they drown it in mayonnaise."

Despite herself, Ophelia snorted.

"There she is," Tilda said softly. "That laugh. Keep it close. We'll need it."

The days after the funeral slid together like one long blur, the hours stitched with casseroles, pitying glances, and the suffocating weight of everyone else's idea of what grief should look like.

On Sunday, Ophelia tried to go to church. She thought maybe slipping into the back pew might feel normal, like she could anchor herself in the hymns. Instead, the entire sanctuary turned to look when she entered, like she was some fragile relic hauled in for display. The whispers started before she sat down.

"That's the poor girl."

"Married one day, widowed the next."

"Bless her heart, she looks thinner already."

Ophelia shrank into the pew, clutching the hymnal as though it could shield her. When the choir struck up "It Is Well With My Soul," she bit her lip until she tasted blood, because it was not well. Not even close. Halfway through the sermon, Tilda leaned over, her whisper sharp. "If one more person looks at you like you're a charity case, I'm throwing my shoe at them."

Ophelia stifled a laugh, her shoulders shaking. That tiny rebellion carried her through to the benediction.

But when she stood to leave, Mrs. Jenkins swooped in like a hawk. "Now, honey, you mustn't waste your youth. God will send another man along, you'll see. Men are everywhere these days."

"Like feral cats," Tilda snapped before Ophelia could answer. "And we don't need another one scratching at the door right now, thank you."

Mrs. Jenkins gasped, scandalized, but retreated.

Tilda looped her arm through Ophelia's, muttering, "They mean well, but I swear, they've got the emotional range of a spoon."

Even at home, there was no escape. The casseroles multiplied like rabbits. Every time she opened the fridge, foil-wrapped bricks threatened to tumble out. The freezer was packed so tightly she half expected it to burst open like a jack-in-the-box, unleashing a tidal wave of lasagna.

One afternoon, she found her grandmother standing in front of the fridge, hands on her hips. "If one more green bean casserole shows up, I'm throwing it straight at Pastor Elmer."

Ophelia almost smiled. But the food came with visitors, and the visitors came with advice.

"You should join a grief support group."

"You should take up quilting."

"You should sell the house."

"You should get out more."

Everyone had a plan for her life, as though grief came with a checklist. She nodded politely, all the while screaming inside. Nights were the worst. Her Grandmother's house was too quiet, too dark. Every creak in the floorboards made her jolt, expecting Charles's footsteps, but instead, it would just be her grandmother walking through. Still Ophelia reached across the bed for him, only to find the cold expanse of sheets.

One night, she curled on the floor by the bed, wrapped in his jacket, inhaling the faint trace of motor oil and cedar that still clung to it. She whispered his name until her throat was raw. The only thing that cut through the silence was Tilda, who had practically moved in. She slept on the couch, patrolled the kitchen like a guard dog, and armed herself with sharp retorts for anyone who dared overstep. When Ophelia apologized for the intrusion, Tilda waved it off. "Honey, this couch has seen worse. Besides, who else is going to protect you from the casserole mafia?"

After a week of pity, casseroles, and suffocating sympathy, Ophelia cracked. She stood in the middle of the kitchen, foil containers stacked around her like a fortress, and shouted, "I can't do this anymore!" Her voice shook the cabinets.

Her grandmother looked up from her crossword. "Do what, baby?"

"This." She gestured wildly. "The casseroles, the whispers, the way everyone looks at me like I'm something to fix. Charles is gone, and all I have left are nine thousand pounds of noodles."

Her grandmother's eyes softened, but before she could answer, Tilda stormed in, heels clicking like gunfire. "Good. Finally. I was wondering how long it would take before you exploded."

Ophelia gaped at her. "Good?"

"Yes, good. Because now we can do something about it. You don't have to stay here, suffocating in pity and starch. You don't have to live in a museum of casseroles. We need to get you out of Woodard, Alabama, at least for a while."

Ophelia's heart thudded. "Out? Where?"

Tilda grinned; eyes gleaming with mischief. "Anywhere. Everywhere. I don't care if it's Biloxi or Barcelona. But you've got to get out of here, Ophelia. Let's cash in that honeymoon."

That night, lying awake, Ophelia replayed Tilda's words. The idea terrified her. Leave Woodard? Leave the only place she'd ever known? But when she closed her eyes, all she saw were casseroles and pity.

Maybe Tilda was right. Maybe she needed to run—if only to find a place where people didn't look at her like a tragedy.

4

The next morning started with the same old routine: doorbell, condolences, aluminum foil. But after the third ding and the second green bean casserole of the day, Tilda put both hands on the kitchen island and said, "Enough."

Ophelia blinked. "Enough what?"

"Enough of this house turning into a starch museum." Tilda swept an arm at the counters like a game show model unveiling a prize. "We are going to reclaim one square foot of countertop, and then we're going to reclaim your air supply."

Her grandmother looked up over the rim of her reading glasses. "If reclaiming the countertop involves throwing Mrs. Yates's tuna surprise into the azaleas, I'll look the other way."

Tilda clapped once. "First good idea of the morning." She opened the fridge, winced at the wall of foil, and began stacking containers with the precision of a field marshal. "Ophelia, get me the largest trash bag you've got!"

After an hour and watching Tilda take three separate trips to the trash, Ophelia opened a bottle of wine and poured them both glasses. They retreated to Ophelia's bed-

room. Sun striped the quilt in warm bars. The wedding dress still lay crumpled on the chair, the veil a matted sigh of tulle. Ophelia moved to pick it up, then let her hands fall. Tilda set her glass on the nightstand and sat on the edge of the bed. When she spoke, her voice was different—softer, careful as a hand on a bruise. "I have something for you."

Ophelia swallowed staring down at an envelope Tilda held in her hand.

"I was supposed to give it to you after your wedding night and you returned to this house but, when he died…"

Ophelia took the envelope from her and looked down at it, hands shaking. CHARLES'S blocky handwriting on the front. Ophelia stared.

Tilda eased the envelope into Ophelia's lap. "If you can't open it, I will."

"I'll open it."

The paper rasped under Ophelia's nail as she lifted the flap. Inside: printed confirmations, a folded itinerary, two luggage tags with little blue anchors. She unfolded the itinerary. Her breath snagged. "Birmingham to Atlanta," she read aloud, voice barely there. "Atlanta to… Podgorica." The letters looked like a dare. "Montenegro."

Tilda whistled low. "Well, I'll be."

There was more—a hotel confirmation, a note about "Kotor—Old Town," the words Charles had scrawled in pen along the margin: *Wait till you see the mountains, Phee. You'll think the sky fell in love with the sea and they decided to live together.* The sentence punched through her ribs. She pressed a hand to her mouth. "He wrote this."

"Then we're listening." Tilda tapped the itinerary.

Ophelia stared at the dates on the page. The flight left in three days. Three days was in the blink of an eye. "I can't just—go," she whispered.

Tilda nudged her shoulder. "You don't have to be brave for a whole trip. Just be brave for the next fifteen minutes. That's about how long it'll take to email the airline and confirm what you need."

Ophelia looked down at the itinerary again, at the neat blocks of time and the strange names. She could almost feel the belly of the plane humming under her feet, the rush of air as she stepped out into a place where no one knew her history. "What if I get there and I still can't breathe?" she asked.

"Then you'll breathe by the sea," Tilda said. "If you're going to gasp, gasp at a view."

Her grandmother crossed the room, took Ophelia's hand, and folded it around the luggage tags. "Your mama used to say there are two kinds of leaving: running away and running toward. Sometimes they look the same for a while." Her mouth trembled, but she kept going. "Charles wanted you to run toward something. Let's not disappoint the dead when they were trying to be kind."

Ophelia's eyes burned so hard she had to close them. In the darkness, she saw Charles's grease-stained hands, his grin when he stole a biscuit, the way he'd said *Mrs. Morrison* like a private prayer. When she opened her eyes, the room was the same and not, tilted a degree toward a future that hadn't existed five minutes ago. "Okay," she said. Her voice was so small it embarrassed her. She tried again. "Okay."

Tilda took the itinerary like a relay baton. "I'll help you make a list. You'll need a plug adapter. And a suitcase that isn't older than both of us. And shoes you can walk in without cussing. And we'll have to find your passport. Please tell me you know where your passport is."

Ophelia gestured weakly to the closet. "Shoebox. With the cougar-pattern scarf Aunt Marlene gave me that one time."

"Of course, it's under the animal print," Tilda said. "Chaos respects chaos."

"Wait, what will my parents think? They will think I've lost my mind."

"We will tell them after you are safely on the plane." Her grandmother put her arms around her.

"Great plan granny!" Tilda agreed.

They spent the next hour prowling the house with purpose for the first time since the funeral. Lists multiplied on scrap paper: medication, sunscreen, a travel-sized bottle of shampoo that wouldn't explode, the good walking sandals instead of the cute ones that would murder her arches. Tilda opened a drawer and discovered a stash of tiny hotel sewing kits Ophelia had apparently been collecting since high school. "Cute," she said. "If your plane loses a wing, you can stitch it back on."

Every so often, they'd stop, both caught by a ghost—Charles's jacket tossed over the chair, the ring dish he'd set by the side of the bed, his scribble of a note on the fridge reminding them to pick up milk. Each sighting was a wave that knocked the wind out of her. But each time, Tilda set another small task in her hands like a life preserver. *Fold these. Pack that. Check this.*

By late afternoon, the list had neat little check marks next to half the items, and Ophelia's suitcase sat open on the bed with a row of T-shirts lined up like well-behaved children. Tilda flopped down beside it and stared at the ceiling fan. "We should celebrate."

"With what?"

Tilda rolled over and grinned. "There's a lemon pie Mrs. Gentry brought that I'm not returning to the casserole vault. We'll eat it with two forks like we stole it."

They did. On the porch steps. The sun lowered itself slowly behind the trees, the cicadas tuning up, the air thick with August and sugar. Grandmother joined them with three plates, because she was civilized and refused to eat anything with a fork straight from a pan. When the first fireflies winked on, Ophelia set her fork down. "What if people talk?" she asked softly. "If I leave so soon."

Tilda didn't even look up from licking pie filling off her fork. "Baby, people are going to talk no matter what you do. Give them something pretty to talk about. 'Ophelia flew across an ocean and sat by a bay that looks like God forgot to stop painting.'"

Grandmother dabbed the corner of her mouth with a napkin. "And if they mention propriety, you send them to me."

They sat in the warm quiet until the pie was gone. Mosquitoes found them, the first stars punctured the sky, and the porch boards creaked under the shift of their weight. Inside, Ophelia packed the itinerary into the front pocket of the suitcase. The sound of the zipper closing was crisp, decisive. She wrote a single line in her notebook, the one she'd been afraid to touch since the wedding:

I am leaving. Not because I don't love you, but because you loved me enough to point me somewhere.

She touched the words, as if she could press them deeper.

That night, the quiet came back as always, but it was thinner around the edges, frayed by the knowledge that it would not go on like this forever. She imagined a map opening out in front of her, the blue seam of the Adriatic stitched beneath mountains, a stone-walled town cradled in an ancient bay. Kotor. The syllables were strange in her mouth and beautiful anyway.

When morning finally eased through the blinds, she woke with the sort of fear that felt like motion instead of paralysis. Her flight now had a date, and a place, and a purpose she could hold in her shaking hands. Down the hall, she could hear Tilda already bullying the coffeemaker into submission and Grandma humming a hymn that had survived a dozen versions of their family. Ophelia swung her legs out of bed and stood, bare feet on cool floorboards, a little steadier than yesterday. She had not wanted to be a widow. She had not wanted to be brave. But she had wanted Charles, and Charles had wanted a world bigger than Woodard for her, and in that algebra, she found the smallest kind of courage. "Okay," she told the quiet room. "Okay."

She picked up her suitcase and set it by the door.

5

The days before she left Woodard, Ophelia felt as though she had signed a contract with fate. Every corner of town seemed to know before she had spoken the words aloud. Small towns were like that—there were no secrets, only delays in distribution.

At the pharmacy, when she tried to pick up motion-sickness pills for the flight with Tilda, Mrs. Jenkins leaned across the counter, lowering her voice like they were co-conspirators. "I heard you're fleeing to Europe, child. Is it true?"

Ophelia blinked. She hadn't told anyone besides Tilda and Grandma. "I... I'm going to Montenegro," she admitted, the syllables still foreign in her mouth.

Mrs. Jenkins gasped. "Montenegro! Isn't that where Dracula lives?"

"That's Transylvania," Ophelia muttered, but before she could elaborate, Tilda materialized behind her like a defense attorney.

"Dracula's got better real estate," Tilda said crisply, tossing a pack of gum onto the counter. "Montenegro's got mountains and a bay that could make you weep, so unless Dracula's picked up a vacation home, I think our girl will be safe."

"How did you know?"

"Well, I'm in bible study with Charles parents and they brought it up for our prayer circle."

"How did they know?" Tilda asked.

"They were the ones that arranged the whole honeymoon, and they mentioned you

33

had reached out to the airline, then the airline contacted them because it was booked on their credit card. I think you are making a huge mistake."

"Oh, um, I guess I should call them." Ophelia murmured.

"You will do no such thing Phee. Shame on you for making her feel guilty. This is exactly why she needs to get out of town. She needs space from people like you." Tilda ordered her, "And you Mrs. Jenkins, for the future I want to kindly remind you that gossip is the devil's phone call. It's best to just hang up."

By the time they left the pharmacy, Ophelia could feel eyes on her, invisible threads of gossip weaving a net around her. Someone at the bank whispered it. Someone at the diner repeated it. By evening, half the town knew Ophelia Morrison was leaving Woodard, and the other half was sharpening their tongues with theories as to why.

"She can't handle the grief."

"She wants to reinvent herself."

"She's running away."

"She's going to come back with some European man in a silk scarf."

Each whisper was a pinprick. She wanted to shrink into herself, to hide until her flight left, but instead she forced her chin up, practiced the art of pretending she didn't hear.

At home, the house turned into a war zone of packing. Tilda stormed through the rooms like a general in combat boots. "Passport?"

"Shoebox under the scarf."

"Walking shoes?"

"I've got sandals."

"You'll need real shoes. Montenegro has hills. Cobblestones. Slopes that could break your ankles."

"How do you know?"

"Oh honey, first thing I did was look up online and read all about this place."

Despite the chaos, Ophelia found herself strangely grateful

for the noise. It left less room for the silence where Charles should have been. The absurdity of it all—her, who had never been farther than Florida, imagining herself striding through an airport in another country—made her dizzy. Tilda plopped down beside her and squeezed her hand. "You've got this!"

Even her parents reached out. They had heard through Charles parent's she would be leaving and much to her surprise, sided with her. They both thought that it was the best plan for her. They thought she needed a breather for a couple weeks and some relaxation. She was grateful to them both for understanding.

Ophelia mustered the courage and called Charles' parents to thank them as well and after speaking with them both they agreed it was a good plan for her. She asked them why Montenegro? His mother said, "Charles never explained why, just that he wanted to take you there. So, we honored his wishes and booked the trip."

Feeling at peace, that Sunday, she tried church one last time. The sanctuary smelled faintly of lilies left over from the funeral, and every person she passed tilted their head like a sympathetic puppy.

After the benediction, Pastor Elmer clasped her hand, his voice oily with piety. "Ophelia, child, remember God is with you, whether you're in Woodard or wandering strange foreign lands."

She nodded, too tired to argue, but Tilda yanked her away with a muttered, "If God's with her, maybe He can carry her luggage."

The night before her flight, the house buzzed with nervous energy. Grandma baked a peach cobbler "for strength," while Tilda stormed around packing emergency snacks into Ophelia's carry-on.

"You never know what they'll feed you on planes," Tilda said, stuffing in a pack of peanut butter crackers, a granola bar, and something that looked like jerky. "And trust me, if you land in another country hungry, you'll make terrible choices."

Ophelia sat on the edge of her bed; suitcase open before her. The little blue luggage tags Charles had chosen gleamed in the lamplight. She ran her thumb across the embossed anchor and felt her throat close.

"Tomorrow," she whispered to the empty room. "Charles, tomorrow I'll go."

That night, she couldn't sleep. She padded barefoot to the porch; the boards cool beneath her toes. The cicadas hummed, and fireflies flickered lazily in the humid dark. Tilda joined her a few minutes later, holding two mugs of tea. "Couldn't sleep either?"

"I keep thinking... what if it's wrong? What if leaving him behind makes it worse?"

Tilda blew on her tea. "Honey, you're not leaving him. You're carrying him. You'll carry him all the way across the ocean. But you can't carry him if you let this town pile casseroles and pity on top of you until you suffocate. You need space. Space he wanted you to have."

Ophelia sipped the tea, hot and floral, and let the words seep into her like medicine. When she finally went back inside, she lay in bed with the suitcase by the door. Sleep didn't come easy, but when it did, she dreamed not of funerals but of a bay cradled by mountains, water sparkling like a promise.

The airport did not care that she was a widow. Birmingham-Shuttlesworth smelled like coffee and disinfectant and a thousand different perfumes fighting for dominance. Families argued gently about boarding groups, businessmen lined up like penguins with identical roller bags, and over the speakers a woman with a smile in her voice announced delays as if they were party favors. It was the ordinary hum of people going places for reasons that had nothing to do with grief, and the sheer neutrality of it steadied Ophelia more than any casserole ever had.

Tilda, however, treated the terminal like a battleground. "Heads up, Phee." she said, shouldering the tote with snacks like ammo.

Ophelia's grandmother had insisted on coming to the airport despite the early hour. She wore her church hat as if warding off all possible calamities, and she kept patting Ophelia's cheek as though it might slide off without frequent anchoring. "You text me when you land in Atlanta, you hear? And then when you get to—what's it called?"

"Frankfurt," Tilda supplied, consulting the itinerary for the sixteenth time. "Then Podgorica."

"Pod-ga-rica," Grandma repeated, mangling it bravely. "And you tell them at each place that your grandmother will haunt them if they lose your luggage."

"I will," Ophelia said, because arguing with a woman who had survived two husbands and three tornadoes felt unwise.

They checked the suitcase—blue tag with the little anchor swinging with Charles's handwriting The agent slapped the sticker on with a cheerful thwack, oblivious to the way Ophelia's heart skipped. Watching the bag slide onto the conveyor felt like watching a small part of her vanish under a rubber curtain. She exhaled carefully, as though breathing too hard might rip something else away.

Grandma pressed a white envelope into her palm. Cash, of course—Grandma didn't trust foreign ATMs any more than she trusted weather reports. "For emergencies," she said. "Or shoes."

Ophelia choked on a laugh. "Shoes are not emergencies."

"Blisters are," Grandma said. "God gave you two feet. Treat them nice."

They hugged. The hug lasted longer than a goodbye and shorter than a rescue. When the boarding call came—zone numbers like bingo—Tilda stood, straightened Ophelia's backpack as if adjusting a shield, and said, "We're not doing the cinematic sob at the gate. We're doing the confident strut. Remember: nod at people like you know things."

Ophelia nodded, even though she knew very few things. She hugged Grandma again, then Tilda, and when she turned toward the jet bridge her knees wobbled and then held. The physical act of walking onto a plane felt like a decision stamped in metal.

The long-haul to Frankfurt felt like entering a new physical law. Lights dimmed to a false night, a false morning dawned six hours later over the black Atlantic, and time itself loosened at the edges. Her seatmates were a father and teenage daughter heading to visit family in Bavaria; the girl wore headphones the size of planets and glanced at Ophelia's tear-reddened eyes only long enough to offer a single tissue, wordlessly, like passing a torch.

Flight attendants served dinner at a time that wasn't dinner. Something with pasta that had forgotten it once had a spine, a roll resilient as a stress ball, and a very chewy brownie. Ophelia ate mechanically, because Tilda had said, "Always eat on planes; you might not get another chance on the ground." She drank water when told, declined wine because the idea of feeling any fuzzier than she already did scared her.

Between movies she couldn't concentrate on and a book she couldn't absorb, she stared at the flight map. A tiny pixel plane crawled across the ocean; its tail of dotted line oddly soothing. *You are here*, it insisted, unromantically. *And then you will be there.*

When sleep came, it was a stitch, a doze against the plastic window. She woke to the pink of a manufactured sunrise and the captain cheerfully informing them the local time in Frankfurt was oh-dark-thirty and the weather was "classic Germany."

Frankfurt airport smelled faintly of bread and jet fuel. Signs shouted in German and English with equal authority. Ophelia followed arrows like breadcrumbs—*Anschlussflüge / Connecting Flights*—and felt a small thrill each time the sign she needed appeared exactly when she feared she'd lost it. She texted Tilda a photo of a pretzel the size of a steering wheel; Tilda replied with: EAT CARBS. THEN FIND YOUR GATE.

The small regional flight to Podgorica boarded from a bus gate; they stood on the tarmac while the plane blinked at them like a sleepy bird. A handful of Montenegrin families chatted around her, consonants tumbling, vowels round and warm. A woman with a baby smiled at Ophelia, and when the baby reached for her necklace, the woman said something musical and apologetic. Ophelia shook her head and smiled back, because kindness translated, and babies were the same in every language: small sovereign nations of need and delight.

As the plane lifted out of Frankfurt's orderly geometry, clouds swallowed the windows, and then—briefly—the Alps appeared, teeth of stone gnawing at the sky. It felt like flying over the bones of a sleeping world. She pressed her forehead to the window, breath fogging the glass, and thought of Charles's note: *Wait till you see the mountains, Phee.* She whispered, "wow, it's so beautiful," and the engines thrummed an answer not in any language she spoke.

Two hours later, the plane dipped toward a patchwork of green and silver. Rivers curled like stray ribbons; hills shouldered close. The announcement came in Montenegrin first, then English: *We will soon be landing at Podgorica Airport.* Ophelia exhaled and felt a tremor in her hands that was not fear, exactly, but readiness with nowhere to sit.

6

Podgorica Airport was small enough to feel personal. They deplaned down steps, the heat wrapping her in a sudden shawl. The mountains stood at the edge of everything like patient ancestors. The terminal smelled faintly of coffee and dust, and the baggage claim was a single belt with an optimism about it. Her blue suitcase appeared miraculously early, the anchor tag swinging like a wink from another life. She made a strangled sound that might have been a laugh, might have been a sob, and grabbed the handle like a handhold.

At the currency exchange, she swapped some of Grandmother's envelope dollars for euros, then stood outside under a sky so sharp it made her eyes water and tried to decide the next right thing. There was no flying directly to Kotor; she knew that much. You didn't step off an airplane into walled towns and postcard bays. You took the long way. You earned it.

Taxi drivers called out—"Kotor? Budva?"—the names rolling like stones. She could have hired a private transfer, and maybe she would next time, but the bus felt right: humble, practical, a way to be a person instead of a project. She found the shuttle to the city center, a smaller bus on to the coast, and paid in cash because her hands understood paper better than plastic in a place where she still didn't know the rules.

Her seatmate was a middle-aged man with weathered hands, smelling faintly of tobacco and citrus. He offered her a wrapped candy without a word. She hesitated, then accepted, peeling the wrapper to find a lemon drop that burst sour and sweet against her tongue. She smiled. He nodded once, as though they had exchanged entire biographies.

The road unspooled west. Flatlands gave way to hills, hills to the first bite of mountains. Villages flashed by—white houses, red roofs, laundry snapped between balconies like flags of domestic nations. The air coming through the half-cracked bus window smelled sharper than Alabama air—less humid, more alive, with a tang of dust and pine. It carried the faintest suggestion of brine, as if the sea itself were leaning forward to welcome her.

Ophelia propped her forehead against the cool window and watched it all pass through her, not just past. Her grief rode beside her like a silent companion, but it wasn't driving. Not anymore. It was a passenger, the way Charles had ridden shotgun on their Sunday drives, flicking the radio between stations until they landed on a song both could hum.

After an hour, the road curved and climbed through a canyon, sun slashing the rock in coins of light. She felt it then, a pressure at the edges of the day, a sense of nearing. She checked the map Tilda had printed from the internet and folded into the exact wrong angles. *Kotor*, it said, an ink dot waiting. The bus rolled around another bend, and though she could not yet see the bay, she felt it like a held breath about to be released.

Outside, Montenegro opened itself in green and stone. The white-walled houses whose red roofs glowed in the landscape. Every few miles, a roadside shrine flashed past, little boxes painted in blue or white, candles flickering inside, a cross atop like a whisper of faith. The mountains were jaw-dropping. The bay shone. The road kept going. And Ophelia went with it.

She closed her eyes, not because she wanted to miss it but because she wanted to meet it with all of herself. When she opened them again, the bus was cresting the ridge, and in the distance, the first gleam of water flashed like something holy. She didn't cry. Not yet. She didn't laugh. Not yet. She just pressed her palm flat to the glass and whispered the only prayer she had that day: "God, if you hear me, don't let me leave."

When the bus hissed to a stop in small towns where clusters of people climbed aboard or disappeared into the folds of the countryside. Children with backpacks, old women carrying plastic bags heavy with produce, young men in soccer jerseys—all slid into the seats around her, the air filling with their conversations, musical with rolling consonants she couldn't catch but loved to hear.

After nearly two hours, the road narrowed, hugging the shoulder of a canyon carved by a river that glittered like glass. The water flashed turquoise where the sun hit, deepened to shadows under the overhanging rock. Ophelia pressed her palm against the glass, feeling the vibration of the engine, the hum of rubber on asphalt. And then the bus crested a ridge, and the world changed.

The mountains fell back, opening like a curtain. The first view of the Adriatic coast spilled into sight—not the full bay yet, but a gleam of water vast and restless, catching light in silver shards. The bus tilted down toward it, and for the first time since Charles's aneurysm, Ophelia felt something inside her unclench. It wasn't joy. It wasn't peace. But it was air—sharp, salted, necessary. She did cry then, quietly, the tears sliding without sobs. No one noticed, or if they did, they pretended not to. That kindness—of being allowed to grieve in public without interference—felt like a gift.

The bus rattled on until finally the driver called out "Kotor!"

She gathered her things, stumbled down the steps, and landed on the pavement in the late-afternoon sun. The station was small, bordered by palm trees and a café with faded awnings. Taxis idled, their drivers smoking and gesturing lazily. In the distance, beyond the low-slung station buildings, the bay glimmered, framed by mountains so steep they seemed to drop straight into the water.

She wheeled her suitcase in a daze, following signs written in Cyrillic and Latin script, both equally foreign and beautiful. The taxi drivers murmured, "Kotor? Budva?" in hopeful tones, but she shook her head, her mouth too dry to answer. She wanted to walk, to approach on her own feet. The pavement was uneven, the air heavy with salt and something floral she couldn't name.

She rounded a corner, and there it was: the Bay of Kotor. It was not a bay in the way Alabama had bays—flat, sprawling, tame. This was a bay carved into the bones of mountains, a fjord in everything but name, the water a deep mirrored blue that caught the sky and doubled it. Stone walls rose along the shore, ancient and stern, wrapping the Old Town like an embrace both protective and watchful. Church towers speared the sky, their bells tolling with a sound that seemed to vibrate through her chest.

Ophelia stopped dead on the sidewalk, suitcase handle still in her hand, and stared. The sun poured gold over the ridges, shadows deepening into velvet in the folds of the cliffs. A small boat cut across the bay, leaving a ripple that caught the light. And all she could think was: *Charles, you were right. The sky and sea really are in love here.* Her knees went weak, and she sat down on the nearest bench, the stone cool under her.

People moved past her: tourists with cameras, locals in sundresses and sandals, an old man carrying bread under his arm. No one paid her any special attention. No one looked at her with pity. She was anonymous, unremarkable. For the first time since the wedding, she wasn't a widow to anyone here. She was just a woman sitting by the sea. And that anonymity was freedom.

Hunger eventually pulled her to her feet. She found a café along the waterfront, its tables shaded by white umbrellas. She sat and ordered by pointing—something that looked like a flaky pastry spiraled and filled with cheese, and a glass bottle of mineral water that fizzed sharply when opened. The pastry was warm, and the cheese was tangy. She ate slowly, watching the bay shift as the sun lowered, turning everything into shades of rose and lavender. Around her, people laughed, clinked glasses, took pictures. Life went on, heedless of her grief, and somehow that too was a gift.

When she finished, she paid in euros and stumbled back up the road toward the station where her accommodations awaited. Just off the bay she entered the small hotel where she was greeted by an impressive woman with dark eyes and a braid thick as a rope. Ophelia greeted her, "Hi, do you speak English."

"Yes, you need room?"

Ophelia fished paperwork out of her bag and handed it to her, "Hi, my name is Ophelia Carpenter. I'm booked here to stay in your guesthouse."

"I am Mira, the proprietor of this hotel." She studied the paperwork. "I confused, I expected Mr. and Mrs. Morrison."

It felt like a punch to the gut.

"Right, things changed. So, it will just be me."

Mira studied Ophelia for a moment and then yelled, "Dino! Come take bags."

A teenage boy appeared quickly and grinned, "I take bags for you."

"Oh, well, thank you."

Mira led her through the back door of the small hotel and into a lovely courtyard with tables. Ophelia grinned looking at the space and flowers that hung from the stone walls. "The kitchen is over on that side of hotel. We have a small cafe and tables inside where our guests have food available to order."

Ophelia nodded along, "Okay great."

Just past the courtyard was a modest guesthouse, made in stone, with a wooden door that looked far older than her hometown. Mira unlocked the door to her guest house. Her room was quaint, with a full-size bed and a small desk. To the left was the bathroom complete with a bathtub with shower nozzle, sink and toilet. Dino set her suitcases down near the bed. Mira pulled back both window's curtains revealing a view of the courtyard in front, and to the back a view of the mountains.

"Again, I am Mira, If you need something, come find me." Mira handed her the key. "If you can't find me, find Dino, he is always around."

"Okay, thank you."

Ophelia handed Dino some euros and as the door shut behind them both she collapsed on her bed with a loud sigh. She turned to her side and looked out the window, curtains open, watching as the last of the sun slipped behind the jagged peaks. The room smelled faintly of stone and lavender soap. She whispered, "I made it." Sleep came faster than she expected, carrying her into a night filled not with casseroles and condolences, but the soft sound of water lapping against stone.

7

Ophelia woke to the sound of bells. At first, she thought she was dreaming—that the noise was the echo of church bells from Woodard, drifting through memory—but then she blinked into the unfamiliar light of her narrow room and realized they were real. The tones rolled across the bay, deep and deliberate, ringing against the cliffs until the whole valley seemed to vibrate.

She lay still for a long moment, heart pounding, the weight of travel pressing her into the mattress. Then she remembered where she was, and a laugh bubbled out of her throat—half disbelief, half awe. "Kotor," she whispered, tasting the word in her mouth like a secret.

She pulled on jeans and a cotton shirt, twisted her hair into a messy knot, and walked outside toward the hotel. The courtyard smelled faintly of coffee and baking bread. Mira greeted her with a slight smile, "Dobro jutro," before pressing a cup of coffee into her hand.

"Good morning, Mira How are you?"

"It's beautiful day in Kotor."

The coffee was unlike any she'd had at home—black, strong, served in a tiny porcelain cup that forced her to sip instead of gulp. The first mouthful hit like a jolt of lightning. She blinked. "Lord have mercy," she muttered. Mira smiled knowingly, as if this was the reaction she expected.

"It's good, no?"

"Well, it's gonna do its job!"

Armed with caffeine, Ophelia grabbed her purse and bravely stepped outside. The morning air was cool, tinged with brine. The mountains loomed impossibly close, jagged shadows against the sky, their slopes still catching wisps of mist. The bay stretched calm and glassy, the reflection of the town blurring as fishing boats stirred the surface. Already, vendors were setting up stalls along the old walls: baskets of figs and peaches, pyramids of tomatoes so ripe they seemed ready to burst, jars of honey glowing like captured sunlight.

Ophelia walked slowly; suitcase-weighted muscles stiff but willing. She let herself drift with the small crowd of locals, listening to their voices—sharp bursts of laughter, vowels that rolled like waves. She understood nothing and everything at once. No one looked at her like she was broken. To them, she was simply another body moving through the morning, anonymous, untethered. At one stall, a woman with a red scarf handed her a plum. "Probaj," she said—*try it.*

"Oh, thank you darlin." Ophelia bit in. Juice exploded down her chin. The sweetness was dizzying, sharper than any fruit back home, as if the tree had funneled all the mountain sun into this single bite. She wiped her chin on her sleeve and stammered, "It's... perfect."

The vendor laughed, understanding without words.

"I'll take two please. One for now and one for later." The vendor didn't understand, so Ophelia raised two fingers. She patted Ophelia's hand and slipped another two plums into her bag. After she paid, Ophelia walked on, cheeks sticky with sugar, heart lifting.

The streets of Old Town were a maze—narrow alleys paved with stones smoothed by centuries of footsteps, walls rising close enough to cast long shadows. Laundry fluttered from balconies; cats lounged on warm steps like self-appointed guardians. Every turn revealed another archway, another square with a fountain, another church tower pointing skyward.

She wandered without plan, letting the streets choose for her. At one point she stumbled into a courtyard where a trio of old men sat playing cards. One looked up, winked, and held up his hand of cards as though asking her opinion. She grinned helplessly. "Always bet on queens," she whispered, and though he couldn't hear her words, he laughed as if he had.

The sound startled her—it was the first time she'd laughed that freely in weeks. She ducked into a café next. The smell hit her like a memory—warm bread, butter, sugar. She thought instantly of biscuits back home, of Charles sneaking them off cooling racks with a grin, of the last batch she'd eaten on that terrible night before everything shattered. Her throat tightened as she approached the counter and stood. The man working behind the counter approached her. "Good morning. What can I get you."

Ophelia was shocked. "How did you know I spoke English?"

Two local women sitting nearby giggled together.

"What?" Ophelia asked confused.

"Just lucky... guess." He smiled.

"Okay? Well, I would love an iced tea please."

"That's all? You don't want any food?"

"Oh no thank you, just a tea would be great. Sweet tea if you have it."

"What is sweet tea? Sugar? You want sugar."

"Yes sir, I want lots of sugar."

He grinned and laughed, "Okay American girl, I give you lots of sugar." He winked and turned around to get her tea.

"Oh no I didn't mean it like that."

As he prepared her iced tea he gestured, "Of course you did."

Ophelia's face burned, "I really didn't" The women giggled behind her, and Ophelia turned around and put her hand on her hip. "Ladies, I *really* didn't."

One of the women spoke up and said, "Hey American lady... what happens when you vacation stays on your vacation."

"They both burst out laughing."

"Lord have mercy." Ophelia muttered as he slid a small glass of tea across the counter and handed her a bowl of raw sugar. "Thank you."

"Pogačice," he said. "Try your tea."

Ophelia noticed there was one ice cube in it.

"Honey, I'm gonna need a little more ice please."

He grabbed two more small cubes and poured them into her glass. "Happy now."

She sighed and put a spoon full of sugar in. She took a sip and her mouth puckered. "Heavens to Betsy, that is strong tea."

"Who is... this Betsy?" he asked.

She thought a moment and softly replied, "I really don't know."

By noon, the square near the cathedral buzzed with life. Musicians played, children darted after pigeons, tourists licked dripping ice creams. Ophelia sat on the fountain's edge, sipping another coffee, letting the noise wash over her. She studied each building and out of the corner of her eye she saw a vacant shop with boarded up windows. She felt something hairy rub against her leg and squealed.

She looked down to find a tabby cat had rubbed lovingly against her leg and was quickly running away. Mortified Ophelia tried not to look at anyone around her and wandered up a side alleyway. She noticed more and more cats and then there it was. "The Cat's Museum."

"No..." She said out loud. "There is a Cat's museum? What on God's green earth."

She had to go. She giggled with delight as she approached the entry and paid a small fee to enter. It was even better when she could ever imagine. Collections of art, antique books, post cards, all honoring Cats. Ophelia smiled wandering through the building. She glanced at other tourists who would wander in and relished in their equal pleasure and fascination. It was a delight to everyone.

When she left, she took immediate notice that all the gift shops had cat merchandise. For some reason she hadn't really noticed it or acknowledged it at least until now. She wandered into to one and found a painted figurine of a tabby cat napping on a bookshelf with its porcelain tail laying over the edge. "This is mine." She grabbed it and paid for it.

～

That evening, after returning to her guesthouse, she sat at the little window desk looking at her new porcelain cat, and lovingly wrote a letter to send to her grandmother.

The bay is even more beautiful than the pictures, more beautiful than Charles's note could prepare me for. I ate a plum that tasted like sunlight and a biscuit that wasn't a biscuit but almost was. I think he would have laughed at me for crying over it. I think he would have drawn every stone in these walls. I miss him with every breath. But I am still breathing. And maybe that's the point.

She signed it simply: *Love, O.*

She set down the pen, folded the paper, and stared at the mountains until the sky turned indigo and the first stars appeared. And when she climbed into bed that night, she felt something strange beneath the grief—a flicker of curiosity. The tiniest spark of wonder at what tomorrow might bring.

8

The first thing Ophelia noticed was the sound. Not bells this time, though they had chimed at dawn, pulling her briefly from a restless sleep. No, now it was the sound of life: the clatter of dishes at the hotel café, the rumble of a scooter down the narrow street, a woman calling to someone in a voice so sharp and melodic it could have been song. Woodard had its own symphony—cicadas, trucks rumbling past the Piggly Wiggly, the hollow *thunk* of screen doors—but this was new, and her brain scrambled to catalog it.

She sat up slowly, the sheets tangled around her legs. Jet lag clung to her like cobwebs. Her body thought it was the middle of the night, her stomach was confused, and her heart thought it might break if she let it. But sunlight streamed through the shutters, and she could smell bread baking. Bread had always been a summons in her life: biscuits from Grandma's oven, cornbread at church suppers, rolls at Thanksgiving. Bread was survival and celebration, both. So, she rose.

The narrow bathroom mirror showed her a woman she barely recognized—hair mussed, skin pale from sleeplessness, eyes shadowed but not hollow. She splashed water on her face, brushed her hair, and whispered to her reflection, "Just walk. One step. Then another."

The guesthouse door groaned as she opened it into the courtyard. She made her way to the hotel's café. Mira greeted her with another *dobro jutro*, sliding a plate across the counter: a wedge of pale cheese, slices of tomato glistening with

51

olive oil, bread so fresh its crust crackled when she tore into it. She blinked. "This is breakfast?"

The woman laughed, nodding. "Good. Yes."

It was good. So good she nearly wept into the bread, the chew of the crust anchoring her to the present moment, forcing her teeth to work, her tongue to taste, her body to remember it was alive.

Suddenly, Ophelia felt her hair being brushed. Surprised she jolted, "What are you doing?"

"I fix you."

"Fix me?"

"Sit, eat, and I do your hair."

Ophelia sat and ate quietly until she finally felt her finish braiding her hair. "Well thank you... I think."

"You will thank me when I am done."

"You really don't need to do my hair."

"Someone needed to." She huffed as she had tied the end of her braid and walked away. Ophelia bit her lip a bit embarrassed, but also pleased. When the plate was empty, she slipped out into the sunlight feeling her newly braided hair with her hands.

Kotor in the morning was alive in a way Woodard never was. The narrow streets of Old Town already bustled with people—vendors wheeling carts into position, children racing pigeons across the squares, café owners wiping down tables in preparation for the day. The scent of espresso drifted like a promise. Ophelia walked slowly, her sandals clicking against stone worn smooth by centuries of footsteps. She felt both invisible and exposed, foreign but not unwelcome. No one stared at her; no one whispered behind their hands. She was simply another body moving through the narrow lanes, and the relief of that anonymity made her dizzy.

She followed the flow of people toward the market. It was held in a square just outside the old stone walls, where stalls were shaded by striped awnings and the air smelled like earth and salt and possibility. Everywhere she looked there was color: heaps of cherries so dark they were almost black, peaches glowing gold, peppers gleaming red and green. Jars of honey lined one table, catching the light like amber gems. Bundles of herbs—sage, rosemary, something sharp she couldn't name—perfumed the air.

She lingered near a stall where an old woman in a headscarf was selling bread. Round loaves, plaited loaves, long slender ones dusted with flour. Ophelia reached out, touched one, and the woman beamed, cutting a slice and pressing it into her hand. It was warm, chewy, with a crust that crunched like a secret. Tears pricked her eyes before she could stop them. *Biscuits, bread, it's all the same thing*, she thought. *It's how the world says you belong.* The vendor said something in Montenegrin, smiling kindly, and Ophelia nodded as though she understood. Maybe she did.

After a while, she bought a small basket of figs and sat on the edge of the square, watching the world move. A man on a bicycle wove through the crowd, balancing a sack of flour on his handlebars. Children tugged at their mothers' skirts, begging for cherries. A fisherman, still smelling of salt and brine, carried a bucket heavy with his catch, setting it down with a grunt near the café.

It was ordinary life, but it felt extraordinary to her, because it wasn't hers. It wasn't steeped in condolences or whispered pity at church. It was life continuing, indifferent to her tragedy.

She bit into a fig, juice sticky on her fingers, and thought *I could get used to this. Maybe.* But then Charles's face rose unbidden, his smile, the sound of his laugh, the way he had promised they'd see this place together. The sweetness turned bitter in her mouth, and she closed her eyes against the ache. Still, when she opened them again, the market was still there, bustling and alive. And she was still here, breathing.

By late morning, she had wandered enough to feel both exhausted and exhilarated. She returned to the guesthouse with a bag of bread and fruit, collapsing onto the bed with the kind of tired that came not from grief but from motion. For the first time since the aneurysm, her fatigue felt honest. Not the bone-deep exhaustion of crying, but the simple ache of walking too far in new shoes. She curled onto her side, cradling the bag of bread against her chest like a child, and let herself drift into a nap, the sound of distant bells cradling her into sleep.

When Ophelia woke from her nap, her stomach was growling like a cranky neighbor. The bread and figs she had bought earlier called to her, but so did the thought of venturing back out. She told herself she'd just "walk around the block," as if she lived in some suburban cul-de-sac instead of a medieval town knotted like a ball of yarn.

The market had grown busier. The late-morning sun had turned the stone walls into golden ovens, and the air shimmered with the heat. The scents were overwhelming: fresh fish glistening on ice, grilled meat sizzling at a stand, herbs crushed underfoot, pastries dusted with sugar. Her senses felt hijacked. She drifted between stalls, trying to look casual. She realized quickly she was failing. Everyone seemed to know exactly what they wanted.

Locals approached with brisk efficiency, speaking in rapid Montenegrin, handing over coins, receiving goods in a seamless dance. Meanwhile, Ophelia wandered like a freshman on the first day of school. She found a basket to buy and new if she started there, she would start making progress in filling it up with.

Clutching her basket like a shield, she approached a stand where the vendor held up a fish as long as her forearm, eyes still glassy, mouth agape. He said something that sounded like "Do you want it gutted?" but could just as easily have been "This fish died nobly, please clap."

"Oh, no, no," Ophelia said, waving her hands. "I wouldn't know what to do with a fish like that. I once set off the smoke alarm cooking pasta."

The man tilted his head, then barked a laugh, slapping the fish down on the table with affection, as though she had told the best joke of the day. He called something to the stall next door, and soon three vendors were laughing, gesturing at her, smiling in a way that wasn't unkind. She blushed crimson and scurried away.

"Congratulations, Phee," she muttered. "You've made your international comedy debut."

The longer she stayed, the more she realized food was its own language. Bread, fruit, cheese—these spoke without words. She bought a wedge of sharp white cheese wrapped in paper, a cluster of grapes that nearly split her bag open, and something that looked like fried dough. The fried dough reminded her of county fairs, of powdered sugar and sticky fingers, of Charles daring her to win him a stuffed bear from the ring toss. She took a bite—crisp, oily, sprinkled with salt instead of sugar— and laughed out loud at the surprise. "Well, you're not funnel cake," she told the pastry. "But I'll allow it."

At one stall, her eye caught on something familiar: small, round baked goods, golden brown, arranged in a basket. They weren't biscuits exactly—they looked firmer, shinier, brushed with egg wash—but they had the same inviting roundness. The vendor, a man with forearms like tree trunks, saw her staring. "Pogačice," he said, offering one.

Ophelia hesitated, then took it. She broke it open, steam rising. The crumb was tender, buttery, almost flaky. She bit in and nearly cried right there in the market. This was it. This was the connection. It wasn't her grandmother's biscuits, it wasn't Charles's favorite breakfast, but it was close enough to feel like kin. Bread, universal and specific all at once.

She bought six, tucking them into her bag. As she walked away, she muttered, "Biscuits, but make it Montenegrin. Phee, you may have found your bridge." The thought startled her. She hadn't expected to think of building anything—bridges, futures, plans. She had only expected to survive. Yet here she was, cradling warm bread in her arms like it was a possibility. Still, the market wasn't all triumphs. She tried to ask for olive oil, gesturing vaguely at bottles, and ended up with something that might have been rakija, the local brandy. The vendor grinned wickedly as she sniffed the bottle, her eyes watering from the fumes.

"Oh, Lord," she coughed. "This could power a tractor."

The vendor pantomimed drinking, then slapping his chest, and the stall erupted in laughter. She shoved the bottle in her bag, vowing to pawn it off on Tilda if she ever visited.

By noon, her basket was overflowing, her arms aching, and her pride both bruised and buoyed. She had made a fool of herself, yes—but she had also been fed, laughed with, and maybe, just maybe, accepted in tiny, crumb-like ways.

She found a bench under a tree, its leaves casting dappled shade. She laid out her treasures like a picnic: figs, peaches, grapes, cheese, bread, and one brave little bottle of rakija. As she ate, she let herself imagine. What if she stayed? Not forever, not yet—but for longer than this first step. What if she baked biscuits here, in this place that already had its own bread, its own pride? Would people laugh? Would they care? Would they taste them and understand something about her, about where she came from? She pictured Charles sketching her stall, teasing her about becoming a biscuit missionary. The thought was bittersweet, but for once, the sweetness was louder.

When the church bells tolled noon, she packed up her feast, crumbs sticking to her fingers, and whispered, "Okay. I could belong here. Just a little." By the time Ophelia left the market square, her arms were aching, and her sandals had rubbed a blister onto her heel the size of a lima bean. She limped through the twisting streets of Old Town, muttering, "This is how it begins. You survive international travel, you survive grief, and then you're taken out by an ill-fitting shoe."

The alleys smelled faintly of stone warmed by the sun, mingled with the sharper scent of coffee drifting from the cafés that had begun to fill with tourists. The square near the cathedral pulsed with life. Musicians played guitars and violins, children chased pigeons like pint-sized gladiators, and waiters balanced trays with the focus of brain surgeons. Her stomach, despite the figs and bread she'd eaten earlier, grumbled again. She drifted toward a café with faded green awnings and wicker chairs spread across the cobblestones. The chalkboard menu out front listed items in Montenegrin and halting English: *Coffee. Cappuccino. Juice. Sandwich with prosciutto. Something we call salad.*

Ophelia smiled. *Something we call salad* sounded both promising and threatening. She slid into a chair, setting her bag of market treasures beside her. A waiter appeared, tall and wiry, with a skeptical eyebrow that seemed permanently arched. "Yes?" he asked in English that was brisk but clear.

"Yes," Ophelia echoed nervously, then flushed. "I mean—um— coffee? Please. And maybe... salad?"

The eyebrow rose higher, but he scribbled something on his pad and vanished. When the coffee arrived—dark, strong, served in a porcelain cup the size of a doll's teacup—she nearly sighed aloud. She sipped, wincing at the strength but determined to love it. The "salad" turned out to be a plate of tomatoes and cucumbers, glistening with oil and sprinkled with salt. Simple, sharp, alive. She ate as though it were a revelation.

Halfway through, the waiter returned, hovering. "American?" he asked, eyes narrowing slightly.

"Yes," she admitted. "From Alabama."

He blinked. "Alabama? This is... football place?"

She nodded. "College football. Yes. Lots of yelling."

The waiter considered this, then nodded gravely, as though she had revealed a national secret. "You like? Or you... hate?"

"Depends on who you ask," she said. "Mostly it's just an excuse to drink more beer."

To her surprise, he chuckled. It was a small sound, but it cracked the air like sunlight breaking through clouds. He tapped her coffee cup. "Next time, rakija. Stronger than football beer."

She shuddered. "I already bought some at the market. I think it could strip paint."

The waiter laughed outright, startling nearby pigeons. He shook his head at her, muttering something in Montenegrin that sounded affectionate, and walked away. Buoyed by that tiny victory, she wandered further. The streets twisted tighter here, shops opening onto courtyards barely big enough for a handful of chairs. She paused at a bookstore tucked into an arched stone doorway. Inside, the air smelled of paper and dust.

The shop keeper, a man with spectacles sliding down his nose, looked up. "Engleski?"

"Yes," she said, tentative.

He nodded, disappearing into a back room, then reemerging with a stack of English-language paperbacks: Hemingway, Austen, Agatha Christie. He placed them in front of her like offerings at an altar. She picked up *The Old Man and The Sea*, the cover worn soft. "This one," she said.

"Good," the man replied. "Love. Always good."

Something about the bluntness made her smile. She bought the book, tucking it into her bag alongside the biscuits. But not every encounter was gentle. At a tiny shop selling household goods—pots, pans, enamel mugs—she attempted to ask about measuring cups. The proprietor, an elderly woman with arms crossed like a general, stared at her as though she had requested plutonium.

Ophelia pantomimed: holding her hands out, making circles, pretending to pour flour. The woman barked something sharp, waved her hand dismissively, and turned away. Ophelia's cheeks burned. She shuffled out, muttering, "Fine. I'll eyeball it like Grandma used to. Who needs accuracy when you have trauma?" A tourist couple passing by shot her confused looks. She waved vaguely at the air. "Don't mind me. Just talking to my failures."

The day stretched hot and bright. By mid-afternoon, she found herself sitting on the low wall overlooking the bay. Boats bobbed gently, their masts like quills scratching the sky. Tourists clambered onto ferries for tours, while locals strolled slowly, unhurried, as if time bent differently here. She took out one of the biscuits she'd bought—Montenegrin pogačice, warm still from the market—and ate it slowly.

A voice startled her. "Good bread?"

She turned. An older man had sat down a few feet away, his fishing rod cast in the water. His English was accented but clear.

"Yes," she said softly. "Very good."

He nodded. "Bread is life. No bread, no... nothing." He gestured to the bay, to the mountains. "All this—better with bread."

Ophelia laughed, blinking back tears. "I think you might be right." She hopped down and walked over and gestured if she could sit with him. "May I?"

The man tipped his cap and went back to his fishing, as if that settled it. And maybe it did. She offered him her bread and her market find and she peacefully watched him fish. Suddenly his rod started bobbing. "Oh, my Lord! You've got a fish."

"He handed her the rod."

"No... I don't know!'

"I will help you."

He smiled and helped her real in a fish. "She squealed with joy!" He helped take the fish off its hook and placed it in his bucket. She gave him a hug and he was taken aback, then politely let her hug him. It was the best hug she had experienced since Charlie was alive.

When she returned to the guesthouse Mira greeted her in the courtyard, "You want me make you dinner... oh... wow... why you smell like fish?" She waved her hand in the air around her.

"I went fishin! It was a ball."

"Yes, I see now."

Mira plugged her nose, "Please go bath before you come have dinner."

"Yes Ma'am." Ophelia skipped to the guest house with joy. For the first time since Charles's aneurysm, she felt the tiniest sliver of belonging. Fragile as a crumb, but real.

Mira served Ophelia mussels for dinner, in white wine, butter, garlic, and tomatoes. She was in heaven. As the sun began to dip behind the mountains, the air had cooled to a softness that Woodard summers never offered. In Alabama, summer nights clung to your skin, humid and relentless. Here, the evening felt like someone had drawn back a velvet curtain, letting in a breeze scented with lavender and sea salt.

Ophelia stood at her window, elbows on the sill, and let the sounds of the town drift upward: the clink of wine glasses at a café below, a dog barking somewhere down the street, the faint roll of church bells announcing the hour. Across the bay, the mountains burned pink, then purple, then a dusky blue that seemed to seep into the water itself. She exhaled, long and shaky. "I wish you could see this Charles."

It hurt—of course it hurt. But the sharpest edge of the grief had been dulled today, not by healing, but by the sheer insistence of life around her. The bustle of the market, the bite of a peach, the laughter of strangers. They hadn't erased her sorrow. They had simply refused to let her wallow untouched. And she realized, maybe that refusal was mercy. She sat at the small desk in her room, pulling out her notebook again. The pages still smelled faintly of paper dust and ink, as though they'd been waiting for her. She turned to a blank sheet and stared at it until her eyes blurred. Finally, she wrote:

Today I embarrassed myself in front of a fish...but than I redeemed myself by becoming a fishermen. She crossed out fishermen and then wrote... *fisherwoman?*

She snorted out loud, surprising herself with the sound. She kept going.

I went to a Cat Museum. I ate a peach that dripped down my chin like I was six years old. A waiter informed me rakija is stronger than football, and I believed him. I may have accidentally bought a bottle of jet fuel disguised as alcohol. I am alive.

She picked up her pen and thought a moment, smiled, and then wrote, *And I think I might stay here longer than planned.*

9

A knock startled her. She opened the door to find the Mira holding a small plate with two cookies dusted in powdered sugar. "For you," she said, smiling holding the plate out.

"Oh—thank you," Ophelia stammered. She took the plate carefully, as though it were something sacred.

Then Mira pulled out a hairbrush from behind her back with the other hand. "I do your hair again and help you find a husband." She closed the door behind her and entered her room before Ophelia could stop her.

"Oh no that's really not necessary." Ophelia blushed biting her tongue.

Mira pointed at the bed, "Sit and eat."

Ophelia sat cross-legged on the bed and bit into one. Sweet, crumbly, a little lemony. She licked powdered sugar off her lip and laughed quietly.

"Why you not married?" Mira asked her as she softly brushed her hair."

Ophelia tried to change the subject, "Why... you not married? And why.... do you keep on insisting on doing my hair?"

Mira scoffed, "My husband died. He drowned in his boat ten years ago during a storm."

"Oh, good gracious, I am so sorry."

Mira continued brushing her hair, "you remind me of him."

Ophelia burst, "I remind you of your dead husband?" Mira pulled her hair and Ophelia yelped.

"Yes. He had character. You have character."

Ophelia tried to understand and finally murmured, "I was married."

Mira kept brushing her hair, "Oh?"

"He also died."

Mira stopped brushing her hair and turned her chin to look into Ophelia's eyes. "It's going to be okay."

"He died very recently... on the night we got married." Mira pulled her into her arms and held her. Ophelia hugged her and wept, Mira rubbed her back and after a few minutes she whispered, "It's okay, I will find you a new husband."

Later that night, after a good cry, she stepped outside into the courtyard. The sky was velvet black now, stars pricking it like sequins on a dress. Fireflies flickered in the shadows, and the bay reflected the lights of the town in shimmering streaks. She sat on a stone bench, her notebook balanced on her knees, the last biscuit from the market in her hand. She nibbled it slowly, listening to the murmur of voices drifting from the café, the low strum of a guitar, the hum of water against stone. She remembered her grandmother's words: *You're not leaving us. You're stretching.*

Maybe stretching hurt. Maybe it tore you a little, like muscles after too much strain. But maybe it was also how you grew. She tilted her head back and looked up at the stars. Mira joined her with a bottle of wine and two cups. "Come, we drink to them. Our men who are up there in the stars."

A couple of hours later she found herself in bed, curled up under the thin blanket, the sounds of Kotor lulling her. She thought of the market's colors, the waiter's chuckle, the fisherman's wisdom: *Bread is life. All this—better with bread.* "Better with biscuits," she murmured, half-asleep, smiling into the dark. She fell asleep with the faintest smile tugging at her lips.

~

The next day she awoke with an itch she couldn't ignore biscuits. It wasn't just hunger. It was memory. Biscuits were how her grandmother said *good morning,* how Charles said *I love you* without words, how church suppers said *you're one of us.* Biscuits were grief and comfort baked into golden rounds. And she needed them. She stared at the ceiling of her guesthouse room, muttering, "You're in Montenegro, Phee. They've got their own bread. You don't need to go dragging Southern traditions across the ocean."

But her body rebelled. It wanted flour and butter and salt. It wanted to press dough with her hands and pull something warm and flaky from the oven. It wanted biscuits because biscuits meant she was still herself. So, she pulled on her sandals, braided her hair, and declared to the empty room, "We're doing this."

She ran out that morning with Mira calling after to her, "What about your breakfast?"

"I'll be back and I'm gonna need to borrow your kitchen!"

"What about my kitchen?" Mira yelled back.

~

The grocery store was a lesson in humility. Unlike the bustling outdoor market, the small shop near the old town walls was fluorescent-lit, its aisles narrow, shelves stacked high with goods labeled in Montenegrin and Italian. Shoppers moved with purpose, plucking items from shelves with the ease of people who understood what they were looking at. Ophelia did not.

She stood in the baking aisle, clutching her basket, staring at bags of powder. Some said *brašno*. Others said *tip 400* or *tip 500*. One bag had a picture of a cake, another of bread. None said, "all-purpose flour." "Tip 500?" she whispered. "Does that mean flour strong enough to build a bridge? Or flour that will make me a laughingstock?"

A woman next to her, petite with sharp eyes, plucked a bag off the shelf and tossed it into her cart without hesitation. Ophelia panicked and grabbed the same one. "When in...Kotor," she muttered.

Next: butter. At home, butter came in neat sticks, wrapped in wax paper, with tablespoon markings like little road maps. Here, it came in giant slabs, wrapped in foil, heavy as bricks. She wrestled one into her basket, nearly dropping it onto her toe.

Salt was easier—so, at least she could read. Baking powder, though—oh, baking powder was an odyssey. She scanned shelf after shelf, finding yeast, sugar, packets of mysterious powders. Finally, she spotted a tin with something resembling the right chemical promise. She clutched it to her chest, whispering, "If this turns out to be Parmesan cheese, I swear I'll move back to Alabama."

Milk came in boxes, unrefrigerated, stacked like juice cartons. She picked one up suspiciously, shook it, and muttered, "Well, you're milk today, buddy."

Eggs weren't in a cold case either—they sat in open cartons on a shelf, room temperature. She stared at them in awe. "Okay, this feels wrong. Y'all should be cold. Don't y'all know you're supposed to be refrigerated?" She glanced around, lowering her voice. "Do eggs expire differently here? Are they magical European eggs?"

An older man standing nearby coughed into his hand, clearly trying to hide a smile. By the time she reached the register, her basket weighed a ton and her pride even more. She fumbled with coins, nearly handed the cashier a token from her Atlanta airport layover instead of a euro. The cashier raised one unimpressed eyebrow but accepted her bumbling with the resigned patience of someone used to foreigners.

Ophelia staggered back to the guesthouse like she was carrying contraband. Her arms ached, her sandals pinched, and she was muttering to herself like a deranged street preacher. She reached Mira's kitchen. Mira appeared, "What is all of this?"

"I'm makin some biscuits!"

Mira made the sign of the cross over her and started quietly "praying," and left the kitchen.

"Good, say a prayer! I'm gonna need it."

The kitchen was small, square, and just intimidating enough to make Ophelia sweat before she even preheated the oven. Which she wasn't entirely sure how to do. The dials on the stovetop looked like they belonged to an alien spaceship—symbols instead of words, temperatures listed in Celsius instead of Fahrenheit. She stood squinting at them. "Alright, 180 degrees Celsius. That's about 350 Fahrenheit. Right? Or is it? Please don't let me burn this building down."

"What did you say about burning. No burning!" Mira popped her head in around the corner.

Ophelia yelled back, "Just ignore me."

Mira walked off again muttering, "Oh dear God..."

She twisted a knob. A faint hum answered. Victory—or possibly impending disaster. She unpacked her groceries onto the counter. Flour in a bag without a measuring spoon. Butter shaped like a brick. Milk in a box that still made her uneasy. Baking powder in a tin whose label she couldn't read. Salt at least felt familiar. Eggs sat smugly in their carton, daring her to question their room-temperature legitimacy again.

"Well," she told the eggs, "you and me, we're about to have words."

She dug into her grandmother's recipe scrawled in her notebook. Except—of course—she had never written anything down with measurements anyone else could understand. The page read:

Flour till it looks right. Butter till it feels right. Milk till it comes together. Don't you dare overwork it. Bake till golden. Pray if you have to.

Ophelia groaned. "That's not a recipe, that's a riddle."

Still, she soldiered on. She dumped a heap of flour into a bowl—too much? too little?—and reached for the butter. It resisted the knife like a frozen boulder. She hacked at it, sending a chunk flying onto the floor. A stray cat, which had apparently slinked in through the back door, pounced on it with glee. Ophelia shrieked. "Excuse me! That's not for you!"

The cat hissed, batted the butter chunk under a cabinet, and vanished.

"Well," she sighed, "guess we're all in this together."

She threw in another slab of butter, tried to cut it into the flour, and succeeded only in coating her hands, arms, and shirt in a ghostly layer of white. The kitchen looked like a cocaine bust gone wrong. Next came milk. She shook the box, tore open the top, and poured too quickly. The dough sloshed into a sticky swamp. She tried to stir with a wooden spoon, but it clung like wet cement. She cursed under her breath, then louder, until she was sure the whole block could hear her. Finally, she dropped the spoon, plunged her hands into the mess, and kneaded desperately. Dough oozed between her fingers like something alive. "Lord have mercy, this is not how biscuits are supposed to feel!"

Shaping the dough was another disaster. At home, she'd have used a biscuit cutter, or at least a drinking glass. Here, she had a chipped teacup and the determination of a woman possessed. She cut lopsided circles, plopping them onto a baking sheet like pale little UFOs.

They went into the oven with a prayer. She set a timer on her phone and leaned against the counter, breathing hard. Flour streaked her face like war paint.

Minutes later, the smell began—not of golden biscuits, but of something... off. Acrid. Smoky. Ophelia bolted upright. Smoke curled from the oven vent. She yanked open the door and staggered back as a wave of burnt flour stench hit her. The biscuits had spread into mutant pancakes, their edges blackening, the tops still raw. Smoke billowed.

"NO NO NO NO NO—"

She flailed for the oven mitts, found none, grabbed a dish towel, and yanked the tray out. One biscuit flopped off and sizzled onto the floor, where the cat reappeared to bat it gleefully across the tiles like a hockey puck. The smoke alarm shrieked, a high-pitched wail that echoed through the guesthouse.

"Oh God, I've killed us all!" Ophelia cried, waving the towel desperately. She fanned the smoke toward the open window, coughing, eyes streaming.

Footsteps thundered in the hallway and Mira returned with a fire extinguisher. "Watch out."

She blocked her, still fanning. "It's fine! Everything's fine! Just a cultural exchange program between me and flour!"

Behind her, two curious guests peeked in, noses twitching. Ophelia gestured weakly at the tray of mutant biscuits, smoke curling upward. "Biscuits," she croaked. "Southern delicacy. Very... authentic."

Mira blinked. Then, slowly, she stepped inside, picked up one scorched biscuit, and sniffed it. She took the tiniest nibble, chewed thoughtfully, then set it down. "Not good," she declared flatly.

Ophelia covered her face with her flour-crusted hands. "No. Not good."

10

hen the smoke cleared and the alarm finally stopped wailing, Ophelia collapsed into a chair, covered in flour, surrounded by charred biscuits and laughing strangers. She looked at the tray and muttered, "Well, Grandma, I prayed, and this is what I got." And for the first time since Charles died, she laughed until her ribs ached.

"Your Grandma is not here. But I am... so you try again." Mira calmly stated.

Ophelia watched as the smoke thinned to a gauze instead of a curtain, the kitchen looked like a crime scene where the victim was dignity. Charred biscuit-shrapnel dotted the tiles, flour drifted through a slanted beam of sunlight like slow snow, and the cat—now dusted ghost-white—wore a crumb beard and the expression of a creature who had finally found its calling.

Ophelia sank onto a chair, elbows on the table, and half-laughed, half-coughed. "I'll try again."

Mira poured Ophelia a glass from the tap and set it in front of her like a prescription.

"Thank you," Ophelia said, mortified and grateful in equal measure. "I swear I am not a menace in every country. Just this one. So far."

Mira's mouth twitched. "You try again," she said. "But maybe... not kill oven."

The cat leapt onto a chair and batted a cooling biscuit in a satisfying arc that landed in the hall. A passing backpacker paused, sniffed, and called back in accented English, "Is there... cake?"

"Not even a little bit," Ophelia answered. "But if you want to risk it, pull up a chair."

Within minutes, the kitchen had become a pop-up tasting room. Travelers from rooms two and four drifted in on curiosity: a German student with a camera strapped to his chest, a Croatian mother and her teenage son, the British couple, and—because fate enjoys a supporting cast—Dino, who claimed with great pride that he could detect oregano in any dish blindfolded. He could not, however, detect politeness, and cheerfully announced, after a bite, "This one is like eating tire from small car."

Ophelia clasped a hand over her heart. "As a creator, I respect your honesty."

"Is good with beer," Dino added, as if to soften the blow.

"Everything is good with beer," the German student observed, photographing the splay of mutant biscuits like they were rare birds. "May I...?" He angled his lens for a dramatic shot of crumbs and sunlight.

"Please," Ophelia said. "If I can't offer food, I can offer ambience."

Mira slid a plate of sliced tomatoes and cheese onto the table, then—God bless practical women everywhere—set down a small jar of local honey. "Try," she instructed, tapping the jar. "Maybe help."

The idea hit Ophelia in the sternum with the soft force of memory. Honey. In Woodard, honey was how you forgave a biscuit its sins. She twisted the lid, drizzled amber over a survivor biscuit, and took a bite. The honey sank into the crumb, found the butter, and together they rose—still lopsided, still singed, but suddenly, surprisingly edible. She pushed the plate forward. "Y'all—sorry, you all—try this."

They did. The British couple hummed. The Croatian teen gave a solemn thumbs-up. Dino, who never met a declarative sentence he didn't want to improve, announced, "Acceptable."

Mira took a careful bite, chewed, and pointed with her chin at the honey jar. "Yes. Without this, no. With this... okay."

"*Okay* is a promotion," Ophelia said, oddly giddy. "Today I will happily be *okay*."

The German student lowered his camera. "What do you call them?"

"Back home?" Ophelia straightened, flour raining from her shirt like confetti. "Biscuits."

"Like... cookies?" the student asked, frowning.

"Not cookies. Different universe. These are... breakfast bread. Soft. Flaky. The thing you make when words aren't enough, and you need someone to feel loved. But mine—" She gestured to the tray with theatrical regret. "Mine are the distant cousins who show up uninvited and drink all the punch."

They laughed, the easy laughter of people brought together by food and failure. The sound loosened something lodged behind Ophelia's ribs. She tucked that sensation away like a warm coin. "Again," Mira said decisively, collecting a clean bowl from the shelf. "You make again. I show you."

Ophelia blinked. "You... you know biscuits?"

"I know dough," Mira replied, with the regal boredom of a woman who had been right a thousand times. "And oven." She pointed at Ophelia's notebook, at the ancestral riddle that passed for a recipe. "This is not recipe. This is poetry."

"Compliment accepted," Ophelia said, and slid off her chair. "Teach me your ways, Oven Whisperer."

They reassembled the battlefield: clean bowl, fresh flour, a measured—not hacked—portion of butter. Mira moved with unhurried economy, her hands sure, her instructions a mixture of gestures and words: "Cold," she said, tapping the butter. "Cold, cold." She worked it in with fingertips, lifting and letting fall so the pieces stayed pebbled, not paste. She sprinkled salt from a height, nodded at the baking powder—*prašak za pecivo*, Ophelia read, committing the phrase to memory like a spell. "Milk," Mira said, and when Ophelia reached for the box, Mira stayed her hand. "Slow. Like—" She mimed rain. "Not storm."

"Gentle hands," Ophelia whispered, the old phrase lighting

in her chest like a candle. She had not said it since the funeral. She had not trusted it. She had not remembered it could apply to anything beyond grief.

They coaxed the dough together until it barely held, tumbled it onto the floured counter, and folded it once, twice—no more. Mira pressed her knuckles to scatter the dough into a thick field. "Now," she said, scanning the tiny kitchen. "Cutter?"

Ophelia lifted the chipped teacup. "We make do."

"Dobro," Mira said, approving, and stamped neat rounds like moons. The room drew in to watch: the British couple, the Croatian teen, the German photographer, Dino pretending not to care and failing. Even the cat, freshly crumb-bearded, perched on a stool with the gravitas of a health inspector.

Into the oven they went. The dial read 200°C because, as Mira explained with a shrug, "Every oven is liar; this one lies less at two hundred."

They waited. Ophelia's heartbeat climbed the temperature scale with the biscuits. The room smelled different this time: not acrid, not panicked—warm and promising, a scent like a door opening. Mira peered through the glass and nodded once. "Now." She pulled the tray and the room leaned forward.

They weren't perfect. The tops were more uneven than Ophelia's hand remembered, the sides not quite as layered as Sunday mornings at Grandma's, but they were risen—honestly, stubbornly risen. Steam sighed from a cracked one as if it had something to confess. Ophelia's throat closed. She felt, obscenely, like crying over flour and fat. Instead, she laughed, a bright astonished sound, and clapped once, flour puffing from her palms like a benediction. "Hello, darlings."

They tasted again. Mira brought out honey and added a dish of local jam the color of rubies. The room hummed with approval like a hive. Dino, who had previously compared her work to automotive rubber, held up two fingers. "Two is good number," he decreed, and ate both.

The British wife dabbed her eyes. "My grandmother was

from Cornwall," she said. "We had scones. These are not the same, but they remind me of... her."

The Croatian teen, mouth full, declared, "Better than tire," and his mother swatted the back of his head without heat. The German student photographed the inside crumb with the solemnity of a war correspondent. Ophelia stood very still and let it happen. Let the validation land. Let the room's warmth press against the cold places. Let the simple miracle of *try again and it gets better* cross the language barrier.

When the second tray went in—because of course there was a second tray; hope is greedy—the door to the courtyard swung open and a neighbor appeared, drawn by rumor and scent. She was a woman in her fifties with red lipstick and the unapologetic posture of someone who could lift a washing machine alone. "Što se dešava?" she asked Mira, hands on hips. What's happening?

Mira gestured at Ophelia. "Amerikanka pravi... kako kaže... biscuits."

The neighbor's red mouth curled. "Keksi?"

"Ne," Mira said, and surprised Ophelia by laying a hand over her heart. "Njeni." *Hers.*

The neighbor appraised Ophelia for a long, alarming second, then held out a small jar tied with string. "Med," she said. Honey. "From my brother's hives."

Ophelia took it like a chalice. "Hvala," she said carefully, the thank you catching in her throat.

They broke bread—hers, theirs—at the tiny table: honey passed from palm to palm, jam replenished, tea poured. The cat, at last sated, sprawled in a patch of sun and offered a single magnanimous chirp.

"I am Vesna."

"Ophelia."

Later, when the last crumb had been argued over and the last laugh shaken loose, the crowd thinned in the gentle way of satisfied people. The British couple retreated to nap, the student to edit photos, the Croatian mother to scold her son for sticky fingers, Dino to boast at the front desk that he had improved a recipe by standing near it. The neighbor with the lipstick tapped the honey jar twice and pointed at the courtyard. "Tomorrow," she said. "Market. You come."

Mira wiped the counter with swift, sure strokes, then set the cloth down and regarded Ophelia. "You cook again," she said, not a question.

"If you'll let me," Ophelia answered. Her voice felt wider, like a road had been cleared inside it. "I... I'd like to try different flours. See what behaves. Maybe... show you how we do biscuits back home."

Mira's mouth quirked. "You show me yours. I show you mine." She nodded at the oven. "Next time—less fear, more butter."

Ophelia saluted. "Yes, Chef."

"Tomorrow, we'll try again. Now get out of my kitchen and go find yourself a husband."

11

phelia found herself wandering back through the Old Town Square and up toward the vacant shop she had seen. She tried to peer in through the edge of the boarded-up windows, but it was dark. "You need something?"

She jumped startled. "Oh no, just peaking in." The local man kept walking and she yelled after him, "do you know what this place was?"

He paused and looked at her up and down and then gruffly spoke, "yes." Then he turned and walked away.

She dropped her shoulders in annoyance and looked back at the building. Then she noticed a little sign to the right of the door that read... ***Izdaje se***

After another afternoon wandering around and buying flowers at the market she returned to her lodging and presented Mira with flowers offering her an apologetic face, "I'm sorry for almost burning down your house."

"Sweet girl. Go have seat. I'll make you something."

Mira started making a plate with cheese and bread and Ophelia asked, "Hey Mira, what does *Izdaje se* mean?"

"For rent. Why you want to leave me and rent something?"

Mira handed Ophelia the plate, "Thank you for the food, but no I am not leaving any time soon."

"Good. You stay forever." Mira sat down.

Ophelia laughed, "Stay forever! Ha. I wish."

"Your wish comes true. You stay. I find you husband and you stay."

"Mira! I don't need a husband to stay." Ophelia was shocked that those words had even escaped her lips.

"Ah... see you want to stay."

Ophelia looked at the plate of food and asked Mira, "Can I take this to the guestroom.?"

"Of course, go call your family and tell them you stay."

Ophelia laughed and then thought about it. Back in her room, she collapsed on the bed, shoes kicked off, hair slipping from its braid. She should have been exhausted. She was exhausted. But her mind buzzed like the bees that had made that honey. She snacked from the plate Mira made and then pulled out her phone. She had not looked at it since she arrived. She was ignoring the condolence messages.

She dialed Tilda, *"Well I'll be damned... I was about to send a search party out for you."*

"Well, I was starting to write some letters."

"Well, hell, we aren't living in the 1800's. Now tell me everything."

Ophelia dove right into everything and after an hour of talking she mustered up the courage to say that she was thinking about staying.

"Staying? Are you out of your mind"?

"I like it here. It feels like home strangely, but without the sympathy. Also, I like not having to be reminded of Charles every single day."

"You can't forget about him, darlin. Escaping isn't going to let you forget. Life just doesn't work like that."

"I know, I don't know. I'm getting tired."

"Okay but promise me you will call again."

"Okay I promise. And do me a favor and tell my parents and Grandma I'm fine."

"Will do. Talk soon. Keep your phone on! Love you Phee."

"Love you."

Ophelia hung up her phone and turned it off.

She pulled out her notebook and stared at the blank page. The urge to write was different tonight. Less of a wound spilling, more of a record keeping. She wanted to remember this, exactly as it was.

She wrote:

Today I burned biscuits so badly they could be classified as weapons. I filled a kitchen with smoke, terrified a cat, and probably shaved five years off Mira's life expectancy. But then—then something happened. People came. They laughed. They ate what I made, and no one spit it into a napkin. One woman even gave me honey from her brother's bees. And for the first time in months, I didn't feel like a woman orbiting grief. I felt... human. I felt like I belonged at a table again.

Her pen hovered. She swallowed, then added:

Maybe biscuits can do that. Maybe they can open doors in places I don't even speak the language. Maybe they can be my way back to the world.

Her throat tightened, but she didn't cry. Not tonight. Tonight, the grief folded itself into the background, softened by laughter, butter, and honey. She set the notebook aside and lay flat, staring at the ceiling. The old plaster was cracked in places, like veins. She traced them with her eyes until they blurred. She thought about her grandmother's kitchen—the sound of the oven door squealing open, the smell of biscuits rising like prayer. Then her thoughts drifted to Charles.

Her heart squeezed. She missed him so fiercely it felt like hunger. But she also realized something startling: today, the ache hadn't swallowed everything. Today, something else had slipped in alongside it—something lighter. It was terrifying. And it was hope. When she couldn't sit still any longer, she padded barefoot to the courtyard. The stones were cool under her feet.

Small moths darted lazily in the shadows. She sat on the same bench as the night before, the honey jar balanced in her lap like a talisman.

The bay stretched out beyond the alley, silvered by moonlight. The air smelled faintly of the sea, of rosemary growing somewhere close, of smoke lingering just enough to remind her she was human. She whispered into the quiet, "I think I could stay here, Charles. Just a little longer. Maybe long enough to bake a proper batch. Maybe long enough to find out what else biscuits can do."

The stars didn't answer, but the water lapped against the shore, steady and unhurried. For the first time, she let herself imagine a future that wasn't only survival. A future with flour under her fingernails, neighbors at her table, laughter in a kitchen that no longer scared her. When she finally went back inside, she tucked the honey jar on the bedside table, next to her notebook. She brushed flour from her hair, crawled under the blanket, and fell asleep smiling.

12

Ophelia carefully measured this time—well, more carefully. She whispered Grandma's advice—*gentle hands, gentle hands*—as she cut butter into the flour. She worked quickly, feeling the dough with her fingers, trying to catch the balance between too dry and too wet. She divided the dough into three bowls, one for each flour type, and shaped biscuits with the chipped teacup.

The oven was preheated—she'd learned that lesson the smoky way. She slid the trays in, shut the door, and crossed her flour-dusted fingers. Fifteen minutes later, the kitchen smelled less like tragedy and more like possibility. Ophelia leaned close to the oven window, squinting. "C'mon, babies. Rise up. Don't embarrass me in front of Mira again."

Mira stood behind her, arms still folded, expression unreadable. "They look... not terrible," she said finally.

Ophelia gasped. "Not terrible? That's basically a Michelin star."

When the timer chimed, she pulled the trays out with trembling hands. The biscuits weren't perfect, but they were *better*. The tip 400 flour batch had spread too thin, pale and flimsy. The tip 500 batch stood proud, golden but a little dense. The pastry flour batch—oh, the pastry flour batch was flaky, layered, the tops browned just enough to look promising.

Ophelia nearly cried. "Look at them! They are looking better!"

Mira broke one open, examined the crumb

with scientific detachment, and took a bite. She chewed. She swallowed. She nodded once.

"Not bad."

Ophelia clutched her chest. "Stop, you're going to make me blush."

She bit into one herself, and the taste nearly undid her. It wasn't exactly like home—different butter, different flour, a subtle tang she couldn't place—but it was good. Not perfect, not Grandma's, but real. And more than that, it felt like victory.

The door creaked open. Vesna, the red-lip sticked neighbor leaned in, nose twitching. "I smell something."

Ophelia waved her in like a proud hostess. "Biscuits, round two. Now with less smoke!"

Vesna sat at the table, accepted a biscuit with honey, and bit in. She chewed, then nodded. "Better."

Mira grunted. "She learns."

Ophelia grinned so hard her cheeks hurt. She didn't care. For the first time since Charles died, she felt like she'd done something right. Small, ridiculous, flour-covered—but right. And as she licked honey from her fingers, she thought, *what if I kept doing this? What if biscuits weren't just comfort? What if they were... a way forward?*

TILDA CALLING flashed on the screen, a tiny pulse of home.

Ophelia dried her palms on her apron and swiped. *"Ma'am,"* she said, already smiling. *"You are on speaker with the international butter authority."*

Tilda exhaled, the sound a mix of relief and opinion. *"What's cookin good lookin?"*

"I am, well baking. I just made biscuits without setting off the smoke alarm." Ophelia leaned her hip against the counter.

There was a beat of silence. Then: *"That's great!"*

"I'm improving," Ophelia said. "Today I managed 'not terrible.'"

"From who?"

"Mira. Say hi Mira."

Mira leaned into the phone. "Hello. Her biscuits- much better today... OH and do not worry, I will find her good husband."

"*Um... Okay,*" Tilda said briskly. "*Can you take me off speaker phone, Phee?*"

Ophelia pressed it off and held the phone up to her ear.

"*Do I need to come save you?*"

"No. I'm fine. What did my parents say?"

"*Well, I went over to talk to them, they said that they think you've lost your mind completely.*"

Ophelia sighed, "I'm sure."

"*Are you going to stay longer?*"

"For now, yes. I'm extending my trip. I'm not ready to come back yet. Just tell my parents I will call them when I'm ready to talk more but for now I'm baking and am taking my time."

"*Alright. Love you! Talk soon and promise to keep your phone on!*"

"I took your call, didn't I? So that's an improvement."

"*Yes! Bye, Phee.*"

Mira smiled at Ophelia when she got off phone. "Your friend."

"My best friend. Her name is Tilda. Hey Mira, I was wondering. Could I... bake for breakfast here? Sometimes? Trade for the room?"

Mira wiped her hands, considered. "Maybe," she said. "If people like. If oven obeys. We try small." She pinched her fingers together: *small.* "No promises."

Ophelia's heart thumped. "Small is fine."

Vesna's voice echoed faintly from the alley—she was bargaining with someone over anchovies with the zeal of a general suing for peace. Dino appeared in the doorway, sniffed like a bloodhound, and spotted the lone biscuit.

"This for me," he declared.

"That one is for science," Ophelia said, snatching it up. "But you may apply to the Bread Bureau for a sample."

He placed a hand to his heart. "I will remember this injustice."

"Bring me oregano," she shot back. "Blindfolded."

He grinned and vanished.

Ophelia broke the biscuit open. Steam ribboned up. She didn't reach for honey this time. She wanted the taste as it was—plain, honest, earnest. She bit in and closed her eyes. It was not Woodard. It was not the morning after the wedding, when she had sat in a new dress and believed in forever because it was in the room with her. It was not her grandmother's kitchen with the window stuck half-open and the radio preaching weather. "Okay," she said to the biscuit, to the room, to the day. "Let's see what you can do."

She sat at the tiny table with her notebook, the honey jar, and what remained of the latest batch—three biscuits, a little sunburned around the edges, proud in the middle. Her forearms were floured to the elbow; she'd rubbed at a streak on her cheek and only succeeded in smearing it artfully like war paint. A cooling breeze slipped in and lifted a corner of the dish towel as if trying to peek.

She dated the page, ("bread diaries or bust"), and began listing the day's evidence like a detective:

- Tip 500 + pastry flour split: 60/40 worked best—rise decent, layers visible.
- Salt adjustment: + ½ tsp woke up the crumb without picking a fight.
- Cream brush: gorgeous color but watch the hotspots in Mira's oven—turn tray at 8 minutes.
- Reaction log: Vesna: "Not shameful." Men at café: jokes ⟶ chewing ⟶ "not pizza." Dino: legacy of automotive metaphors continues. Market kids: sticky approval.

She paused and set the pen down. The list was practical, useful, something she could test tomorrow. But the current running under it pulsed louder: that feeling at the café table when the mocking had melted into chewing; the quiet nod from the card-playing king who decided her biscuits didn't need to be pizza to matter; the unexpected weight of an onion pressed into her palm like coin.

She pushed the biscuits together on the plate so their sides touched—like a little family huddled on a ship's deck—and let herself see it clearly: a stall at the market with a hand-lettered sign, Vesna's honey shining like captive sunlight, Mira's coffee steaming in paper cups, a basket lined with a checked towel, people she didn't know reaching for food she had made and laughing with their mouths full. Not pity. Not condolence. Just appetite and pleasure and opinion.

The picture lit her chest in a soft, steady way. It didn't feel like replacing Charles. It didn't feel like betraying Woodard. It felt like finding a place to set all the love that had nowhere to go. She picked up a biscuit and split it; steam unfurled in a thin ribbon. She ate the heel plain—honest, without the kindness of honey—and thought of the first weeks after the aneurysm, when everything had tasted like cardboard. Taste was back. Hunger was back. Wanting was back, in small, manageable portions.

"Well?" said a voice, dry as the good corner of a pan.

Mira stood in the doorway, a ledger tucked under one arm, her gaze taking in the notebook, the biscuits, the woman at the table who looked like she had crawled out of a flour avalanche and decided to build a house on the slope.

Ophelia smiled. "Status: stubborn."

Mira grunted, which in Mira-speak could mean anything from *the toilet is broken* to *I am pleased for you as one would be for a niece who has finally found a functional partner.* She crossed the room and sat, setting the ledger down like a chaperone. "Tomorrow," she said, "I need small things for breakfast. Not many. Ten? Twelve?" She pinched the air to indicate modesty. "We try to sell. If sell, then more."

Ophelia blinked. Her heart, which had been behaving like a reasonable organ for the last hour, sprang up and did a clumsy two-step. "You mean... my—?"

"Your biscuits," Mira said, as though explaining gravity. "With honey. Maybe small jam." She tilted her chin at the jar. "Vesna will stand like lion and guard the sugar."

Ophelia laughed, a helpless little sound. "I don't have proper cutters. I don't have—"

"You have hands," Mira said. "You have teacup. You have brain. Enough." She flicked a crumb from the table toward the cat, who had materialized from nowhere with the resigned entitlement of a duke. "Also, you have cat. Important."

"I have named him Goliath," Ophelia said solemnly. "We have reached a detente. He only steals butter designated for chaos."

Mira stood, already bored with gratitude. "In morning, come early. We test again."

Ophelia agreed, "We test again!"

13

awn undid the dark with quiet fingers. The bells counted a tender hour, and Ophelia woke before they finished, heart already working on the day's math. She dressed in the good shirt—the one that made her feel like she had a collarbone worth rooting for—and tied her hair back with a strip of cloth that had once been the lining of a gift bag. Shoes: sensible, purchased yesterday under the combined terror of Mira's glare. She bounced on the balls of her feet and did not wince. Victory.

In the kitchen, the air was cool, the counter bare and expectant. She laid out tools like talismans: bowl, pastry cutter (okay, knife), teacup, measuring spoons that didn't measure quite right but close enough if you squinted. Ingredients followed: pastry flour and tip 500 in their chalked jars, salt, baking powder with its stern Montenegrin label, butter in cubes she'd chilled in a metal bowl like jewels, the thick cream, the milk that no longer offended her by being warm on the shelf. The honey jar watched from the corner like a small sun with opinions.

"Gentle hands," she said aloud, and felt the words settle her shoulders.

She worked. Butter into flour until it felt just right. Salt scattered like good gossip. Baking powder sifted in a tiny hiss. Milk slow as weather, cream folded like a secret. She turned the dough onto the counter and coaxed it; she did not argue with it. Fold, turn; fold, turn. Teacup, stamp—hello, moon. Arrange on the tray so the sides touch: let them help one another rise.

Brush the tops with cream. Whisper something soft for luck, even if luck is just the memory of other hands doing this same ridiculous, ordinary magic in another kitchen on another morning.

The oven, primed and stern, received them without complaint. She cleaned because cleaning was prayer. At eight minutes, she turned the tray; at twelve, she peered in; at fourteen, she pulled them: gold at the tips, tender in the middle, one with a crack that looked like a grin. Steam rose and carried a smell that had crossed an ocean to find her.

Mira appeared, as she always did when judgment and plates were required. She lifted one, tore it, nodded once. "Good enough," she decreed, and set three on a saucer with Vesna's honey and two little jars of jam. "Front desk," she said. "We see."

Ophelia walked the plate out like a crown on a pillow. The lobby was a morning diorama: a pair of hikers tying boots, a mother whispering threats of love to a child resisting socks. Dino pretending to polish the desk bell while scrolling his phone. One of the hikers sniffed the air and looked up at Ophelia. He wandered over to her and politely asked, "Ah," he said, "what is this?"

"Breakfast," Ophelia said sweetly. "For our paying customers."

He took one, bit, and did not fake his nonchalance well. "Okay," he said, mouth full. Then, with a cough, "Price?"

Ophelia blinked. She looked to Mira. Mira named a number that did not embarrass either side of the counter. The hiker agreed and then pulled an extra euro out of his pocket and gave it to Ophelia. "For the bread."

"Biscuit and thank you." Ophelia slipped the Euro back to Mira and winked.

Pretty soon there was a sign out that said **Biscuits 1 Euro.** The second buyer was a woman with a guidebook and a kindness in her eyes that looked like morning light. She paid, took a bite, closed her eyes, and reached for the honey with the reverence of a believer. "Oh," she said. "Oh, that tastes like... Sunday."

"Which one?" Ophelia asked, startled.

"All of them," the woman said, smiling, and the coin chimed in the dish.

Two hikers bought one to split. A businessman took one to go and came back exactly six minutes later for a second with jam. Vesna swept in, kissed Ophelia on both cheeks as if she'd invented bread, pointed at the card, and said, "Raise price," like a threat. Ophelia laughed and didn't. Not yet.

By ten o'clock, the plate was empty. By ten-fifteen, Ophelia had to sprint back to the kitchen for another batch, Mira's eyebrow at her back like a riding crop.

"Small," Mira reminded, but her eyes were bright.

Between batches, Ophelia ducked into the courtyard, leaned against the cool stone, and let herself feel it—properly, fully—without bracing for it to be taken. Not a dream. Not yet a bakery. But a table where her work sat and became part of other people's mornings. The ache for Charles flared hot and clean—he should have been here.

"I'm doing it," she told the slice of bay she could see through the alley's throat. "You pointed, and I'm walking."

A shadow moved; Vesna slid into the light with the quiet of a cat burglar. She thrust a small, battered tin at Ophelia. Inside: recipe cards, the old kind, grease-soft, stained with fingerprints. "My mother's *pogača* notes," Vesna said. "You don't copy. You... hm." She tapped Ophelia's chest. "You read. You learn. You make your own." Her red mouth softened. "We are not same bread. But we are same hands."

Ophelia blinked away the thin, traitor tears. "Hvala," she managed.

"Don't say thank you," Vesna sniffed. "Say *come for coffee.* I bring gossip."

"I will," Ophelia said, laughing. "Bring salt opinions too."

"Always," Vesna promised, and vanished like a stage magician.

In the kitchen, Ophelia laid the cards beside her grandmother's lawless page. Two women, strangers, living in different languages, were suddenly shoulder to shoulder on her counter. She copied nothing. She folded their presence into the dough with the butter, lifting and letting fall the way Mira had shown her, the way Grandma would have approved of without saying so.

By noon, she'd learned the rhythm: mix, bake, sell, breathe. Dino had a running tally of "research samples" that would shame a rat in a maze. A backpacker had asked if she did savory ("cheese inside?"), and Ophelia had scribbled *cheddar? local? herbs?* in her notebook. And when it finally slowed, when the saucer was empty a second time and the coffee urn hissed its last humility, Ophelia slipped into the alley with her notebook and wrote the only thing that mattered:

Today I sold ten. Then twelve. People ate what I made and paid for it, and my heart remembered a word I had not trusted: possible.

She underlined it. Twice. She added, smaller:

I am not okay in the way people mean when they ask kindly and don't want the real answer. I am okay like a dough that's still shaggy but will come together with two more folds. I am okay like a biscuit that's leaning but will rise if you tuck it against its neighbor.

She closed the notebook, rested her palms against its warm cardboard, and lifted her face to the slice of blue that hung between stone walls. A gull careened through, noisy and entitled. Somewhere, a bell tripped over the hour. The bay kept breathing like a good example.

"Alright," she said to the air, to Charles, to the oven that was teaching her and being learned in return. "I won't quit."

It felt less like a vow and more like a muscle moving the way it was designed.

Back inside, she washed bowls and set them to drying. She

lined up the teacup with a small reverence that made her want to roll her eyes at herself and didn't. She tucked Vesna's tin on the highest shelf like a relic. She left her notebook open on the counter to the page where the word *possible* glowed like a pilot light.

When she turned toward the doorway, Goliath blocked it with the bone-deep entitlement of a cat who had outlived empires. He inspected her ankles, then the counter, then—grudgingly—accepted a tiny flake of biscuit like a monarch allowing fealty. "Don't get used to it," she told him.

He blinked, which was agreement in cat law.

The rest of the day unfolded in ordinary ways that felt miraculous because she had a place inside them. A run to the market where a child announced "biskvit lady!" and she did not correct him. A stop at the shoe shop to thank the owner for saving her heels from mutiny. A text to Tilda of the little price card; Tilda responded with a voice note of herself whooping and crying and threatening to sue anyone who said *scone.* A message from Grandma—just a heart and a biscuit emoji that one of the cousins had surely taught her to find.

When the light went gold again, Ophelia stood by the water and watched a boat lay a white stitch across the bay's blue fabric. She touched the anchor tag on her suitcase in her mind the way you touch your throat to feel your own pulse.

"Stubborn as a biscuit," she said, smiling. "And rising."

14

By the third morning of the experiment, the guesthouse breakfast table looked like a low-stakes miracle. The saucer of biscuits was gone before the second coffee pot emptied, and Dino was forced to start keeping a written tally because Mira caught him with crumbs on his shirt and accused him, correctly, of "sampling" too many.

Ophelia baked twelve. They sold twelve. She baked sixteen. They sold sixteen. By the time she made twenty, she thought she was clever, but a bus tour deposited hungry Germans in the lobby and she had to sprint back to the oven mid-bake, flour streaking her cheek like war paint.

She moved like a woman in a sitcom: sprinting, dodging hikers with backpacks, sliding into the kitchen like a baseball player, pulling trays out with an oven mitt in one hand and her phone buzzing in the other. Her hair frizzed into a halo of humidity and heat, and Mira, watching with the flat amusement of someone who has seen Americans self-destruct before, occasionally muttered, "You need bigger bowl."

At 10:15, Ophelia leaned against the counter, fanning herself with a folded recipe card. Mira was tallying coins in a small tin with the kind of precision that suggested each cent had to explain itself.

"We sold out again," Ophelia said, voice half astonishment, half plea.

"Yes," Mira replied, not looking up.

"This is... this is real."

"Yes."

Ophelia laughed, giddy. "You could show a little more enthusiasm."

Mira glanced at her; one eyebrow raised. "Enthusiasm doesn't wash dishes."

Ophelia giggled so hard she had to cover her face with the recipe card.

When Dino appeared, already reaching for the empty plate, Mira slapped his hand

"Gone."

"Tomorrow?" Dino whined.

"Yes," Ophelia promised, finding herself suddenly in the role of town carb supplier.

"Tomorrow."

She scribbled in her notebook between batches, her handwriting messy with heat:

Third day running: sold out. Word of mouth traveling faster than I can knead. Mira pretending to scowl but counted the coins twice, and I swear she smiled when she thought I wasn't looking. Dino angling for free samples like a raccoon in a tie. Tourists asking if I'll open a shop. A shop. As though I'm capable of anything beyond keeping my hair out of the dough. Still, I didn't hate the sound of it. A shop.

She closed the notebook before she could terrify herself further.

By early afternoon, the kitchen was clean, and the guesthouse smelled faintly of butter, honey, and coffee—an accidental advertisement to every passerby in the alley. Ophelia carried a plate of the last two biscuits into the courtyard, collapsed into a chair, and let the sun slap her in the face.

Vesna materialized, as she often did, like a well-accessorized ghost. She plucked one biscuit off the plate, sniffed it, and took a bite. "Better," she announced. "You put soul in this one."

Ophelia laughed. "I also put more butter."

"Same thing." Vesna licked her fingers. "What will you do when you leave?"

The question landed with the weight of an anchor. Ophelia stared at the last biscuit on the plate. "Leave?"

"Yes. You are tourist. Tourists leave."

Ophelia's stomach tightened. She thought about her return ticket, about the word *temporary* like a stamp across her forehead. She thought about her grandmother's house back in Woodard, the empty rooms, the pitying eyes at the church. She thought about how, for the first time since Charles's death, she felt the air moving through her lungs without protest.

"I don't want to leave," she said quietly.

Vesna raised one eyebrow, a mirror of Mira. "Then don't."

"It's not that simple."

Mira appeared, "What are we talking about?"

"I want to stay here in Kotor" Ophelia stated.

Mira announced, "But wanting and doing—different. You have visa?"

"Uh..." Ophelia's stomach swooped. "A tourist one. Ninety days."

Mira nodded once, decisive. "Then you cannot stay. Not without paper. Not without plan."

Vesna rolled her eyes. "Always with paper. Sometimes life is more than stamps."

"Sometimes life is prison if you don't have stamps," Mira retorted.

Ophelia leaned forward, voice thin. "So, what happens if I just... don't leave? I mean, hypothetically."

Both women looked at her with matching expressions of horror. "Do not be stupid," Mira said flatly. "They fine you. They ban you. They put you on plane. Then no more biscuits here. Only in your sad American town."

Ophelia flushed, caught between laughter and panic. "I don't want to be banned."

"Then you ask," Mira said. "Tourist office. Government building.

Find out how. You want to work? You need paper. You want to live? You need paper. This is not complicated."

Vesna waved her cigarette. "She could marry someone."

Mira's head whipped around. "What are you saying?"

"It is the oldest trick in the book," Vesna said innocently. "Find handsome fisherman, say vows, boom—paperwork done."

Ophelia nearly choked on air. "Oh my God."

"You said you were married already," Vesna reminded her with a shrug. "You know how it works. Why not practice again?"

Ophelia pressed her palms to her cheeks, torn between hysterical laughter and a sob. "I cannot even think about that."

Mira, surprisingly, softened. "She is right. Not now. But there are ways. Work visa. Residency. You must look."

Ophelia clutched the edge of the table, staring at the stone beneath her feet. She had thought grief was complicated enough—how to breathe, how to eat, how to make it through one day without cracking. Now she was contemplating immigration law, as though her heart had dragged her into a bureaucracy she had not studied for.

"I just... I don't want to wake up in Woodard," she admitted, her throat tight. "I want to wake up here. With the bells. With the biscuits. Even if it's hard, I want here."

Mira watched her for a long moment. Then she nodded once, as if the case had been presented and accepted. "Then go to tourist office. Say you want to stay. They will laugh. Then they will give you paper. Then we see."

Vesna stubbed out her cigarette and leaned back. "And if they do not give you paper, you make biscuits so good the government begs you to stay."

Mira stood, gathering her ledger. "Ask first. Bake second. Paper and promises. In that order." She paused at the doorway, then added, "But don't stop baking."

The door shut behind her. Vesna reached across the table and squeezed Ophelia's hand with a lacquered grip. "She is right. You are afraid. But you are also stubborn. Stubborn women find ways."

Ophelia stood up and pat down on the table, "There is nothing more stubborn that a woman from the south!"

Mira grinned and patted her on the arm, "Yes! I like *this* Ophelia."

15

The next morning, Ophelia marched out of the guesthouse armed with two weapons: determination and a tote bag full of biscuits wrapped in a towel. The biscuits weren't for bribery, she told herself—they were for emotional support. Portable courage. Like an edible therapy dog.

The "Tourist Information Center" was only two streets away, tucked between a gelato shop and a jewelry store that displayed necklaces in velvet boxes as though they were auditioning for royalty. The center was fronted by a cheerful blue awning that promised guidance to lost travelers, but the moment she pushed inside, Ophelia realized she was entering another world: the sacred temple of bureaucracy.

The air smelled faintly of paper and disinfectant. A fan turned lazily in the corner, making more noise than wind. Behind the counter sat a woman in her forties with sharp cheekbones and nails painted the exact color of a stop sign. She was scrolling through her phone with the focus of a surgeon, occasionally nodding at something only she could see.

"Dobar dan," Ophelia said, trying to summon every bit of courage her Southern upbringing and three biscuits could provide.

The woman glanced up, unimpressed. "Yes?"

"I, um." Ophelia stepped forward. "I'm an American. And I... well, I really like it here." Her voice cracked. "A lot. And I was wondering what the, uh, legalities are... for staying longer. Maybe working."

The woman blinked. Then she sighed, pushed

aside her phone, and reached under the counter. She surfaced with a pamphlet so thin it could have been a cocktail napkin.

"Residency information," she said flatly.

Ophelia unfolded it. The text was in Montenegrin on one side, English on the other. The English side read:

HOW TO STAY IN MONTENEGRO: A SIMPLE GUIDE

Step 1: Apply for residency.
Step 2: Fill forms.
Step 3: Provide documents.
Step 4: Wait.
Step 5: Success.

Ophelia stared. "Um. This seems... vague."

The woman shrugged. "It is simple."

"But what forms? What documents?"

The woman leaned back, as though bored by the concept of specificity. "Passport. Money. Proof of purpose. Or..." She smiled faintly, as though amused at an inside joke. "You marry."

Ophelia almost dropped the biscuits. "Excuse me?"

"Many Americans marry. Easy."

"Oh no, no, no." Ophelia's hands flapped like birds. "I'm not—I mean, I just lost my husband. I'm not ready to—this is not about marrying someone, this is about—biscuits."

The woman tilted her head. "Biscuits?"

Ophelia thrust the towel-wrapped bundle forward. "Yes. I bake them. Southern-style. Fluffy, buttery, sometimes edible. People like them here. I thought maybe... I could, you know... make a business."

The woman's stop-sign nails drummed on the counter. Then, slowly, she unwrapped the towel, plucked a biscuit, and took a bite.

Silence.

Ophelia held her breath.

Finally, the woman said, "Not pizza."

Ophelia exhaled. "Correct! Thank you!"

The woman finished chewing, then shrugged. "For business, you need business visa. You make company. Papers. Taxes." She waved her hand as though these were minor inconveniences, like gnats. "Go to Podgorica for details."

"Podgorica?" Ophelia squeaked.

"Yes. Capital. Very simple."

Ophelia thought about trains, buses, forms. She thought about standing in another office where someone would hand her another pamphlet that said, "Step 1: Have documents." Her stomach dropped.

"Or marry, I have a brother who is single. He good looking. Make you very happy and you will have many sons," the woman added helpfully, as if circling back to her favorite solution.

Ophelia grabbed her biscuits, mumbled thanks, and bolted into the street.

She sat on a stone bench in the square, staring at the pamphlet. Tourists drifted around her, snapping photos of the clock tower, licking gelato, adjusting wide-brimmed hats. She felt like she was in the wrong play, a background extra with flour in her hair.

Step 1: Apply for residency. Sure. Easy. Just like *Step 1: Fix your heart.*

She unwrapped a biscuit, tore it in half, and ate both pieces too fast. The butter hit her system like a small prayer.

"Complicated?" a voice asked.

Ophelia looked up to see Mira standing there, as though the universe had sent her. Mira glanced at the pamphlet, snorted, and sat down. "They give this to everyone. It means nothing."

"Great," Ophelia said weakly. "So, I'm still just a tourist with a dough addiction."

"You need lawyer," Mira said matter-of-factly. "Paper is always paper. But lawyer can put paper in right pile."

"A lawyer," Ophelia repeated.

"Yes. Maybe accountant. Maybe both. Depends. But first, you

decide. Do you want to stay one year? Two? Forever? If forever, more paper."

Ophelia pressed her hands over her face. "This is so overwhelming."

Mira patted her knee once, the emotional equivalent of a gold medal in Mira-lympics. "Everything new is overwhelming. First batch of biscuits. First day after he died. First morning here. You did those."

Ophelia's throat closed. Mira's bluntness always landed like a blow and a balm at the same time.

"I just..." She swallowed hard. "I want to belong here. Not just sneak around on a ninety-day countdown. I want to be... allowed."

Mira nodded once. "Then you fight paper. Same as you fight dough. Stubborn."

Ophelia wiped her eyes, laughed wetly. "Stubborn as a biscuit."

"Yes," Mira said. "And biscuits rise. Come, I take you somewhere."

"Somewhere?" Ophelia asked confused.

"Yes, follow me."

~

Mira guided her to a building with peeling paint and windows that reflected the bay.

"Go inside and say you want residency." Mira demanded.

"You're not coming?"

"Something you need to do for you. This is learning." Mira pointed at the door.

Ophelia nodded, and slowly walked inside. The clerk's desk was stacked with folders in pastel colors that looked more decorative than functional.

"Hi, do you speak English?" Ophelia asked a young man with gelled hair that looked friendly. He greeted her with suspicious cheer.

"Yes, hello! How can I help?"

Ophelia clutched her tote. "Residency? I'd like to know how an American can stay. Legally."

The man grinned. "Ah! Very good. Many ways. Marriage. Job. Investment. Marriage easiest."

Ophelia groaned. "Does everyone here think marriage is like ordering a sandwich?"

The man blinked. "You do not like sandwiches?"

She pressed her palm to her forehead. "Never mind. Let's say... job. Baking. I would like to open a bakery."

He tapped his pen thoughtfully. "You open company. Pay tax. Hire people. Very good for Montenegro."

Ophelia perked up. "Yes! That's what I want!"

"Okay." He reached into a drawer and pulled out... another pamphlet. This one even thinner.

It said, simply:

HOW TO OPEN COMPANY IN MONTENEGRO

Step 1: Forms.
Step 2: Notary.
Step 3: Bank.
Step 4: Tax.
Step 5: Profit.

Ophelia stared at it, then at him. "That's... that's it?"

"Yes!" He beamed. "Very easy."

Her laugh came out like a sob. "Easy? That's the least helpful thing I've ever read, and I once tried to assemble IKEA furniture using only the Swedish side of the instructions."

The man shrugged, unbothered. "Lawyer will help."

His phone started to ring, and he picked it up and started speaking in Montenegrin, Ophelia whispered, "How do I find a lawyer?"

He shushed her away flinging his hand at her like she was a fly bothering him. Ophelia shoved the pamphlet in her tote, thanked him, and stumbled outside before she dissolved completely.

Mira grinned. "Marriage is still best option."

Ophelia pointed at her. "Do not start with me."

Mira, unbothered, "So. Paper. Lawyer. Slow. But possible."

Ophelia dropped her head into her hands. "I don't know whether to laugh or cry."

"Both," Mira said simply. "It helps."

"Why are you helping me?"

"Because I like you first and most, because like you I know what it's like to lose husband and be scared. Feel alone. So alone. All alone." Mira sighed and looked off to the distance, but before Ophelia could speak Mira put her hand on her shoulder and said, "You make good biscuits. I see new business opportunity for us."

"For us?"

"Yes. I have gotten, how you say? Tired? Borrred."

"Bord."

"Yes, bord with hotel business. It was husband's dream. Not mine. I think I want new business."

"New?"

"Yes, so, I help you start your bakery, because I like food, I like making food."

Ophelia was shocked. "You want to help me open this bakery."

"Yes. I invest in you."

"Really? That's amazing!"

"I spoke to my dead husband's family and they say they will help run hotel for me until we get you going on your two feet."

Ophelia hugged her tightly. So tight Mira gasped.

Mira hugged back, "I know you need me. Maybe, I need you most... more...most?"

Ophelia, "Either one! Oh, my stars! I'm so excited. Let's get back to the hotel. We have so much to talk about."

"Let's buy wine first. I need drink."

"Great idea Mira!"

16

Ophelia sat outside staring at the pamphlets spread out in front of her like a bad poker hand. They flapped in the breeze, taunting her with their minimalist steps: *forms, bank, tax, marriage.* "Ridiculous," she muttered. The truth was, for the first time since Charles's death, she had a goal. A ridiculous, bureaucratic, paperwork-laden goal. Stay. Not visit. Not linger. Stay. It terrified her.

Back in Woodard, she'd barely been able to fill out her husband's death certificate forms without collapsing. She'd barely done anything with her life. Marrying Charles was the beginning of her life and now that he was gone, she had nothing there. Now she was contemplating navigating an entire foreign legal system with pamphlets written by minimalists who clearly thought humans could intuit tax codes. She laughed out loud, startling a pigeon off the wall.

"I bring wine and ledger. Make notes" Mira declared, setting her ledger on the table with two full glasses of wine.

Ophelia nodded and pulled herself together like a soldier going to battle. She took a long drink and stated, "I'm staying. Paperwork, business, whatever it takes. I'm not going back to Woodard. I can't go back."

Mira studied her for a moment, then gave the faintest smile. "Good. I already called lawyer."

Ophelia exhaled, almost giddy. "You did?"

Mira shrugged. "Yes, and good news he is single. So, if he can't get you to stay and fix your problem. He can always marry you and then problem fixed no matter what!"

"Oh, for heaven sakes, Mira!"

~

Later that day, she texted Tilda: *Bad news: I need a lawyer. Good news: I'm officially plotting to stay. I even have an investor. You'll have to come to Montenegro if you want to drag me home.*

Tilda responded with thirty-seven celebratory emojis and a voice memo that said simply, *"HELL. YES."*

Ophelia laughed so hard she had to stop rolling dough. She looked out the kitchen window at the bay, glittering under the sun, and felt something she hadn't trusted in a long time: permanence. Maybe not legal yet. Maybe not simple. But real.

~

The next day both Ophelia and Mira arrived at a building that looked like it had been assembled from spare parts of three other buildings. The plaque on the door read: **LEGAL & OTHER MATTERS – Dragan Popović, Esq.** The "Esq." was scratched, as though someone had questioned it.

Inside, the waiting room smelled faintly of cigarettes and copy toner. A dusty plant leaned against the wall like it had given up years ago. A secretary with bubblegum-pink nails gestured for them to sit. Mira sat. Ophelia perched, clutching her tote like it was a life vest. After ten minutes, a man in his fifties appeared, tall, balding, with glasses that slid dangerously low on his nose. He wore a suit that might once have been navy but had surrendered to a vague grayness. "Ladies," he said grandly, ushering them in. "Welcome. I am Dragan. I solve problems."

"I am Mira," Mira said, not bothering with pleasantries. She shoved Ophelia forward. "She is American. Wants to stay. You help her stay."

Dragan clasped his hands together. "Ah. Residency. Easy."

Ophelia blinked. "Really?"

"Yes. Easy." He leaned back in his chair, which squeaked ominously. "First, you marry."

Ophelia dropped her head down on his desk.

Mira crossed her arms. "She will not marry."

"Fine, fine." Dragan waved his hand. "Then business. Very easy also. You create company. Pay tax. Hire people. Provide documents. Done."

"That doesn't sound easy at all," Ophelia said weakly.

"Of course, not easy," Dragan said cheerfully. "But easy."

Ophelia stared. "That doesn't make sense."

"Law never makes sense," Dragan replied.

Mira, unamused, leaned forward. "Tell her steps. Clear."

Dragan adjusted his glasses, rummaged through a drawer, and pulled out a stack of forms. They looked like they had been photocopied during the Cold War. He spread them across the desk like playing cards. "Step one: bank account. Step two: notary. Step three: application. Step four: wait. Step five: celebrate."

Ophelia squinted. "This is almost identical to the pamphlet."

"Yes, but bigger font," Dragan said proudly.

Mira glared. "What about documents?"

Dragan ticked them off on his fingers. "Passport. Birth certificate. Proof of address. Proof of income. Police clearance." He paused, then added, "Possibly blood type."

Ophelia's jaw dropped. "Blood type?!"

"Maybe not," Dragan admitted. "Depends on the mood of the officer."

Ophelia buried her face in her hands. "I can't do this."

"You can," Mira said firmly, "and she will."

Dragan leaned across the desk. "Or, you marry."

"Mira, I swear—"

Mira held up a hand. "No marriage."

Dragan shrugged, as though disappointed in their lack of imagination. "Then business." He tapped the forms. "Do not worry. Everyone confused. Even Montenegrins confused. Confusion is part of culture."

Ophelia peeked through her fingers. "Confusion is a culture?"

"Yes," Dragan said solemnly. "We drink coffee, we argue, we fill wrong forms, we try again. This is Montenegro."

She wanted to scream. Instead, she laughed. The sound came out high and shaky, but it was laughter, nonetheless. After half an hour of incomprehensible explanations—something about notarizing her late husband's will, something about needing "company stamp" even though she didn't have a company, something about taxes being due "yesterday but also never"—Ophelia staggered out into the street, Mira at her side. "I am doomed," she muttered.

"You are not doomed," Mira said briskly. "You are American. Americans never doomed. They just loud."

Ophelia clutched her tote. "He said I might need my blood type."

Mira actually snorted. "He lies. Or jokes. Hard to tell."

"Great. So now I don't just need a lawyer, I need a lawyer translator."

"I translate," Mira said.

They stopped for coffee at a tiny café tucked in the wall. The waiter placed two tiny cups in front of them. Mira sipped hers in silence. Ophelia stirred too much sugar into hers and stared at the bay beyond the narrow alley. "What if I can't do it?" she whispered.

Mira didn't answer right away. She tapped the edge of her cup, her expression unreadable. Finally, she said, "You will."

"Why are you helping me?"

"Because I like you... and I don't like anybody."

"That might just be one of the best compliments of my life."

17

The morning after her meeting with Dragan-the-Lawyer-or-Magician-of-Confusion, Ophelia woke with a headache made of paperwork. She had dreamed of endless forms chasing her through Kotor's alleys, each page demanding her blood type while a notary shouted "STAMP! STAMP!" like a deranged cheerleader. She sat up in bed, clutching her tote like a teddy bear, and muttered, "I need more butter."

By the time she stumbled into the kitchen, Mira already had flour measured out and her hair tied back like a general preparing troops.

"You look dead," Mira observed.

"I feel dead," Ophelia croaked, tying on her apron. "But biscuits wait for no woman."

"Yes," Mira said. Then, softer: "Good."

And so, they baked. The smell of butter lifted her spirits enough that when the first knock came at the door—a pair of British honeymooners demanding "the famous biscuits" before they climbed the fortress wall—Ophelia found herself laughing instead of panicking. She slid them a bag of biscuits, pocketed the coins, and thought: *Maybe fame is good currency, too.*

After the morning rush, Vesna appeared in the courtyard, her honey jars gleaming like amber suns in the light. She plopped herself into a chair with all the grace of a cat that knew it owned the place. "You look like woman who lost fight with dragon," Vesna said, watching Ophelia collapse into the opposite chair.

"Close," Ophelia sighed. "I lost a fight with Dragan. The lawyer."

"Pfft." Vesna waved her hand. "He is not dragon. He is mosquito. Annoying, not dangerous. You need better lawyer."

"I don't need a better lawyer," Ophelia said miserably. "I need a miracle."

Vesna leaned forward, eyes glittering. "Sometimes miracle is just woman who refuses to stop." She tapped the biscuit in her hand. "Like you."

Ophelia felt heat rise in her cheeks. "I'm just... baking. Anyone can bake."

"No." Vesna shook her head fiercely. "Anyone can burn. Few can bake. You make people smile. You make me sell more honey. You make Mira... well, not smile, but less frown. This is power."

Ophelia blinked at her. "Power?"

"Yes," Vesna said firmly. "Biscuits are power. Use them."

Ophelia laughed, because what else could she do? But later, as she swept flour off the counter, she thought maybe Vesna was right. Maybe biscuits could be more than comfort food. Maybe they could be leverage.

That afternoon, Dino swaggered into the kitchen with his usual aura of trouble.

"Auntie," he announced, "I have idea for your business."

"I'm not your aunt," Ophelia said automatically.

"Details," Dino said with a dramatic shrug. "Listen. You need name. Very important. All great businesses have name."

Ophelia raised an eyebrow. "Like what?"

"Like... Biscuit Kingdom." He spread his arms wide as though unveiling a palace.

"That sounds like a children's board game," Ophelia said.

"Okay, okay. What about... Queen of Dough?"

Ophelia snorted. "That sounds like a bad romance novel."

Dino frowned, undeterred. "Fine. Butter Empire?"

She shook her head.

"Okay... Biscuit Baba?"

Ophelia wheezed with laughter. "That sounds like a fairy tale witch who lures children with carbs."

Dino grinned. "Exactly. Memorable."

"Dino, stop tormenting her," Mira called from the doorway, but Ophelia was still laughing, and for the first time all week, it wasn't nervous laughter.

Later that evening, she ventured into the small café by the square where a cluster of older men always played cards and gossiped in rapid-fire Montenegrin. She had walked past them a dozen times, always feeling like an outsider intruding on a secret club. But tonight, armed with a basket of leftover biscuits, she decided to risk it. "Dobro veče," she said, setting the basket on their table.

The men paused mid-card, eyeing her suspiciously. One of them muttered something that sounded like "tourist."

Ophelia pushed the basket closer. "Biscuits. Try."

They exchanged glances. Finally, the oldest man—a wiry fellow with eyebrows that could have hosted small birds—picked one up. He sniffed it, broke it in half, and took a bite.

Silence.

Then he nodded once, slowly, like a judge delivering a verdict. "Good."

The others dove in. Soon the table was littered with crumbs, and the men were grunting approval. One even raised his glass of rakija in her direction. Ophelia smiled so hard her cheeks ached.

"See?" Vesna's voice rang out from the doorway. "Biscuits conquer."

The men muttered in agreement, and one even said something that sounded suspiciously like "better than pizza."

Ophelia nearly fainted. That was practically sainthood in Kotor.

"What do you know about that shop in the Old Town Square that is for rent?" She asked. Surprised the men all looked at each other and started whispering in Montenegrin. "English please?"

Finally, one of the men spoke, "Was café and closed. Haunted."

"Did you say haunted."

"Yes ghosts. Boo..."

Taken completely by surprise Ophelia thanked them and started to wander in the direction of the shop. When she arrived, she tried to peer under the corner of the board and barely see through the dusted-up windows. *Ghosts?* She thought. Her stomach started to turn. Then she pondered, *Could Charles now be a ghost?* She gulped wondering if he would haunt her. Then two cats nearby hissed in an argument, and she jumped with a loud "Ahhhhh."

Everyone in the square was staring and whispering in her direction. Ophelia shook it off and stuck her chin up and tried to walk back to her guesthouse remaining calm. Before she made it, she stopped by the water recognizing her favorite fisherman. He recognized her and waved her over to sit. She took her shoes off and dipped her feet in the cool water.

She joined him and shared her remaining biscuits. "Good." He grinned.

"Do you love living here?" She asked him.

Nodding along with her he waved at their surroundings, "Nowhere better."

The water felt amazing on her feet, and she took a long breath in and closed her eyes. She felt him looking at her curiously and she met his eyes and announced. "I'm staying."

He grinned, "Good, you stay. I trade you fish for your special bread." He held out his hand to shake hers. She took it and shook it, "It's a deal."

⁓

Ophelia barged into the kitchen holding a large fish. Mira stopped peeling her potatoes and demanded, "What is that?"

"It's a fish, silly. You are going to have free fish for life because I'm staying."

"What? Why?" Ophelia plopped the fish in Mira's sink happily. Mira's eyes glowed open, "You find nice Fisherman to marry!"

"No...Mira." She replied dryly.

"You smell, time to wash." Mira pointed at door with her knife.

"No time for that Mira."

Ophelia exited the door replying full of joy, "I'm going to finish all my paperwork! Did you hear that Kotor? I'm staying!"

Mira grinned and continued peeling her potatoes.

18

The next morning, Mira found her already awake, hunched over the notebook, hair sticking up in twelve directions.

"You look like raccoon," Mira said.

Ophelia grinned sheepishly. "Stayed up too late."

"Why?"

Ophelia turned the notebook around. On the page was a shaky drawing of a storefront: crooked shutters, a sign over the door that read **Biscuits by the Bay.**

Mira, "Perfect." Today we meet with your accountant."

Ophelia blinked. "Accountant?"

Mira nodded. "Paperwork needs numbers. We fight numbers next."

Ophelia groaned, covering her face with floury hands. But under the groan, she was smiling.

"Then after you meet with bank."

"I do?"

"Yes."

"Okay?" Mira hovered over her with her hands on her hips watching her. "What?"

Mira clapped her hands together, "Well, what you wait for! Go get ready!"

"Oh, okay!" Ophelia ran off with a puff of flour that poofed off her into the air.

"And bath!"

"I already did!" Ophelia yelled

"Bath again!" Mira called after shaking her head.

They set off through Old Town with combat energy: Mira in front, ledger under her arm like a weapon; Ophelia hustling behind with a tote bag of meticulously labeled papers and a sacrificial Tupperware of biscuits. The sky was a perfect Adriatic blue that seemed personally offended by the idea of spreadsheets.

The accountant's office lived above a shop that sold ceramic cats in a variety of judgmental poses. A hand-painted sign on the door read: **MARIJA MARKOVIĆ – ACCOUNTING, TRANQUILITY, & SOMETIMES MIRACLES.** Ophelia loved her immediately.

Marija was in her forties, short, with hair the color of espresso and glasses on a chain. Her desk was a friendly battlefield of folders, stamps, and a calculator the size of a small raft. She stood to shake hands, clocked the biscuit Tupperware, and said, "Good. I think better with butter."

"Finally," Ophelia whispered, "a scientist."

They sat. Marija clicked her pen like a metronome and said, "Tell me your dream."

Ophelia did, in a rush—how the biscuits had started by accident, how the guesthouse sold out most mornings, how Vesna's honey now had a fan club, how Dino believed she should name the business either *Butter Empire* or *Biscuit Baba*.

Marija nodded, scribbling. "Excellent. First rule: Dino does not name things."

"I told you," Mira said without looking up.

Marija unfurled a neat list. "You have three tracks: one, sole proprietor—simplest, but limited. Two, LLC—a company, safer for you, more paper. Three, run and hope no one notices—fun until it isn't. We will not choose three."

"I love that three exists," Ophelia admitted.

"For foreigners, LLC is usual." Marija tapped the list. "We

will need: passport, proof of address, opening capital, bank account, notary, company stamp, tax registration, and a saint to watch over us."

Ophelia slid over her folder like a student hoping for mercy. Marija paged through it, humming. "Very organized."

"I stayed up all night labeling things," Ophelia confessed. "It felt like promising the universe I'm serious."

Mira made a low approving sound (rare; collect these like comet sightings).

"I see you have a house in Alabama."

"Yes."

"Are you going to sell it?"

Ophelia's heart sank, and then she knew she would never be able to step foot in that house again. "Yes. I will contact my late husband's parents and let them know we need to list it to sell right away."

"Okay," Marija said briskly. "To the bank!"

Ophelia expected a dragon. The bank gave her a glass door and a burst of air-conditioning that nearly made her weep. A row of tellers gazed out with identical polite expressions, like lilies in a vase. Muzak tinkled. A security guard regarded everyone with the benign boredom of a saint in a niche.

Marija took a number and handed Ophelia a pen. "When they call, breathe. Answer only what they ask. Do not offer poetry."

"I would never," Ophelia lied.

Their number pinged. The banker who beckoned them wore a pinstripe suit and the air of a man who had once wrestled a spreadsheet and won. His name tag said Marc. He smiled like a postcard. "How can I help you ladies?"

"We open account for company," Marija said. "Future company. Today she deposits initial capital."

Marc nodded, tapping his keyboard. "Name of company?"

Ophelia froze. Panic hit like an incoming tide. She had not officially picked a name. Every possibility she'd scribbled sounded like a soap brand or a 1920s speakeasy. She glanced at Mira. Mira arched an eyebrow that said: *Decide like a grown woman.*

"Biscuits by the Bay," Ophelia blurted. "No... Kotor Biscuit & Honey. Wait." She saw Vesna's grin in her mind, the jars gleaming. "Biscuits by the Bay" She exhaled. "That one."

Marc typed, nodded. "Biscuits by the Bay. Nice."

Marija underlined something twice in her notes. "We will file the name reservation after. For now, bank account under applicant."

Marc requested documents in a soothing tone: passport (check), proof of address (Mira produced a letter with the unforgiving precision of a bailiff), tax number (Marija promised to file), first deposit (Ophelia slid a modest stack of euros across the desk, her savings shrinking in her mind like a puddle in sunlight).

"And company stamp?" Marc asked gently.

Ophelia blinked. "A... stamp?"

"Of course," Marc said. "Every company in Montenegro has a stamp. It makes documents feel loved."

"It's true," Marija said. "We'll get you a beautiful one. Round. Chic. Very official."

Mira murmured, "Dino will try to stamp his forehead. Hide it."

Paper rustled. Signatures blossomed. Marc stamped things with a satisfying thunk that made Ophelia feel like progress had a sound. He handed her a small stack: IBAN, account details, a debit card application.

"Congratulations," he said. "Biscuits by the Bay is one tiny step closer to reality."

Ophelia's eyes stung. "Thank you for treating my ridiculous dream like it's not ridiculous."

Marc shrugged, kind. "We see many dreams. The ridiculous ones are usually best."

They left the bank buoyant until the heat in the alley reminded them paperwork cannot be leavened by enthusiasm alone. Marija marched them two doors down to a tiny shop that sold... stamps.

Only stamps. The window display was a still life in bureaucracy: ink pads, embossers, engraved circles that declared things into existence.

A man with a walrus mustache emerged from behind a curtain. His name was Boris, and he looked personally responsible for stamping half the coast for the last thirty years. "Design?" he grunted.

Marija nudged Ophelia. "Choose."

On the wall hung samples: circles, ovals, austere fonts, fancy curls. Ophelia felt like she was picking a tattoo for her business soul.

She chose a clean circle: **BISCUITS BY THE BAY** arcing along the rim, a tiny, stylized wave and a little dot that might be a biscuit (or a moon; she decided both).

Boris nodded, vanished, and returned ten minutes later with a stamp that felt heavier than it looked. He rocked it once on a scrap of paper and slid it across. Ophelia clapped a hand over her mouth. The little circle was absurdly moving. *Oh,* she thought, giddy. *I exist on paper now.*

"Hide stamp from Dino," Mira repeated.

They celebrated with gelato because capitalism is easier with pistachio. On the way back, Vesna intercepted them like a joyful pickpocket.

"Report," she demanded.

"Bank account," Marija said.

"Stamp," Ophelia beamed, producing it like a magician. "Look!"

Vesna gasped as if shown a newborn. "She is beautiful! We must stamp something."

"Not living things," Mira warned.

They stamped a napkin. Then Vesna's honey price list. Then, solemnly, the back of Ophelia's notebook, where **BISCUITS BY THE BAY** landed like a seal on a letter to the universe.

Back at the guesthouse, Dino sniffed the air, clocked the stamp box, and reached for it with the languid confidence of a cat reaching for a roast chicken. Mira smacked his hand faster than physics. "No."

He pouted, then brightened. "We stamp receipts! We stamp foreheads! We stamp—"

Afternoon drifted into golden heat. The kitchen called, as it always did, and Ophelia answered mix, cut, bake, while the stamp sat on the counter like a tiny planet of authority. Between trays, she practiced pressing it on scrap paper—thunk lift, admire—until she could do it with her eyes closed. Power, Vesna had said. She believed it now: not the power to bulldoze, but the power to say *I'm here. This is mine. Please and thank you.*

When the last batch cooled, she carried a plate into the courtyard where Mira and Marija were whispering over forms, their heads inclined like generals plotting a gentle coup. Vesna swept in with a bottle of something that had the color and caution label of rakija.

"To Biscuits by the Bay!" Vesna toasted.

"To opening a bank account without crying," Marija amended.

"To hiding the stamp from Dino," Mira decreed.

"To all of the above," Ophelia said, and they drank.

The rakija burned like an affectionate dragon and then unfolded into warmth. Ophelia set her glass down and, because she couldn't stop herself, pressed the stamp onto a napkin again. **BISCUITS BY THE BAY** smiled back. Real. Ridiculous. Hers. Ophelia wiped butter from her thumb and thought, with a fizz of delighted terror: *Fun begins when fear and paperwork shake hands.* She looked around at her accidental board of directors—Mira the enforcer, Marija the translator of numbers, Vesna the queen of sweet bribes, Dino the chaos intern—and laughed out loud.

"Alright, team," she said, raising her biscuit like a gavel. "Tomorrow, we take on the notary."

Mira winced like someone remembering an old war wound. "Wear comfortable shoes."

"I have learned," Ophelia said solemnly.
"And bring the stamp," Vesna contributed.

19

If the bank had felt like air-conditioning and progress, the notary's office felt like purgatory with folding chairs. Mira insisted they arrive half an hour early, which meant they spent that half hour sweating in a hallway painted beige sometime in the 1970s. The walls were lined with frowning portraits of what Ophelia assumed were past notaries, each one staring like they disapproved of her passport photo.

"This is... formal," Ophelia whispered.

"This is necessary," Mira corrected, adjusting her ledger like armor.

Dino had insisted on coming "for moral support" but had so far provided only commentary. "I think your stamp needs glitter ink," he whispered.

"No," Mira snapped without looking at him.

"Or maybe gold foil."

"No," Mira repeated.

Ophelia rubbed her temples. "Dino, stop trying to brand me like a nightclub."

"I'm just saying," he shrugged. "Biscuits by the Bay deserves sparkle."

Before Ophelia could respond, the secretary called their name. They were ushered into a room where time had stopped somewhere around Tito. The air smelled faintly of ink and bureaucracy. A woman in her sixties sat behind a desk stacked with files, her hair a

formidable helmet of auburn. Her nameplate read: **NOTARY –
LJILJANA VUKOVIĆ.**

She peered over her glasses at Ophelia like she was about to
administer an oral exam. "American?"

"Yes," Ophelia squeaked.

"Purpose?"

"Biscuits," Ophelia blurted before she could stop herself.

Mira coughed violently into her sleeve, disguising it as a throat
clear. Dino, unhelpfully, gave a thumbs-up.

Ljiljana squinted. "Biscuits?"

"Yes," Ophelia said, finding her courage. "I want to open a
biscuit shop here. In Kotor."

The notary regarded her as though she had announced plans
to open a moon colony. Then, with a sigh that sounded centuries
old, she said, "Paperwork."

Paperwork, it turned out, was less a stack and more a small
mountain. There were affidavits, declarations, sworn statements,
and sheets that required signatures in triplicate. Each time
Ophelia signed her name, Ljiljana stamped it with the precision
of a sniper, the ink thunk reverberating through the room like
the gavel of judgment.

Halfway through, Ophelia's hand cramped. "I feel like I'm
autographing the Constitution," she muttered.

"Keep writing," Mira ordered.

"Carpal tunnel is how you know you are official," Ljiljana
said dryly.

Dino leaned over to watch. "You should make your signature
bigger. More dramatic. Like Elvis."

"Dino," Mira hissed, "leave."

"No, no, it is true," Ljiljana said, surprising them all. "A signature is a brand. Bigger is better."

Ophelia blinked. "Really?"

"Of course," Ljiljana said, stamping another page with feroc-
ity. "When you sign, you say: *I am here. I matter. Look at me.*"

For the first time all day, Ophelia smiled at the advice. She signed the next form with an extra flourish, looping the "O" in her name like a banner. Dino clapped. Mira looked pained. Ljiljana nodded, satisfied.

At the end, the notary stacked everything into a neat pile, thumped it twice, and handed it to Mira. "Done."

"Done?" Ophelia asked, barely daring to believe it.

"Done," Ljiljana confirmed. Then, unexpectedly, she held out her hand. "Biscuit?"

Ophelia blinked. "What?"

"Biscuit. You talk so much about them. Bring me some next time."

Ophelia grinned so hard her face hurt. "Deal."

The relief lasted until they stepped outside into the blinding sunshine.

"Now," Mira announced, "we must register with tax office."

Ophelia groaned. "Does bureaucracy ever end?"

"Yes," Mira said. "When you die."

"Comforting," Ophelia muttered.

But Dino, still giddy from the glitter idea, said, "We should do PR."

Ophelia nearly tripped on the cobblestones. "What?"

"Public relations. You are a brand now. You need exposure. I can handle it."

Mira gave him a look that could curdle milk. "You will not."

Dino ignored her. "I'll tell everyone at the café that Biscuits by the Bay is coming. Hype it up. Make it legendary."

"I don't want hype," Ophelia said. "I want paperwork that doesn't give me hives."

"You want customers," Dino countered. "Customers need hype. Trust me, I am visionary."

"You are pest," Mira said flatly.

"Visionary pest," Dino corrected with pride.

Later that afternoon, Ophelia went with Vesna to the market. She needed fruit for jam experiments, and Vesna insisted on escorting her as "brand ambassador." The vendors had begun to recognize her by now—the American with flour on her nose who always bought too many peaches. One fisherman waved. A woman selling plums called her "biscuit girl."

But the real surprise came at Vesna's stall. Two tourists from the Netherlands were hovering near the honey jars, whispering. When Ophelia approached, one pointed and asked, "Are you the one making the biscuits everyone talks about?"

Ophelia nearly dropped a jar. "I—uh—maybe?"

The woman beamed. "We tried some yesterday at the guesthouse. Best thing we've eaten here."

The man nodded enthusiastically. "We told friends. They want to try, too. Where's your shop?"

Ophelia's heart stuttered. "I don't—uh—I don't have one. Yet."

"Soon," Vesna cut in smoothly. "Biscuits by the Bay." Coming soon."

The tourists clapped like they'd been handed golden tickets. They bought three jars of honey and left promising to return. Ophelia stared at Vesna. "What did you just do?"

"Marketing," Vesna said smugly. "Better than Dino."

"Everyone is better than Dino," Mira muttered, appearing with apples.

Ophelia laughed helplessly, cradling her peaches like treasure. It was absurd—ridiculous even—but maybe, just maybe, her dream was already leaking into the world faster than the paperwork could catch up.

The very next day, Mira and Ophelia arrived at the Tax Office. "Don't fight door," Mira said, pulling her free. "It always wins."

Inside, the air smelled like coffee, ink, and collective suffering. A digital number board beeped overhead, but the numbers jumped in no logical order. People sat slumped in plastic chairs, their expressions ranging from resignation to spiritual defeat.

"This is where hope goes to die," Ophelia whispered.

"No," Mira corrected. "This is where hope gets taxed."

They took a number—87—and waited. The board read 65. Ophelia slumped next to Mira, clutching her tote of documents. Dino bounded in five minutes later, breathless and grinning.

"Why are you here?" Mira demanded.

"Moral support," he chirped, sliding into the chair beside Ophelia. "And also—networking. I brought flyers."

Ophelia blinked. "Flyers?"

Dino pulled a crumpled stack from his backpack. The top one read:

COMING SOON!
BISCUITS BY THE BAY — BUTTER, HONEY, AND HOPE.

Mira snatched the flyers and stuffed them under her ledger. "You will not hand these out here. Officials will not like. They not happy people."

"Exactly why they need biscuits," Dino argued.

Before Mira could strangle him, the board beeped—87.

"Oh God, that's us," Ophelia hissed, standing so quickly she nearly toppled her tote. "I thought we would have to wait." Mira steadied her. Dino darted after them, carrying himself with the swagger of a man about to close a deal. The tax official behind the desk was a thin, severe man with round glasses and the face of someone who had not smiled since 1998. His nameplate read: **Vlado Petrović.** He gestured at the chairs.

"Name?" he asked, monotone.

"Ophelia Carpenter," she said, handing over her passport.

"Purpose?"

"She is opening business," Mira explained. "Biscuits by the Bay."

Vlado typed slowly. "Nature of business?"

"Biscuits," Ophelia said.

Vlado's brow twitched. "Bicycles?"

"No," Ophelia said quickly. "Biscuits. Food."

Vlado squinted. "Bread?"

"Not exactly bread," Ophelia said. "Smaller. Fluffier. With butter. And—"

"She sells food," Mira cut in firmly.

"Ah. Food," Vlado said, typing.

Dino leaned forward suddenly, extending his hand. "I am her assistant."

Ophelia choked. Mira dropped her forehead into her palm.

"Assistant?" Vlado repeated.

"Yes," Dino said smoothly, as if the lie had been rehearsed. "Marketing, delivery, morale. Very important. I ensure biscuits reach hearts of our people."

To Ophelia's horror, Vlado nodded seriously and typed something.

"Oh no," she whispered. "He's putting you in the system."

"Yes," Dino whispered back gleefully. "I am official."

The process dragged on. Vlado asked for copies of documents they didn't have, forms that contradicted the forms they'd already filled, and at one point, a receipt from the notary that seemed to have evaporated from the tote bag. Ophelia's stomach knotted. She fumbled through folders, muttering, "I'm going to be deported because of missing stationery."

Vlado raised a brow. "Stationery is important."

Just when Ophelia thought she might cry, Dino slid a biscuit across the desk. "Morale," he whispered. Vlado stared at it. The office went very quiet. Finally, he picked it up, sniffed it, and took a bite.

Silence.

Then, very slowly, Vlado typed again. "Approved. Conditional."

Ophelia gawked. "Did... did a biscuit just bribe the tax office?"

"No," Vlado said calmly. "It reminded me life is short. Conditional approval."

Mira muttered under her breath, "We live in strange times."

"You single?" He asked.

Ophelia gagged, "Oh no. I'm so sorry..."

"Not you... your friend."

Ophelia's jaw dropped and Mira cracked a smile. She took her finger out and shook it to scold him. "You very naughty man."

He grinned, "I am."

Dina and Ophelia nudged each other with eyes wide open overjoyed. Mira shrugged her shoulders, "Naughty naughty." She took her purse and casually walked away.

He called after her, "What is your name!"

Ophelia turned around and yelled, "Mira!"

"Mira! I will come find you!"

"Ophelia. I can't believe you gave him name." Mira nudged her as they finally staggered out into the sunlight, Ophelia was dizzy with relief and giggling at Mira. "He's got a crush on you!"

She fixed her hair casually and happily, "Of course, he does. I strong beautiful woman. He crazy not to."

"Mira! I have never seen this side of you!"

Dino strutted ahead, triumphant. "Ummm. Did anyone forget about Assistant Dino saves the day. You're very welcome."

"You're fired," Mira snapped.

"You can't fire me," Dino said cheerfully. "I'm your nephew."

Ophelia laughed so hard she doubled over in the alley. The laugh came out wild and tear-streaked, the kind of laugh that only grief survivors know—half hysteria, half joy at still being alive to make a fool of yourself. Mira shook her head, muttering something in Montenegrin that sounded like a prayer for patience. But even she was smiling faintly.

That night, back at the guesthouse, Ophelia collapsed on her bed with her notebook. She stamped the page with her official seal and scrawled beneath it:

Today, I survived the tax office. Dino declared himself my assistant. Mira nearly killed him. A biscuit may have saved me from fiscal doom. This country is absurd. This dream is absurd. But maybe absurd is what I need.

She closed the notebook, rested her head on it, and whispered, "Charles, you would have loved today."
And somehow, she knew he would have.

20

y Sunday, the town seemed to be gently humming her name. Not *Ophelia*—that was too many vowels for a lazy Adriatic morning—but "the biscuit lady," which slipped down alleys like steam and drifted across the bay with the gulls. She wasn't famous, not really; she was useful. Kotor, it turned out, had a soft spot for people who showed up in the morning with something warm to eat.

She woke before the bells and lay still, letting the sounds assemble: a scooter backfiring, a shutter banging, a dog announcing the dawn as if it had invented it. Somewhere below, someone laughed. She smiled into her pillow. Later, Mira would march in with a ledger, Dino would materialize with a brand-new disaster, and Vesna would whirl through like a persuasive storm. But this moment was hers: the quiet before butter.

Downstairs, she set out her tools like talismans: bowl, whisk, teacup cutter, a chipped plate that was lucky. She breathed in the flour—a fresh bag, "tip 500" scrawled on the side—and measured with a precision that would have startled her grandmother and thrilled Marija the accountant. Butter, cold as a dare. Milk, patient. Salt, generous. Baking powder, stern.

"Gentle hands," she murmured, and smiled when the dough came together without argument, soft as a promise. She folded, turned. Folded, turned. Stamped out moons. Arranged them shoulder to shoulder so they could help each other rise. Mira slipped in silently,

preheating the oven by touch alone, like a pianist finding middle C in the dark.

They worked without commentary until the kitchen smelled like victory. When the first tray came out—golden, proud, and fluffy like a cloud—Ophelia's chest pulled tight. The sensation felt suspiciously like joy.

By eight-thirty, a line had formed—hikers and honeymooners, a grandmother with a tote bag, two teenagers pretending not to care but very much caring. Dino stood at the front desk as if conducting a symphony of coins, taking orders with solemnity undercut by the smudge of flour on his cheek. Mira dispensed coffee like penance and tampered enthusiasm with exact change.

Ophelia handed a biscuit to a little girl who cupped it like a small bird. The child took a bite, eyes widening, and whispered to her mother, "Cloud bread." Ophelia blinked hard and turned away before anyone could detect she was the sort of person who cried because a five-year-old had poetically misidentified her product.

"More," Mira said simply.

"Already," Ophelia answered, sliding a second tray into the oven.

By ten, the saucer was empty. By ten-oh-five, Vesna arrived with a fresh battalion of honey jars and a rumor: "People at the market say you open shop soon."

Ophelia sputtered. "I—who—why—maybe?"

"Good," Vesna said, ignoring grammar. "We lean into myth."

Dino clapped once. "Hype cycle!"

Mira tossed him a look that could crack rock. "You will not speak in cycles."

The day spooled out: a couple from Prague bought biscuits "for the road" and then sat down at the first bench and ate them immediately, guiltily happy; an old man with eyebrows like retired caterpillars brought her a jar of olives as tribute; the card players from the café ambled over with an air of diplomatic inspection and left with honey-slicked fingers and the fatal admission that biscuits improved rakija if consumed responsibly. The words "Biscuits by the Bay" began to echo in places she didn't expect: a shopkeeper waving, a taxi driver asking, a pair of students debating whether a biscuit could be a sandwich (it could; Ophelia lied).

That afternoon she and Mira walked to the market to replenish. The heat backed off a little; clouds smudged the sky the soft gray of newsprint. As they threaded through stalls, vendors lifted chins at her, the shorthand greeting she was learning to love. Vesna's table glowed, amber beehives catching the light. A chalkboard leaned against her crates: HONEY FOR THE BISCUIT LADY with a wobbly arrow. Ophelia covered her mouth.

"You did this?" she asked.

Vesna fluttered a hand. "Brand alignment. Also, truth."

A family approached with the shy momentum of fans. "Excuse," the father said, accent careful. "You have biscuit shop?"

"Soon," Vesna said, before Ophelia could inhale.

The mother clasped Ophelia's hands, warm and dry. "We come next summer. You be here, yes?"

Something shifted behind Ophelia's ribs—an anchor tug, a little ache that wasn't grief for once but the weight of being expected. "I'll be here," she said, surprised to hear certainty in her own voice.

At the plum stall, the farmer refused payment for a kilo of fruit. "For jam," he said. "For your... how to say... empire."

"Don't you dare," Ophelia whispered, delighted, and scandalized.

"Biscuit empire," Dino murmured, appearing at her elbow like an omen. "I told you."

They stopped at a herb table where a girl with nail polish the color of the bay held out a bunch of rosemary. "For savory," the girl said shyly. "Cheese and rosemary, maybe?"

"Maybe," Ophelia repeated, and felt ideas pop like corn.

On the walk back, Mira carried the flour like it weighed nothing and said, without preamble, "Accountant filed tax registration. It will be... some time."

"How much time?" Ophelia asked.

Mira shrugged. "Government time. Elastic."

Ophelia exhaled. "Elastic I can handle. As long as it snaps back to me."

"It will," Mira said, as if she could will it so through bone.

～

Evening slid in on velvet feet. The bells counted the day gently, as if reluctant to interrupt. Ophelia carried a plate of "end of day" biscuits to the café men, who pretended not to care until the plate touched their table and then devoured them with the stealth of raccoons. One of them—the eyebrow patriarch—handed her a folded newspaper scrap with neat script: a phone number. "For cousin," he said. "He knows landlord of your shop... it's haunted."

"Perfect," Ophelia said gravely. "I like a shop with a personality."

The men raised their eyebrows at each other and then grinned at her as they watched the number written down and handed over to the brave American girl. She tucked the number into her notebook. That notebook had become more than paper: ledger, diary, recipe graveyard, sketchbook, talisman. It held the stamp impression of Biscuits by the Bay and the scrawl of her new life: *possible, stubborn, rise.* She added: *haunted okay* and underlined it. Twice.

～

The next morning Ophelia eagerly called the number provided and inquired about the shop. Happily, he agreed to meet with her that afternoon. Mira insisted on coming. Ophelia had expected haunted places to look more... haunted. Maybe a flickering lantern. Maybe a broken shutter slapping in the wind. Maybe a faint chorus of "ooooooh" the minute she stepped inside.

"This is it!" Ophelia proudly showed Mira.

Mira nodded. "It does look haunted. That's why rent so cheap and looks small. The landlord, or rather the landlord's cousin, materialized in the form of a cheerful man named Marko who had a belly like a wine barrel and a handshake that lasted three beats too long. "Welcome, welcome! Good bones, this shop. Very good bones."

"Bones," Ophelia repeated faintly, exchanging a look with Mira.

Marko produced a key that looked like it could double as a weapon and twisted it in the lock. The door gave a theatrical creak as if auditioning for the part of "Spooky Door #3" in a horror film.

Inside, it smelled of dust, old wood, and faintly of lavender, which was not nearly as frightening as she'd prepared for. A single lightbulb dangled from the ceiling, glowing weakly. The space was narrow but deep, with stone walls and a low arch at the back that looked like it had survived three centuries of gossip.

"There is storage behind," Marko said, gesturing grandly. "And cellar. You like cellar."

"Cellar?" Ophelia squeaked.

"Yes," Marko said. "Cool in summer. Perfect for flour, butter. Maybe ghost."

Mira was already prowling, tapping walls like she was testing defenses. She pulled a notebook from her bag and began measuring with the intensity of a military strategist.

Ophelia drifted toward the counter—an ancient wooden thing scarred by time. She ran her fingers along the grooves, imagining trays of golden biscuits lined up like soldiers, honey jars catching the light, the air warm and yeasty with butter. She saw herself behind the counter, laughing, flour in her hair. The vision jolted her so hard she swayed.

"You okay?" Mira asked, not looking up from her measurements.

Ophelia nodded quickly. "Yeah. Just... picturing."

"Good," Mira said. "Pictures mean you want."

Marko launched into a sales pitch that seemed to be less about the shop and more about his cousin, the actual landlord. "He is very reasonable. Very honest. A little deaf in one ear, but not about money. Ha! Utilities are separate. Roof leaks only when rain is biblical. Very charming."

Ophelia raised an eyebrow. "Charming leaks?"

"Rustic!" Marko corrected. "Adds character. You tourists love character."

"I'm not a tourist," Ophelia said softly, almost to herself.

But the words felt important. The stone walls seemed to hear her. The back room was smaller, with shelves that tilted like they were drunk. A cracked mirror leaned against the wall. When she peered into it, her reflection looked older than she expected, tired but curious. She touched the glass, half-expecting it to ripple. It didn't.

"Cellar," Marko declared, producing another key. The trap-door groaned as it opened, revealing a steep set of stairs. Cool, damp air drifted up.

"Nope," Ophelia said instantly.

"Yes," Mira said firmly, already descending.

Marko followed, humming cheerfully. "Maybe little mouse. Nothing more."

Ophelia stood at the top, muttering, "This is how horror movies start. This is how Americans die in Europe. I'm going to be a cautionary tale on TripAdvisor."

But she followed, one cautious step at a time, gripping the railing that wobbled ominously. The cellar was, in fact, not horrifying. It was stone-walled and cool, with a faint earthy smell. It would have been a wine cellar once, maybe. There were niches in the wall that could easily hold sacks of flour, crocks of butter, jars of Vesna's honey. "This is perfect," Mira said, clapping her hands once.

"Perfect for what?" Ophelia asked.

"Inventory."

Marko nodded sagely. "And maybe ghost. But friendly ghost."

Ophelia squinted at him. "You keep saying that."

"Yes," Marko said. "Because tourists like story. If shop is haunted, better business. People come. They buy biscuit. They meet ghost. Everybody happy."

She couldn't tell if he was joking.

Back upstairs, Marko began to talk rent. Numbers that sounded high to Ophelia but made Mira purse her lips in a way that suggested she was already mentally cutting them in half. "Too much," Mira said flatly.

"But location—" Marko began.

"Too much," Mira repeated, her eyebrow doing the work of three lawyers.

Ophelia hovered, nervous, until Marko glanced at her with a look that said, *Please rescue me from your terrifying friend.* She smiled awkwardly. "Um. I really like it. I think... I think I can see it. The shop. My shop." Her throat tightened. "But the rent has to be possible. I'm not... I don't have endless—"

Marko held up a hand. "We talk. Cousin likes dreamers. Cousin has soft spot. He say, 'We make deal with the biscuit woman.'"

Ophelia blinked. "The...what now?"

Marko beamed. "Already, people call you biscuit woman. See? Reputation. Ghost not needed."

Mira muttered, "Yet."

Ophelia wandered one last circuit, fingertips brushing stone. She could already hear the scrape of chairs, the clink of coffee cups, Vesna laughing at the register, Mira sighing over receipts, Dino scrawling nonsense slogans on napkins. She could almost hear Charles too, teasing her for picking the haunted one, insisting he'd set up fairy lights across the beams. Her chest ached, but not with the sharpness of before. This ache felt... possible. Like something stretching into shape. When they stepped back outside, the late afternoon sun turned the street gold. The green door closed behind them with a thunk.

"Well?" Mira asked.

Ophelia exhaled. "I think it's mine. Or will be. Haunted or not."

"Haunted," Marko confirmed cheerfully. "Very good business."

Ophelia laughed until she bent double, the sound bouncing off the stones. She straightened, wiping her eyes, and said it again, firmer this time.

"It's mine."

21

The next afternoon, the town was buzzing Vesna stood in the courtyard with a bottle of rakija like a herald announcing the birth of a prince. "Congratulations," she sang, eyes glittering. "On your haunted palace."

"It is not a palace," Ophelia said, dazed and smiling. "It's a stone shoebox with a roof that gets emotional when it rains."

"Palaces are just shoeboxes with delusions," Vesna replied, kissing both her cheeks and pressing the bottle into her hands. "For courage. We go now."

"Go where?" Ophelia asked.

"To meet cousin," Mira answered, already grabbing her ledger. "We meet him today."

"Wait," Ophelia protested. "Shouldn't I… I don't know… prepare?"

"You prepared when you made biscuits people won't shut up about," Vesna said, stealing the bottle back for a 'test sip.' "Now we negotiate. I will wear lipstick. Dino will not speak."

"I absolutely will speak," Dino said, suddenly materializing in the doorway with a stack of comic-sans flyers and the aura of a chihuahua detecting drama. "I will speak truth to landlord."

"You will speak air only," Mira told him, her tone the sort of soft that meant steel.

They set off like a small, ill-advised parade: Mira at the front, ledger tucked under her arm like a sword; Vesna striding like a general whose perfume could topple governments;

133

Dino carrying a tote bag of "branding materials" no one had asked for; and Ophelia gripping her notebook and the rakija bottle as if both could be notarized courage.

Marko was already waiting on the narrow street, beaming, a hand spread theatrically toward the green door as though presenting a game-show prize. "Ladies! And... Dino. Excellent. Cousin will arrive shortly. He is late because he is always late. This is his brand."

"His brand needs a watch," Mira said.

Inside, the shop looked less dusty than before, either because the light had shifted or because Ophelia's heart had decided it was hers and therefore could not be dusty. She could smell lavender again, faintly, as if the walls had learned manners. Vesna slipped behind the old counter like she owned it, winking at Ophelia. "This is good height for commanding customers," she announced. "Also good for hiding secrets."

"What secrets?" Ophelia asked, alarmed.

"Discounts for neighbors. Smuggling cookies to children. We will plan our benevolent corruption later."

The bell over the door clanged, and a man stepped in with the slow gravity of a minor planet. He was in his sixties, compact, bald on top with a silver ring of hair, and he wore a suit jacket over a T-shirt printed with a wolf under a moon. He had dark, heavy-lidded eyes that suggested he could spot a liar at a thousand meters. Marko snapped to attention. "Cousin!"

The cousin—Rade, as he introduced himself with a short nod—shook hands all around, including Dino's, who introduced himself as "Assistant to the Biscuit Vision." Rade's mouth twitched, which, in this room, counted as a laugh.

"So," Rade said, hands in his pockets, surveying the space. "You want my store."

"I do," Ophelia said, trying to keep her voice steady.

"Sense is optional," Rade said. "Rent is not." He gestured to Marko, who produced a folded paper with numbers handwritten in a precise, teacherly script. The figure at the bottom made Ophelia's heart attempt a quiet swan dive into her shoes.

"Too much," Mira said, without a beat.

"It is the market," Rade replied.

"Markets lie," Mira said. "Roof leaks."

"Only in biblical rain," Marko chimed, cheerful as a weather report.

"Biblical is common in November," Mira shot back. "And December."

Rade's heavy-lidded gaze slid to Ophelia. "You cook."

"I bake," Ophelia said, clutching the bottle of rakija. "Biscuits. With honey. People seem to like them."

"We like money," Rade said mildly.

"I will give you both," Vesna inserted, beaming. "Honey and money. She fills stomachs. I fill jars. You get rent."

Rade studied Vesna, then Ophelia. He pointed at the bottle. "Rakija?"

"For courage," Ophelia said. "And negotiation."

Rade took it, sniffed, and passed it back. "We will need both."

Mira opened her ledger like a fan and began. "The shop is small. The roof 'is rustic.' The door sticks. The light is not light, it is a suggestion. The cellar steps wobble. We will fix some, you fix some. We need months of grace while she establishes business. We need rent reduction for first quarter—"

"Half," Vesna suggested magnanimously. "For charm."

"Not half," Rade said, as though swatting a fly. "Fifteen percent."

"Twenty-five," Mira countered.

"Nineteen," Rade said, his mouth now definitely amused.

"Twenty-two," Mira said.

"Twenty-one," Rade said, and there it was: the dance, the numbers moving like chess pieces while Ophelia tried not to hyperventilate.

Dino lifted his hand. "As assistant to the vision, I propose an exchange: rent reduction for exclusive biscuit access. First pick. Lifetime discount."

Rade looked at him. "You eat for free anyway."

Dino placed a hand on his heart. "I feel seen."

Mira pressed on. "Maintenance—your responsibility. Cosmetic—ours. We need permission for new wiring. She needs a small oven, maybe two. Vent must be discussed with your cousin neighbor at café because coffee people are dramatic."

"Coffee people are always dramatic," Rade agreed.

"Also," Vesna added, "we will host a monthly honey tasting. Your name on sign as patron of small business. For charm."

"Charm does not pay tax," Rade said.

"Neither do leaks," Mira replied.

Rade's gaze cut to Ophelia again, quieter this time. "How long you stay?"

Ophelia's throat tightened. She thought of the ninety-day clock, the forms, the notary's thumb, Vlado's biscuit-induced mercy. She thought of Charles, of Montevallo, of the way the bay looked at dusk like a coin you could trust. "I'm fighting the paper. I don't know how long I'm allowed. But if you rent to me, I will do everything I can to make this street smell like butter for a long time."

Silence. The lightbulb hummed. Somewhere, in the alley, a scooter coughed.

Rade scratched his chin. "My sister says her grandchildren talk about 'the biscuit lady.' They are fat children. I trust their judgment." He looked at Mira, then at Vesna, then back to Ophelia. "Okay. Terms: one-year lease, renewable if taxes do not hurt me. Twenty-one percent reduction first three months, because I like odd numbers. Maintenance for roof: I will send a man who is good with roofs, bad with people. You pay utilities. You do not paint door a stupid color. Deposit... two months."

"Too high," Mira said. "One and a half."

"Two," Rade said.

"Two, but spread over two months," Mira countered. "She is new."

Rade considered. "Two, spread. Okay."

"Add access to cellar included, no extra fee," Mira said.

Rade shrugged. "Cellar comes with ghosts. No one pays for ghosts."

"Ghosts are value-add," Vesna said. "We will name him. Or her."

"Leave ghost alone," Rade said, but there was a smile in it.

Dino raised a finger again. "We will also need permission for sign: BISCUITS BY THE BAY. Clean font.

"Sign okay," Rade said. "But small. You are in old town. If sign is loud, preservation people come and shout."

"We will make sign humble," Vesna vowed, lacquered to the gods.

Mira closed the ledger with a small, satisfied click. "We have terms."

Rade nodded. "We have terms."

Ophelia had the distinct sensation of standing on the lip of a cliff and deciding to enjoy the view. Her palms were damp. Her heart thudded with a tempo she recognized now as *the beginning of something and also nausea.* "Can we... put it in writing?" she asked, trying to sound like a woman who did contracts before breakfast.

"Pre-lease," Rade said. "Simple paper. Then full lease when your lawyer stops being drunk with stamps."

"Marija is drunk with spreadsheets," Ophelia said. "A different vice."

Rade extended his hand. "Shake on this. Then we drink. Then we sign."

They shook—Mira first, because respect must be measured in eyebrows; Vesna next, because she would have hugged him otherwise; Ophelia last, her grip surprisingly steady. She felt the odd shock of recognition: of Rade as a man who had lived in these stone rooms longer than she had been alive, who had seen waves of summer people ebb and flow and had no patience for fantasy without rent attached. She respected that. He respected that she could say *I don't know how long* and still look him in the eye.

Marko produced small glasses from somewhere (this was a national magic trick—glasses appeared in pockets and drawers like birds). The rakija went around. They toasted to small businesses, to roofs that only cried in November, to ghosts who paid in rumors, to numbers that behaved, to ovens that obeyed, to patience.

When the toast made its warm ribbon down Ophelia's throat, the door creaked, and a draft slipped across her ankles. She glanced at the ceiling. The weak bulb swayed once like a wink.

"Did you feel that?" she whispered to Mira.

"Wind," Mira said.

"Ghost," Vesna corrected, delighted.

"Draft," Rade said, practical.

But Ophelia, because she needed the extra courage, whispered, "Charles?" and let herself imagine he'd followed her here today to see if she would sign her name.

Rade tucked a folded page onto the counter: the pre-lease, brief and stern. It had blank lines where numbers would go, and one long line where a signature would anchor the dream to ink. "You sign," he said. "Big. Like you mean it."

The notary's words returned: *When you sign, you say: I am here. I matter. Look at me.*

Her hand trembled over the first curve, smoothed at the second. She did not apologize to the paper. She did not make herself small. She wrote Ophelia with the banner O and the comet tail the pen liked to give her when she wasn't afraid.

Mira added her witness signature, precise as a ruler. Rade counter-signed with a line that looked like a mountain range. The page became heavier, not with ink but with intention. Outside, the town kept doing what towns do: hawking gelato, arguing over parking, letting gulls get away with petty crimes. Inside, Vesna dabbed her lipstick on the corner of a napkin and pressed the kiss next to the signatures. "For luck," she said solemnly.

"That is not legal," Rade said.

"It is binding," Vesna said.

Dino, vibrating with the need to participate, held up the stamp like a relic. "We should...?"

"Not on this," Mira said, smacking his hand lightly. "On the copy."

They stamped the copy with satisfying authority: BISCUITS BY THE BAY — KOTOR. The circle shone like a coin.

"Now," Rade said, "you rest. Tomorrow, I send roof man. Few days more, we discuss electrician who owes me a favor because his brother married my ex-wife's cousin."

Ophelia blinked. "That's... tangled."

"It is Montenegro," Rade said, not unkindly. "Everything is cousin."

They walked back into the alley blinking at the brightness, as if they'd emerged from a cave with treasure. The air tasted like stone and sea, and Ophelia's fear, which had been flapping like a trapped bird, settled on a perch and looked, almost, like excitement.

Mira squeezed her shoulder once—quick, nearly anonymous. "Good," she said.

Vesna linked arms. "We need curtains. And a ribbon to cut. And a playlist for opening morning. I have opinions."

"You always have opinions," Mira said.

"They are excellent opinions," Vesna returned. "We will source a bell that rings only when decent people enter. We will train the ghost to chase away the rude."

"I will design uniforms," Dino proclaimed. "Aprons with tiny, embroidered waves and biscuits. Perhaps berets."

"No berets," three voices said in weary chorus.

At the corner, Ophelia paused. She turned to look back at the green door, the windows that would soon be clean, the space she had just promised to. She tried a new sentence out loud, just to hear it. "I signed a lease."

Vesna whooped. Mira allowed herself a thin, real smile. Dino threw confetti made of illegal flyers into the air until Mira confiscated the rest. The bells somewhere in the city counted an hour as if to notarize her claim. She imagined the first morning the door would open, and the smell of butter would tumble over the threshold and people would step in on purpose.

22

Ophelia giggled excitedly when she stepped through her green door this time, it felt like the threshold of a church. The air smelled faintly of damp stone and lavender still, but also of possibility. She walked the length of the narrow space slowly, her hand brushing the wall as though introducing herself.

The shop was still dusty, still shadowed, still a little too damp in the corners, but Ophelia's eyes no longer saw it that way. The boards outside had been removed and there was light, filled with dusty particles floating around, but light no less.

Here, near the counter, she imagined the register, a glass case, little cards handwritten with names of biscuits in English and Montenegrin. She pictured Vesna leaning across, convincing tourists to buy honey "for health, for love, for protection against heartbreak." She pictured Mira counting coins into neat stacks while sighing dramatically.

Halfway down the wall she paused and shut her eyes. When she opened them, she could see it clearly: shelves with jars of jam, small packages of biscuits wrapped in paper with twine. Maybe postcards. Maybe recipe cards for sale, though her grandmother would've said recipes were meant to be given, not sold. She wrote the thought in her notebook anyway: *Recipe cards?*

At the back, under the low arch, she imagined a chalkboard with daily specials. "Today's biscuit: rosemary & cheese. Try with Vesna's

141

honey." She smiled, thinking Charles would've teased her mercilessly for pairing cheese and honey. *That's a charcuterie board in disguise, darling,* he would've said, and then eaten four.

She stepped through the arch into the back room, where the cracked mirror still leaned. Her reflection caught her off guard: hair messy, shirt streaked with flour, eyes tired but alive in a way she hadn't recognized for months. She studied herself as if she were both stranger and architect.

The door creaked open, and she jumped. Expecting the roof man, it was Marija. "We celebrate with solvency, your tax number, and your bank card is printing. Also, your landlord's cousin sent a text promising he would be here.

Ophelia clapped and her body hummed with a sugarless sugar high, the kind that came from signing a thing that could not be un-signed. "You are amazing!"

She ran over to hug her. Marija looked around the shop. "I hope you are sure about all this."

A sound from the back of something dropping made them both jump. Ophelia giggled in fright, "Well I think our ghost is sure. So yes! It's going to be amazing."

Marija opened the folder and slid a simple budget toward her with the serenity of a midwife. "We have *a plan.* Down payment from savings. Rental discount for first quarter. We'll stagger purchases. You will sell out most mornings if you don't get silly with batch size. Cash flow is a river: do not dam it; do not drown in it."

"I won't."

The green door creaked its goodbye for Marija and Ophelia continued to wait for the elusive Roof Man. Was he just invented to keep foreigner's hopeful? The street outside rattled with the sound of a battered van that coughed more smoke than an overworked barbecue pit. Out tumbled a man in overalls so patched they looked like a quilt. He was thin, wiry, with a cigarette glued to his lip and hair that might once have been black but now resembled the color of burned toast.

"Roof man," he announced in a gravelly baritone, as if auditioning for a one-man show.

"Yes," Ophelia said cautiously.

He squinted at her. "You the biscuit widow?"

Ophelia blinked. "I... excuse me?"

"Word travels," he said with a shrug. "You bake biscuits. You widow. People talk. Better than weather."

Ophelia's jaw flapped like a broken hinge. Somewhere in her chest, grief and indignation held hands and hissed. "I suppose that's me. And you are...?"

"Vuk... means WOLF," he said simply, and with the gravitas of someone who had never needed a surname. "I fix roofs. Sometimes. When the spirit moves me."

Mira arrived just then, clipboard in hand, expression set to *storm warning*. "You are late."

"I am here," Vuk replied, as if that were the same thing. He tossed his cigarette butt into the gutter with a flick that suggested centuries of practice, then hauled a dented ladder out of the van. It looked older than the Venetian walls.

Ophelia stepped back, visions of insurance claims dancing in her head. "Is that... safe?"

Vuk stared at her as though she'd asked if the sun planned to rise tomorrow. "Ladder never killed me yet."

"Yet," Mira echoed darkly, writing something on her clipboard with a stab of pen that nearly tore the paper.

The ladder was propped, the cigarette replaced with another, and Vuk ascended with the slouchy grace of a man who considered gravity an inconvenience rather than a law. He vanished onto the roof, muttering curses in Montenegrin that Mira did not translate but Ophelia suspected included words like *idiot tiles* and *what fool signs a lease in November.*

They heard him stomp, bang, pause, and then bellow down through the hole where a tile had given up on life: "It leaks because it wants to."

Ophelia shaded her eyes. "Excuse me?"

"Some roofs," Vuk said, face appearing upside down through the gap like a reluctant gargoyle, "they leak because water finds path. You can fight, but water always wins. You respect water, you respect roof."

"That's very philosophical," Ophelia said weakly.

At that moment, Dino appeared, late as usual but with boundless enthusiasm, carrying a bag labeled **'Roof Snacks.'**

"What," Ophelia demanded, "are roof snacks?"

"Every craftsman works better with snacks," Dino said proudly, unveiling a paper sack of stale crackers and what might have been beef jerky. "Fuel for vision!"

"Biscuits would've been better," Vuk said from above.

"You've never tasted mine," she called.

"Town talks," Vuk said with a shrug.

Ophelia turned pink, half-embarrassed, half-pleased.

Then, inevitably, Dino decided to "help." He grabbed the bottom of the ladder. "Stability check!" he announced, shaking it like a carnival ride.

Vuk lunged. "Do not—"

It was too late. The ladder wobbled, Vuk cursed loudly enough to frighten pigeons, and Ophelia's heart stopped somewhere near her ankles. Miraculously, Vuk did not plummet to his death, but a cascade of roof dust rained down, covering Dino like powdered sugar on a beignet. From above, Vuk spat out his cigarette and roared: "Do not touch ladder! Ladder is religion! You respect ladder!"

Ophelia buried her face in her hands, torn between hysterical laughter and the urge to run back to Alabama. This, apparently, was what starting a business in Montenegro looked like: chaos, dust, and a roof philosopher screaming about religion.

After several more bangs, curses, and one suspicious crash that made Vesna (who had shown up purely to spectate) cross herself dramatically, Vuk descended. He stood in the doorway, covered in grit, holding a broken tile like a holy relic.

"Roof is tired," he announced. "But not dead. Needs patch, not funeral. I fix. You pay. I'll be back in morning."

He left quickly and decidedly.

Ophelia sagged against the counter and looked over to Dino. "If the oven man is anything like him, I'm doomed."

"Oh no," Dino said grimly. "The oven man is worse."

A few days later and a semi-fixed roof. Ophelia met Mira at the bus stop like a woman reporting for a duel. The destination was Herceg Novi, and the weapon of choice was cash flow. Mira wore her "don't test me" cardigan and carried a folder labeled *OVENS* with the bleak optimism of a field medic. Ophelia carried a tote bag with two biscuits (for morale), a notebook (for panic), and the official stamp (for power, and because she liked to press it onto things when terrified).

The bus coughed up the road with the cheerful death rattle of a metal dinosaur. Ophelia snagged a window seat and watched the bay unfurl beside them, the water a calm, smug blue that made budgets feel silly. Mira flipped through her folder as if she could will the numbers to behave.

"Explain the plan," Ophelia said, because hearing a plan out loud made it less like a cliff and more like stairs.

Mira obliged. "We go to store. We ask many questions. We do not buy the first shiny thing that hums. You will try a deck oven and a convection oven. We talk ventilation. We talk amps. We negotiate like wolves in cardigans."

Ophelia made a strangled sound. "Amps?"

"Electricity," Mira said. "Your shop has feelings. It cannot support an oven that thinks it is a small sun. We pick heat you can feed."

Ophelia stared at her biscuit as if it might have the answer printed in crumbs. "What if— bear with me—what if I just buy a nice home oven and bake like a pioneer?"

Mira didn't glance up. "Then you will sell four biscuits a day, cry, and I will take away your stamp."

Ophelia hugged the stamp protectively. "Rude."

The bus rattled past stone terraces and bougainvillea clinging to walls like cheerful trespassers. Ophelia pressed her forehead to the glass and whispered, "Please let the right oven be on sale and emotionally supportive."

"Emotionally supportive ovens are extra," Mira said.

They got off at a dusty stop near a strip of industrial shops that all smelled faintly of oil and ambition. First on Mira's list: KITCHEN KINGDOM—a warehouse with a sun-faded sign and a row of stainless-steel appliances gleaming inside like a spaceship showroom. The air-conditioning hit them like an absolution.

A salesman materialized, slick hair, slick smile. His name tag read NIKOLA – SOLUTIONS. He shook both their hands with a fervor that suggested commission.

"Ladies! What do we build today? Café? Restaurant? Empire?"

"Shoebox," Ophelia said. "With ghosts."

Nikola laughed, but his eyes flicked to Mira for confirmation. Mira's look said *she is not joking, proceed anyway.*

"We need oven for biscuits," Mira said. "Not pizza. Not bread. Something with soul and reliability."

"Ah," Nikola said, pivoting with the grace of a ballerina and the zeal of a televangelist. He ushered them to a line of ovens like a proud father at graduation. "This is the Falcon 6:12—convection, programmable, gentle steam, glass door for romance. And this is the Atlas Deck—stone decks, old-world charm, weight of a small tank. People bake bread that makes grandmothers cry."

Ophelia's heart tugged treacherously toward the Atlas Deck. It looked like a stone hearth had slept with a bank vault. "Deck oven," she whispered, reverent. "Romance."

"Deck oven," Mira countered, "electricity hog. Heat like furnace. Your shoebox becomes sauna. Biscuits become tantrum."

Nikola patted the Falcon. "Convection is kinder. Air circulates. Even bake. She sings."

"She sings?" Ophelia asked.

"All good ovens sing," Nikola said with a straight face.

They loaded a tray of test "biscuits" (Nikola's freezer contained an uncanny collection of dough units for demonstration) and ran both machines: the Atlas humming low like a dragon, the Falcon whispering like a diligent librarian. Ten minutes later, they tasted: the deck oven's biscuit was proud, crustier, dramatic; the convection oven's was tender and consistent, a reliable friend who remembered birthdays.

She swallowed. "Falcon."

Mira nodded once. Nikola beamed. The list exploded like confetti. Ventilation required ducting and a fan with the personality of a fighter jet. Power required a three-phase supply, which Mira had already anticipated like a weather witch. Warranty required promises in two languages. Delivery required something called a CMR, which Nikola explained was a document for logistics—and which Ophelia wrote down as "Sea Monster Form" because her hand was shaking, and her brain had left her body.

"And of course," Nikola added smoothly, "we will need a customs clearance if we bring in the unit from our warehouse in Zagreb. It is simple. Many stamps."

Ophelia clutched her own stamp like a talisman. "I have one stamp."

"You will need... more," Nikola said gently.

Mira steepled her fingers. "Price."

He named one. Mira named a smaller one. He tried to flirt with math. Mira flirted with homicide. They finally landed in a valley called *possible with nausea.* Ophelia did quick arithmetic in her notebook and tried not to measure the total in biscuits. (Answer: too many. Always too many.)

Nikola leaned closer, confiding. "There is also... Aunt Unit."

Ophelia blinked. "I'm sorry?"

"Floor model," Nikola said in a whisper. "Used gently. Demonstrations only. She is... aunt. Not mother, not baby. Reliable. Cheaper."

Mira's eyes narrowed, calculating. "How much cheaper?"

He named a number that made Ophelia's pulse unstick. Mira shot her a look: *This is mercy disguised as metal.*

"We'll take Aunt Unit," Ophelia said before she could talk herself into poverty with a newer machine.

"Good," Nikola said, clapping his hands once. "She likes butter. She is kind."

They moved to mixers (too big, too loud, too proud), to cooling racks (surprisingly expensive towers of honesty), to sheet pans (Ophelia chose the ones that felt like they wouldn't wobble under pressure, which she took personally). Mira asked about lead times, installation dates, and whether Nikola's cousin in customs was feeling generous this month.

"Always generous to people who feed me," Nikola said, eyeing the tote bag.

Ophelia produced the biscuits. He bit. He closed his eyes. He exhaled like a man remembering his first love. "Yes," he said, reverent. "We will move mountains."

"Move paperwork," Mira corrected.

"Mountains of paperwork," Nikola amended.

That night, Ophelia crept into her bakery holding her folder with Aunt Unit's details. and stood in the dark for a full minute to let her eyes adjust to the dimly ridiculous bulb. She whispered to the empty room, "Aunt Unit is coming," and felt foolish until the echo—soft, real—returned to her in the stone. She walked to the counter, laid both palms flat, and pressed her cheek to the cool wood the way people press their cheeks to their children's foreheads to check fever. The fear was still there, but it was changing shape. It had edges now. It could be measured in amps and centimeters and euros and time.

On her way out, she paused under the arch and looked at the cracked mirror. She lifted the stamp and pressed it to a scrap of paper she'd stuck in her pocket. Biscuits by the Bay circled itself into being. She tucked the scrap behind the mirror frame like a tiny, silly blessing.

"Be kind," she told the shop. "I'll bring you an oven that sings."

24

Word in Kotor traveled faster than electricity, especially when it involved biscuits, foreigners, or anything vaguely scandalous. Within two days of Ophelia and Mira returning from Herceg Novi, the town seemed to know about Aunt Unit—the oven, the deal, the fact that the biscuit widow had "adopted" it. Ophelia couldn't walk ten paces without someone poking their head out of a doorway to comment.

The first was her neighbor, Petar, who ran the nearby café. He leaned on his counter, espresso in one hand, cigarette in the other, and eyed her green door with suspicion. "Don't paint it yellow," he warned solemnly. "Tourists like yellow. But yellow attracts bees. Then everyone blames Petar."

Ophelia blinked. "I... wasn't planning yellow?"

"Good," he said, and vanished back into his café, where his radio immediately resumed playing the same melancholy ballad it always seemed to play.

A few steps later, she met Ivana, who sold lace out of a tiny stall and wore glasses that magnified her eyes to startled proportions. "Your biscuits," Ivana said, gripping Ophelia's arm like a prophetess. "They must have rosemary. Always rosemary. My grandmother said rosemary makes a man stay faithful."

Ophelia coughed. "Well, I... I'm not baking for fidelity."

"Then bake for tourists," Ivana said, unbothered, and handed her a sprig of rosemary as if bestowing a relic.

By the time she reached the courtyard, she had also been told by one fisherman that she absolutely must invent "sailor biscuits" (with anchovies, heaven forbid), warned by a taxi driver not to sell coffee stronger than Petar's (apparently there were turf wars), and advised by an elderly woman that "if you put too much butter, people will slip on the street."

Ophelia dumped the unsolicited herb bundle onto the table where Vesna was already waiting with jars of honey like ammunition. "Does everyone in Kotor have an opinion about my biscuits?" she demanded.

"Yes," Vesna said cheerfully. "And they will keep giving them until you are dead. Maybe after." She tapped a jar. "Good. Free marketing."

"Free suffocation," Ophelia muttered, collapsing into a chair.

"Consider it tradition," Vesna said. She unscrewed a jar, dipped a spoon, and shoved it under Ophelia's nose. "Now—taste. This is linden blossom honey. Tourists love linden. Say the word: *lin-den.* It feels expensive."

Ophelia obediently tasted. Sweet, floral, faintly citrus. It did, in fact, taste like something you'd pay too much for in a fancy New York bakery.

Vesna smirked. "See? Honey sells story. Biscuits sell belly. Together, we make empire."

Mira arrived in the middle of this pronouncement, her arms full of folders, her patience already eroded. "What empire?" she asked.

"Biscuits by the Bay," Vesna said grandly. "Also, Ghost Tourism Incorporated."

Mira groaned. "We do not monetize ghosts."

"We absolutely monetize ghosts," Vesna countered. "American girl loves haunted stories. Americans pay extra for haunted biscuits."

"I am the American girl," Ophelia said faintly. "And I don't know how to bake haunted."

"Easy," Dino said, bursting into the courtyard with yet another sketch. He slapped it on the table: a logo featuring a cartoon biscuit with vampire teeth. *"Bite into fright!"*

"Absolutely not," Mira said, already flipping open a folder like she was filing a restraining order.

"Maybe," Vesna said, tapping her chin.

Ophelia groaned into her hands.

Marija appeared last, serene as ever, balancing a tray of paperwork on one arm and coffee on the other. "I bring forms," she announced, like a benevolent bureaucrat. "And deadlines. And this coffee is stronger than Petar's, so don't tell him."

They gathered around the table like a council convening. Papers spread, honey jars gleamed, Dino's cursed logo fluttered in the breeze, and Vesna commandeered a biscuit sample tray to lure passing neighbors into "taste testing" while dropping not-so-subtle hints about the opening.

One tourist paused, chewing. "This place will be cute," she said. "Like a secret."

Ophelia flushed. A secret—that she could live with.

The rest of the afternoon became a circus of opinions: Vesna lobbying for a honey shelf in the corner, Dino campaigning for branded napkins with bad puns, Mira sketching electrical outlet placements like she was planning a military campaign, Marija calculating startup costs against likely tourist traffic, and three separate neighbors offering heirloom recipes "for free" as long as Ophelia promised to name them after their grandmothers.

At one point, Ophelia slipped away into the shop, leaned against the counter, just to breath in the dust and lavender. Outside, voices rose and fell in affectionate argument. She realized she didn't need to ask if Kotor would accept her; Kotor had already barged in, rearranged the furniture, and demanded rosemary.

For the first time, instead of panicking, she laughed. The rest of the day they practically broke their backs cleaning the place. Scrubbing it looked a little brighter. That evening exhausted from cleaning; after Vesna finally ran out of honey metaphors, after Dino had been threatened with bodily harm if he ever drew another vampire-biscuit logo, after Marija had packed away her clipboard and Mira and Ophelia walked back together.

"I'm ready for glass of wine." Mira announced.

"I'm ready for bed, Ophelia moaned. I am physically and emotionally exhausted."

"Go to bed and I bring you some soup."

"Oh no but thank you. I'm going right to bed."

That's what she did. She made it to her bed and kicked off her shoes and pulled the cover over. Falling deeply into sleep. So deep that she slept through the bells, the breakfast, cats scratching at her door. She slept. By the time she woke up it was noon. She gasped! "Oh, good Lord." She scrambled to find her shoes and then she saw the tray of food and a note that read...

"Rest. Eat. Then come to your bakery." –Mira

As soon as Ophelia's heart finally settled down, she sat, and she did just that. She ate and rested more for a bit. She took her time getting ready and when she felt ready to face the day, she made her way to town. But when she pushed open the green door, it wasn't empty. Mira was already inside, wielding a tape measure like a sword, barking dimensions at a nervous electrician who scribbled notes while sweating into his collar.

Vesna swept in moments later with a bundle of curtains under one arm and a basket of fresh figs under the other. "For atmosphere," she declared, holding up the fabric. "And for sugar crashes."

Dino skidded in behind her, breathless, clutching a new sketch. "Apron number eight! This time with *detachable* pockets. For biscuits!"

Marija arrived last, unhurried as always, holding a ledger so thick it could have doubled as a weapon. "The customs office called. Aunt Unit will clear the border tomorrow. I have arranged the fee to be... survivable."

Ophelia stood in the doorway, blinking at the chaos. The electrician cursed under his breath, Vesna draped curtains against the wall like it was a theater stage, Dino made oven noises under his breath, Mira measured distances with the authority of an architect, Marija was already balancing the next two months of her life in neat columns.

And in the center of it all, her shoebox shop no longer looked like a tomb or a gamble. It looked like a beginning.

Ophelia laughed—loud, a little cracked, but real. Everyone stopped, startled, then smiled (or in Mira's case, smirked).

"What?" Vesna demanded.

"Nothing," Ophelia said, wiping her eyes. "Just—everything. You all. This. It's amazing."

"Of course," Mira said briskly. "Amazing."

Ophelia walked in, set her bag down, rolled up her sleeves. "All right then. Let's build a biscuit shop."

And for the first time, the words didn't sound like a dare. They sounded like the truth.

25

The day the painter came, Kotor decided to perform weather like a soap opera. Sun, cloud, dramatic shadow, sudden brightness—repeat. It made the faded green door wink like it had secrets. Ophelia stood under it watching him slowly paint. He looked down from his ladder at her. "You are biscuit widow, no?"

Ophelia rolled her eyes, "Yes, that's me, I guess. But you mind your manners and finish painting my sign!"

"You feed me, I paint faster," he said, businesslike.

"I'll go make a tray now," Ophelia said, "but when I get back, I want that sign finished and you starting on the front door and remember, it's gotta be green. Absolutely no yellow."

"Oh yes."

Her heart suddenly racing with the cozy dread of performance. Aunt Unit hadn't arrived yet; this would be a guesthouse-kitchen batch, one last victory lap before the oven came home.

While she hustled back to the guesthouse, Mira and Branko measured the over-door board with the solemnity of a treaty signing. Dino slunk off to "conceptualize" aprons in peace (a

merciful lie). Vesna roped two passing tourists into an impromptu focus group by feeding them honey on spoons and pointing at Branko's paper sketch. The tourists, high on sugar and vacation, declared it "charming" and "very Instagram," which made Mira almost, almost smile.

By the time Ophelia returned with a warm plate wrapped in a towel, the lane had gathered a small audience: Petar leaning in the café doorway, two lace-stall aunties clucking approval, a pair of kids with soccer balls scuffing the stones, the electrician smoking like a chimney on break, and, inexplicably, the notary from three streets over, who had appeared with the radar of a woman who could sense signatures from afar.

"Biscuits," Ophelia announced, setting the plate on an upturned crate. Steam rose.

The painter took one, bit, closed his eyes, then nodded with a gravity that bestowed both blessing and deadline. "I finish painting everything today," he said. "You open soon."

"Soon is good," Ophelia echoed, dizzy.

The preservation officer materialized the way bureaucrats do: quietly, but with an aura of carbon paper. Her name was Milena, and she wore a linen dress the color of approval. She studied the sketch, then the door, then Ophelia. "Small. Good. No neon," she said. "No metal letters that blind pigeons."

"Never," Mira said, horrified by the very idea.

Milena's gaze snagged on the microscopic bee. Silence stretched. Vesna's lipstick seemed to hold its breath.

Milena leaned closer. "Dot of i," she said finally, deadpan. "Acceptable." She signed a form with a flourish that would have impressed the notary. "Install with two screws. No drilling the soul of the stone."

"Who would do such a thing?" the painter asked, genuinely offended.

"Tourists," Milena said, as if this answered all questions, and slipped away like a satisfied cat.

Dino reappeared with a new sheet of apron ideas and an alarming hat sample he refused to admit was a beret. "It's a *biscap*," he said, proud. "Half biscuit, half cap."

"No," Mira said, not even looking.

The painter finished the last flourish of the door and leaned back. Even Petar clapped, one dry smack of palm to palm that sounded like a grudging blessing.

A tiny cheer went up—Vesna's, the kids', someone's dog barked approval because dogs are patriots of joy. Petar muttered something that might have been "not bad." The notary dabbed at her eye, then pretended she had dust in it.

At the end of the day as the painter packed his brushes, accepted a second biscuit and a jar of honey payment "on account," and doffed his cap at Ophelia. "Tomorrow, I bring varnish. Today you look." He tapped the sign with one paint-slick finger the way a priest taps a bell.

He left them staring up. Mira set a hand on Ophelia's elbow. "You chose well."

"I think it chose me," Ophelia said, surprised to find it true.

Vesna looped her arm through Ophelia's. "Now we must plan window. Lace or linen? Jars or flowers? A discreet bowl of rosemary sprigs so the faithful can bless themselves?"

"No rosemary font," Mira said, but she was smiling, the rare soft one that lifted only one corner of her mouth.

Dino held the hat aloft hopefully.

"No," the chorus returned, but it was kind this time, rounded by laughter.

The bells rang, the sign was hung, and for the first time the green door no longer looked like an unanswered question. It looked like an entrance.

Ophelia took a step back until the lane framed the shop just so—the cream board, the navy letters, the shy bee—and snapped a photo for Tilda with hands that barely shook. **It's real,** she typed. **We have a sign.**

A heartbeat later: **TILDA** — *CRYING AT MY DESK. Also, please tell me you vetoed vampire biscuit.*

Ophelia laughed out loud, and laughter, as always, drew the town like sugar draws ants. People peered, pointed, drifted closer; Vesna began an unlicensed tour; Mira permitted herself the indulgence of pride in two syllables—"Good sign."

Petar crossed the lane, squinted at the letters, and nodded once. "Not yellow," he said. "Excellent."

"Coffee alliance?" Ophelia ventured, heart in her mouth.

He considered. "We see," he said, which in Kotor, she was learning, was practically a vow.

～

The very next afternoon Ophelia stared at her sign that had dried perfectly. Aunt Unit arrived like a visiting dignitary. The delivery truck rumbled into Kotor, grumbling through the narrow stone streets as if the city itself resented the intrusion. A small convoy followed—neighbors, curious tourists, and one confused goat that had wandered too far uphill. It was less an appliance delivery and more a parade.

The driver, a red-faced man who introduced himself only as Goran, leapt down from the cab and demanded papers with the solemnity of a border guard. He carried a clipboard like a weapon. Mira, prepared as always, produced a folder thick enough to stun a bear. Goran flipped through the documents, grunted at acronyms, and asked for one more form: the CMR, which Ophelia was still convinced stood for *Sea Monster Report*.

Mira handled it like a champion. She signed, stamped, and barked instructions in a rhythm that had Goran sweating within five minutes. Ophelia just clutched her own official stamp like a rabbit's foot, terrified he'd suddenly demand a new species of paperwork she hadn't invented yet.

At last, Goran relented. "Fine," he said. "Unload."

What followed was a ballet of brute force and shouted instructions. The oven was swaddled in plastic and strapped to a pallet like a dangerous prisoner. The delivery men grunted, strained, swore, and argued in three languages as they guided Aunt Unit down the ramp. The crowd applauded when the pallet jack squeaked onto the cobblestones.

"Careful!" Vesna cried, wringing her hands. "That oven is family!"

"It's an appliance," Mira corrected.

"It's an aunt," Ophelia and Vesna said firmly.

Ophelia couldn't breathe until the pallet finally squeezed through the green door with a centimeter to spare. The oven settled into its corner like it had always lived there, squat and proud, stainless-steel glinting against the stone walls.

She touched the metal reverently. "Hello, Aunt Unit," she whispered. "Please be kind."

The electrician muttered about amperage, Mira supervised the hookup with an expression that could curdle milk, and Vesna fussed around draping tea towels as if the oven might catch a chill. Dino tried to christen it with a ribbon but was physically stopped.

Finally, with a triumphant hum, Aunt Unit came to life. Lights flicked on, fans whirred, and heat rose into the shoebox air like the exhale of a dragon.

"Test," Mira ordered.

Ophelia had already prepared. She pulled from her bag a tin of biscuit dough she'd mixed the night before in the guesthouse kitchen. Butter, flour, milk, a pinch of salt—simple, humble, ready to rise or fail. She cut rounds with trembling hands, set them on a tray, and slid them into the oven.

Everyone seemed to hold its breath.

Minutes ticked. Heat shimmered. Butter perfumed the air. Vesna fanned herself with a honey brochure. Dino made oven sound effects under his breath until Mira threatened him with bodily harm. Marija tapped figures into her ledger with a precision that could measure hope. When the tray emerged, golden biscuits stood proud on the sheet, their tops kissed with brown, their edges flaked like whispered promises.

Ophelia's throat closed. She'd made biscuits a thousand times before, but never here, never with her future clattering against the pan in twelve perfect rounds. She set the tray on the counter. "Taste."

The first bites were chaos. Mira dissected hers with surgical precision. Vesna bit, moaned, and immediately began planning honey pairings. Dino nearly choked because he insisted on eating too quickly, then declared through crumbs, "These biscuits could stop wars." Marija ate silently, then nodded once. "Viable product."

"Viable?" Ophelia croaked.

"Viable and profitable," Marija amended, which in her language meant *delicious.*

Ophelia sagged against the counter. Relief, grief, joy—these feelings tangled until she couldn't tell one from the other. She didn't stop at one tray. Soon the oven ran like a heartbeat, tray after tray sliding in and out: rosemary biscuits (to please Ivana), honey biscuits (to fuel Vesna's empire), plum jam biscuits (messy, glorious, a hit with the kids), and butter-only classics that made Petar grudgingly admit, "Not bad."

Ophelia felt her phone vibrate in her pocket and pulled it out. **TILDA** *"Good news."*

Ophelia replied quickly, *"What is it?"*

"The House Sold."

Both grief and relief hit her all at once. *"Thanks for letting me know. Love you."*

"Love you too Phee."

By late afternoon, the courtyard smelled like a festival. The neighbors lingered with plates in hand. Tourists followed their noses. Even the sign painter, returned, varnish brush in one hand and a biscuit in the other, declaring, "Sign is dry, biscuits are not—perfect balance."

Ophelia stood amid the chaos, flour on her shirt, hair damp with steam, face aching from smiling. For the first time since Charles had collapsed, since the hospital, since the funeral, she felt not only alive but necessary. She was feeding people. And they were laughing with their mouths full.

When the last tray cooled, she tucked one biscuit aside, slipped upstairs, and sat at her little window overlooking the bay. She broke it in half, let the steam curl into the air, and whispered to the quiet water: "We did it, Charles. First batch."

A gull wheeled overhead, screaming like an idiot. It made her laugh, tears wetting her cheeks. Downstairs, Aunt Unit purred softly, like a cat that had decided to stay.

26

The day after Aunt Unit's triumphant arrival, Ophelia thought she might get a moment to breathe. She thought wrong. Branding day arrived like a thunderstorm with lipstick. It began when Dino skidded into the courtyard, his arms stacked with poster board, markers, and something that looked suspiciously like glitter. "I have slogans!" he declared, slapping one sheet onto the table. In thick bubble letters it read: **BISCUIT ME BABY ONE MORE TIME.**

Mira groaned audibly, her forehead hitting her clipboard with the force of a gavel. "No."

"Wait, wait," Dino said, flipping to the next. **ROLL WITH IT.** A sketch of a rolling pin grinned idiotically.

"No," Mira repeated.

"Okay, but look at this one—" Dino grinned, revealing **DON'T BE CRUMBY, EAT HERE.**

Ophelia snorted before she could stop herself. Mira turned on her like a teacher catching a student mid-giggle. "Do not encourage him."

Vesna arrived mid-slogan parade, carrying a basket of wrapped jars tied with ribbons. "Branding day!" she sang, setting them down like treasure. "I have designed tourist gift boxes. Honey jars, biscuit samples, postcards with our sign painted on them. Very chic. Very irresistible. Americans will faint."

Ophelia reached for one. "They're beautiful."

"Expensive," Mira corrected, flipping to her expense sheet. "Ribbon alone—"

"Ribbon sells fantasy," Vesna cut in smoothly. "Do not murder fantasy with numbers."

Marija arrived next, ledger under her arm, eyebrow already raised. She took one look at Dino's poster board and said, "No." Then she inspected Vesna's gift boxes, scribbled a figure, and announced, "Possible, if markup is three hundred percent."

"Three hundred percent!" Ophelia choked. "That's robbery."

"It's retail," Marija said serenely.

Meanwhile, Dino had climbed onto a chair, holding up another poster: **BISCUITS BEFORE BUSINESS.** Underneath, a cartoon biscuit winked.

"Absolutely not," Mira said without glancing up.

"Fine," Dino muttered, sitting down. "But you can't kill my creativity. It multiplies in the dark."

Ophelia pressed her palms to her eyes. "Can't we just... be called Biscuits by the Bay, bake good biscuits, and let people eat them?"

"That is too reasonable," Mira said. "Therefore impossible."

Vesna looped an arm around Ophelia's shoulders. "People come for biscuits, yes. But they stay for story. They want to take a little piece of Kotor home. A jar of honey. A ribbon with your logo. Maybe even..." She lifted one of Dino's glittered sketches, ignoring Mira's strangled sound. "...a silly apron."

"Aprons!" Dino perked up. "Yes! I have designs." He rifled through his stack, unveiling options: **KISS THE BISCUIT, I GOT BAKED IN KOTOR,** and, inexplicably, one that just said **HOT CROSS FUNS** with a drawing so anatomically confusing it made Ophelia choke on her coffee.

"Confiscated," Mira said, snatching it and shredding it into lethal confetti.

"Collector's item!" Dino wailed.

"Lawsuit waiting to happen," Mira corrected.

Marija tapped her pen. "Tourists will buy aprons," she

admitted. "Even bad aprons. Especially bad aprons. But we must control Dino."

"That is impossible," Vesna said airily. "Better to harness him, like a donkey who thinks he is a racehorse."

Ophelia laughed, clutching her stomach. "You people are insane."

"Yes," Mira said flatly. "But functional."

They argued for hours—over fonts for the menu, colors for the wrapping paper, whether biscuits should be served in baskets or plates, whether honey should come in jars or squeeze tubes. Dino suggested a biscuit mascot costume and nearly got tackled. Vesna suggested branded candles that smelled like butter and rosemary. Mira suggested bankruptcy. Marija suggested insurance.

In the middle of it all, Ophelia realized something strange: she wasn't panicking. Yes, her head spun with numbers and slogans, but underneath, she felt steady. For the first time, this wasn't just *her* dream wobbling on the edge of disaster. It was theirs too—Mira with her budgets, Vesna with her ribbons, Dino with his idiotic aprons, Marija with her ruthless logic.

She thought of Charles then, sudden, and sharp, the way he used to brainstorm with her late into the night. He would have loved this circus, would have egged Dino on, would have whispered to her afterward that she was the only one who made the whole thing work.

Her throat thickened. She blinked fast, smiled anyway, and when Vesna demanded her opinion on whether the gift boxes should smell faintly of lavender, Ophelia said, "Yes. Why not. Let's make biscuits smell like memory."

The courtyard exploded in fresh argument. But it was the good kind—the kind that felt like movement, like momentum. By the time the sun dipped low, and the last ribbon had been tied (against Mira's better judgment), the shoebox was cluttered with prototypes: mock menus, biscuit wrappers, stacks of aprons, towers of honey jars. Ophelia looked around at the mess and thought, *this is what a beginning looks like.*

Not clean. Not orderly. But alive.

By the time evening fell over Kotor, the bakery looked like the inside of Ophelia's brain: chaotic, overstuffed, and oddly beautiful. Biscuit crumbs dotted the counter like confetti, glitter clung to the cracks in the stone floor courtesy of Dino's "vision boards," and ribbon ends fluttered from Vesna's abandoned scissors like festive streamers. The sign above the door glowed softly in the last light, BISCUITS BY THE BAY steady against the dusk.

Her friends had finally dispersed, leaving her with silence that hummed like the sea in her ears. Mira had left muttering about receipts; Vesna had gone to hunt more tourists for honey trials; Dino had sulked off with three rejected apron sketches tucked under his arm, swearing they'd be collector's items someday; Marija had drifted away like a calm tide, ledger under her arm, promising to return in the morning with "further strategies." Now, only Ophelia remained. Alone with the smell of butter, sugar, and lavender dust still clinging to the air, she leaned against the counter and felt her body finally sag.

The day had been endless—sign debates, oven inaugurations, branding madness—but it was also the first day she truly believed she was building something. Not just for herself, but with a web of people who had tethered her to this place without asking her permission. A place that had gone from foreign stone and suspicion to something resembling a family. She wandered over to Aunt Unit, who still radiated faint heat from the day's marathon. She pressed her palm against the cool steel of the door. "Good job," she whispered, as if the oven were a teammate. "You and me, Aunt Unit. Let's not let each other down."

The broom that had been standing up in the back suddenly fell making Ophelia jump in fright. "And you.... Mr. or Miss Ghost. You, me, and miss Unit." She slowly approached the broom and put it back. "Lord, have mercy." She whispered.

On the counter waited a single biscuit she'd tucked aside—plain, golden, humble. She picked it up, broke it in half, and carried it her small desk She stared out at the mountains hunched close around the town, protective and immense, their shoulders draped in twilight. Somewhere a dog barked, somewhere a boat engine coughed. Life kept happening, indifferent and eternal.

She ate half slowly, the butter dissolving on her tongue, the salt reminding her of Alabama's summer sweat and Kotor's Sea air all at once. With the other half resting warm in her palm, she spoke to the night. "Charles," she whispered, voice cracking. "It's real now. We have a sign. We have an oven. People ate my biscuits and didn't die. Some of them even smiled. And" her laugh broke through tears "—one man tried to brand them with vampire teeth, but I vetoed it. You'd have loved that disaster. You'd have laughed until your face hurt."

The ache rolled through her, steady and unbearable, but she let it. For months she had tried to run from it—through airports, through narrow lanes, through stacks of paperwork—but here, under a sign that bore her dream's name, she let the ache sit beside her like an uninvited but permanent guest. She imagined Charles in the chair opposite, legs crossed, crooked smile waiting for her to finish. He would have teased her about overthinking. He would have eaten four biscuits in one sitting and declared himself the official quality control officer. He would have told her—seriously, finally, in that voice that cut straight to her bones—that she was capable. That she was enough.

Her throat closed. She set the half biscuit on the sill, like an offering. Maybe to him. Maybe to the bay. Maybe to herself. The silence stretched, not cruelly, but like a blanket she was learning to live under. Then, from outside, she heard laughter—a couple strolling arm in arm, a group of kids still chasing a soccer ball across the stones. Life pressed in, unrelenting and ordinary. She was part of it, whether she wanted to be or not.

She leaned her head against the glass. "I'm scared," she admitted softly. "The biscuit cooled beside her. The bay breathed. The town, this strange stone embrace, held her without even knowing it.

At some point, exhaustion pulled her under. She woke briefly when a breeze nudged the curtains, lifting them like a hand. The biscuit crumb trail still dotted the counter, the ribbon ends still littered the floor. It wasn't perfect, it wasn't polished, but it was hers. And for the first time since the wedding, since the aneurysm, since she had boarded a plane with grief as her only luggage, Ophelia felt not just like a widow surviving, but a woman beginning.

27

The green door greeted her with its familiar theatrical creak. The sign above it looked impossibly calm and steady as a benediction. Aunt Unit glinted in the corner like a friendly spacecraft. The room smelled faintly of paint and rosemary and the ghost of yesterday's butter. She flipped on the lights and pulled out her notebook. It was the day before opening.

"I thought we'd start with candles and a playlist," Ophelia said weakly.

"Candles burn. Playlists distract. Bleach saves businesses," Mira said, already scrubbing the counter with the kind of vigor that suggested she'd had caffeine and an argument on the walk over.

Vesna swept in ten minutes later with a bucket of flowers and a roll of linen. "We will seduce the eye while Mira seduces the germs," she declared, kissing Ophelia's cheek and leaving a lipstick crescent shaped like good luck. "Also: I bring 'soft opening' ribbons." She unfurled a spool the color of honey. "We tie bows on bags. People will imagine childhood. They will tip."

Dino arrived last, breathless, carrying a cardboard box labeled **APRONS – APPROVED** and another, smaller box labeled **APRONS – ILLEGAL (FOR HISTORY).** "I took the liberty of laundering the legal ones," he said proudly. "And hiding the illegal ones under my bed, where art belongs."

"Burn them," Mira said, without looking up.

"Art cannot be murdered," Dino said, clutching his chest.

Marija glided in on the top note of that drama, ledger beneath her arm, eyes already on tomorrow's cash flow. "I secured a small change float," she said, setting down a tidy tin. "Do not accept goats or mysterious coins from the Ottoman period. We are not a museum."

"We are a vibe," Dino corrected.

"We are a business," Mira and Marija said, in eerie harmony.

Ophelia smiled, nervous and grateful all at once. "Team," she announced, mostly to convince herself she had one. "Today, we do everything but panic."

"Panic at two," Vesna suggested. "Just a little. For circulation."

"Hiring," Marija said, tapping her pen. "We need hands."

Ophelia nodded, stomach pinching. She'd avoided the question by pretending she had eight arms. "Do we... know any hands?"

Vesna snapped her fingers. "Nika."

"Who is Nika?" Ophelia asked, braced for a cousin of a cousin who was secretly a violin prodigy.

"A niece of my neighbor. Or a goddaughter. Or just a child who needs money," Vesna said airily. "Sixteen. Quick. Polite. Terrifying to boys. I will fetch."

Mira gave the tiniest shrug, which, translated from Mira, meant *acceptable risk.* "She learns, she stays. She whines, she goes."

Within twenty minutes, Vesna reappeared with Nika in tow: a sharp-eyed teenager in a black T-shirt and a braid down her back, who surveyed the shop with the cool appraisal of a visiting auditor. "Rules?" she asked.

Mira fell a little in love on the spot. "Number one: wash hands. Number two: cash accuracy. Number three: never argue with Aunt Unit."

"Aunt Unit?" Nika deadpanned.

"Our oven," Ophelia said.

Nika considered, then nodded once. "Okay."

They plunged into prep. Mira carved the space into zones with tape and purpose: register here, tray landing there, honey shelf tucked under the rosemary sprig painted on the sign (Vesna's triumph). Nika shadowed Ophelia through a mock service run, memorizing the choreography of plates and words: "Dobro jutro—good morning. Classic or rosemary? Honey or jam? Cash or card?" She practiced the smile that was polite but not apologetic. Ophelia wanted to give her a medal.

Dino set up the window display under Vesna's supervision—linen runner, a neat stagger of jars, a sprig of rosemary in a tiny vase, and a single biscuit under a glass dome like a saint's relic. He tried to tuck a glittered "soft opening" sign behind it; Mira removed it with chopsticks, as one might handle a biohazard.

Midmorning, Ophelia squared her shoulders and made the pilgrimage across the lane to Petar's café, palms sweating. The coffee alliance could still make or break her mornings. Petar looked up from his espresso machine with his usual air of mild mourning, as if every latte were a eulogy.

"Truce?" Ophelia asked, hands up, absurdly. "I don't want to fight. I want to feed people and send them to you for coffee. We could... be allies?"

He studied her a full ten seconds, then reached under the counter and slid a small stack of coffee tokens toward her—paper chits he gave to locals when he had overpoured. "You put tokens in biscuit bags," he said. "Half of them. They come to me. I send people to you when they ask, 'what is that smell.'"

Ophelia blinked. "That's—are we—did we just—"

He held up a hand. "Do not thank me. It makes me itchy." Then, in what could only be called a flourish by Petar standards, he added a tiny bag of his house roast ground for moka pot. "For testing."

"Alliance," Ophelia breathed, AL-LI-ANCE, and tried not to cry on a man who likely only cried in the presence of soccer.

Back in the bakery, she tucked the tokens into a little dish near the register as if they were precious stones. Mira approved, which was rarer than rain in August. "Good. Kotor prefers symbiosis."

"Big English word," Dino said, impressed.

"It means 'no one murders anyone over espresso,'" Mira translated.

By noon, the place gleamed. Aunt Unit hummed like a basso singer clearing his throat. The sign caught a forgiving patch of sun, the tiny bee casting its microscopic shadow right where Ophelia liked it. The price cards sat in a neat stack, hand-lettered the night before: **Classic Butter – 2.50€; Rosemary & Sea Salt – 2.80€; Honey Brush – 2.80€; Plum Jam – 3.00€; Savory "Fisherman's Friend" (no anchovies, calm down) – 3.20€.** Vesna had vetoed anchovies but insisted on the name: "Fishermen will feel famous."

They were mid-rehearsal—Nika practicing bag-folding; Ophelia teaching the art of honey drizzles; Dino wearing an apron like a sash—when the Inspector arrived.

He was compact, dapper, with a clipboard and the calm demeanor of a man who had watched grown adults weep over sink placement. His name tag read B. Kovačević. He nodded at each of them, glanced at the sign as if it might confess something, and stepped inside.

"Pre-opening compliance," he said. "We check. We are kind if you are prepared."

Ophelia's stomach attempted a cartwheel. Mira moved into the pocket like a point guard. "We are prepared," she said.

The next twenty minutes were a slow-motion tango between fear and readiness. The inspector checked the washing station (approved), the trash area (approved), the ingredient storage (approved after Ophelia moved a rebellious sack of flour a full two centimeters to the left), Aunt Unit's electrical hookup (approved with a grunt), and the thermometer in the small refrigerator (approved after tapping it twice like a barometer). He examined the allergen notice Mira had posted in both languages. He read the price cards with grave interest, nodded at the absence of Comic Sans as if this were a moral victory, and finally, finally, clicked his pen.

"Open soft," he said. "Not loud. Learn your rhythm. Do not

let Dino name anything." He signed a form with a signature that had beaten many kitchens into submission. "Good luck."

As Ophelia took the form from him the room exhaled as he left. She waved the form at her face, "Good Lord, I sweating more than a hooker in church?"

"Be happy. You did it." Mira encouraged Ophelia placing her arm around her.

"We did it!" Ophelia brought in Mira, Vesna, Nika, and Dina for a hug.

They were officially approved to open. After their embrace, Ophelia leaned on the counter and laughed, a little wild. "Emergency biscuit!" she declared, and they ate one each as if it were communion.

Afternoon ebbed into late light. They split to run last errands. Marija took Nika to the bank for change larger than the national debt. Mira hustled to the hardware store for two more extension cords. Vesna promised to return with "tasteful flowers and also a tiny bell." Dino swore to print a modest announcement flyer and was threatened with exile if he disobeyed the word "modest."

Left alone with Aunt Unit and the sound of her own blood in her ears, Ophelia rolled dough. The counter became a landscape of flour. She folded, turned, pressed, and when the cutter bit down, she felt that old, secret thrill: circles emerging where there had been none. She set them on trays in twinned rows, little moons ready to rise.

TILDA called on video just as Ophelia slid a test batch in. *"Face!"* Tilda demanded, and Ophelia obliged, aiming the camera badly so Tilda mostly saw a chin and a sliver of sign. *"You look alive,"* Tilda said, delighted. *"And also, like someone who has threatened several officials today."*

"Only softly," Ophelia admitted. "We passed inspection. Petar formed an alliance. We hired a teenage assassin named Nika."

Tilda cheered. *"Put me on the counter so I can see the first tray."*

They counted down together. When Ophelia pulled the biscuits, Tilda clapped on a tiny screen in Alabama, and Ophelia cried in a bakery in Montenegro, and the distance between them felt like a string they were both holding.

Evening drew a soft shawl over the lane. The ribbon on the window swayed as if nodding. Vesna trotted back with a bouquet of olive branches and wildflowers that looked exactly like "tasteful" and exactly like "from a ditch"—which was perfect. She wedged them into a jar by the door. "For prosperity," she said. "And because leaves make everything look intentional."

Mira returned with more cords and the grim news that Dino had been seen at the copy shop. Ophelia texted him *NO FLYERS*, and he responded with a halo emoji, which meant catastrophe. Marija messaged a photo of the change tin, meticulously organized like a tiny city.

They cleaned again because cleaning was a coping mechanism. Ophelia wrote **SOFT OPENING TOMORROW – MORNING HOURS – BE KIND** on the chalkboard in her handwriting. She practiced unlocking and re-locking the till, counting coins. She set aside a tray—first batch of the morning—labeled with a sticky note that said **FOR PETAR** (diplomacy). She tucked coffee tokens into paper bags—every other one, as promised. She placed the stamp near the register, because circling her own name gave her courage.

When the others finally pried the mop out of Mira's hands and shepherded her to the gate, when Vesna kissed the sign and declared it photogenic, when Marija set an alarm and Dino swore an oath of flyer chastity on Aunt Unit (which no one believed), Ophelia stayed a minute longer.

She turned off the overheads and left only the little lamp by the counter. The shop glowed like a snow globe. Outside, the bay inhaled and exhaled; somewhere, the clock tower cleared its throat. She leaned both hands on the counter and spoke to the room the way one speaks to a faithful animal. "God, if you are listening, help a southern girl out. Make tomorrow a success, and please, keep Aunt Unit happy. Amen."

A noise from the back of the shop made her jump. "...and Mr or Miss Ghost please behave."

The silence felt approving. She locked the green door, double-checked it, triple-checked it because anxiety is thorough, and walked into the blue-black lane. The sign held the moon like an accent. The tiny bee's shadow had gone to sleep. Across the way, Petar's café was closed, but a single light burned in the back—a vigil for espresso.

28

The morning cracked open with the sound of bells, gulls, and Aunt Unit's gentle roar. Ophelia was already in the bakery by five, apron on, hair tied back in what she hoped was a "competent baker" knot. The air smelled of flour and butter, sharp and comforting all at once. The counter gleamed. The chalkboard sign outside declared:

SOFT OPENING TODAY – MORNING HOURS – BE KIND.

By 6:45, Mira had arrived, crisp as a fresh page, clipboard in hand. Nika followed close behind, looking more awake than anyone had the right to at that hour, braid swinging like punctuation. Vesna swept in soon after with a small armful of wildflowers for the counter. Dino appeared last, dramatically, carrying nothing but mischief.

"Remember," Mira said as she positioned herself by the register like a sentry. "No giveaways. No chaos. Control flow. Soft opening means small. Quiet."

"Subtle," Vesna echoed.

"Elegant," Marija added, sliding in just as the bells struck seven.

The shoebox glowed with readiness. Trays of biscuits sat steaming on the counter: plain butter, rosemary, honey-brushed, plum jam tucked in the middle like secrets. Ophelia felt her pulse in her wrists, her ears, even in her knees. She had half a second to breathe before the first customer appeared.

It was Petar. Of course, it was. He stood in the doorway like a reluctant king, hands behind his back, the faintest trace of a smile tugging his lips. "Smell is strong," he announced, as though delivering a verdict.

"Good morning," Ophelia said, throat dry. She handed him a paper bag with a single biscuit inside, carefully labeled FOR PETAR. She added one of his coffee tokens, tucked like an olive branch.

He opened the bag, took one bite, chewed slowly, then nodded. "All right," he said. "We are allies." And he left without fanfare, bag in hand, his loyalty as tacit as his espresso shots. Her knees nearly gave out. "First sale," she whispered.

"Not sale," Marija corrected. "Diplomatic trade. Still counts."

The next customer was a tourist couple—sunhats, sandals, cameras swinging like pendulums. They peered at the chalkboard sign, then stepped inside. "What's a biscuit?" the woman asked, puzzled.

Ophelia's brain nearly emptied. Nika saved her by sliding a butter biscuit onto a small plate and presenting it with the kind of gravitas that made it seem like a national treasure. "Fluffy bread," she said. "Better."

The tourists laughed, bought two, and left chewing happily.

After that, the trickle began. An elderly woman in a kerchief bought rosemary biscuits "for memory." A fisherman stopped by, eyeing the *Fisherman's Friend* flavor suspiciously before buying three and grumbling, "At least no anchovies." A pair of teenagers bought plum jam biscuits and immediately smeared them across their faces, posing for selfies with the green door.

Dino, assigned to tray-running, insisted on narrating every transaction like a sports announcer. "AND SHE GOES FOR THE HONEY BRUSH—OHH, AN EXCELLENT CHOICE—TEXTURE'S LOOKING GOOD, CROWD LOVES IT—" until Mira physically smacked him with her clipboard.

Vesna floated around like a maître d', offering napkins, complimenting accents, sliding honey jars into conversations with the skill of a politician. Marija hovered discreetly near the register, making small ticks in her ledger, occasionally murmuring, "Raise plum jam to 3.20. Demand is strong."

Ophelia, at the counter, rolled dough, cut circles, and fed Aunt Unit like she was stoking a fire that kept her alive. Each tray slid in, slid out, golden and fragrant, the rhythm steadying her heartbeat. With every bite someone took, every smile, every crumb dropped onto her clean floor, the fear loosened.

Mid-morning, a group of schoolchildren came barreling in, lured by the smell. Their teacher tried to herd them, but Vesna waved her off, handing out tiny biscuit halves like communion. The room filled with chatter, laughter, crumbling edges. For a moment, Ophelia just leaned back and watched: the shoebox alive, humming, full.

"Look at you," Tilda texted when Ophelia snapped a quick photo of the chaos and sent it across the ocean. "You're feeding a town."

Ophelia typed back with flour-stained fingers: I think I'm feeding myself too.

By eleven, the tray racks were nearly empty. Aunt Unit wheezed softly but gamely, and Ophelia realized with a shock: they had sold out.

Nika counted the till with military precision, lips pressed into a thin line of approval. "Successful," she pronounced.

"Viable," Marija added, which was her version of confetti.

"Delicious," Vesna corrected, licking jam from her finger.

Ophelia pressed both hands to her apron, closed her eyes, and let the truth of it sink in: *her biscuits, her shop, her beginning.*

By noon, Ophelia had convinced herself they'd coast through the rest of the day. The trays were empty, the till was balanced, and Mira had declared "adequate performance" in a tone that, for Mira, meant *near miracle.* Ophelia thought maybe they could sweep, restock, breathe. Maybe even—imagine this—have lunch. She should have known better.

Because Kotor had ears, and those ears had mouths, and those mouths had already whispered: *The American's biscuit shop is open.* By 12:15, the whisper had turned into a rumor. By 12:30, the rumor had become a migration.

First came two fishermen with weathered hands and skeptical faces. "Heard you make food that isn't bread, isn't cake," one of them said. Ophelia handed them rosemary biscuits straight from the tray, and their expressions melted like butter. They bought six each and promised to return "with cousins."

At 12:45, three German tourists appeared, snapping photos of everything from the sign to the honey jars. One of them asked if Vesna came with the biscuits, to which she replied, "Only if you buy a dozen," before upselling them three jars of honey.

At 1:00, a line formed out the door. A *line.* Ophelia stared at it, horrified, and delighted in equal measure. "But this was supposed to be soft!" she wailed.

"Soft is for bread," Mira muttered, grabbing the mop to mark a queue line on the floor. "This is commerce."

From there, the afternoon unspooled like a slapstick play. Aunt Unit wheezed under the constant flow of trays; Ophelia rolled dough until her arms shook; Nika darted between register and counter like a shadowy warrior.

Dino, drafted into "customer entertainment," set up near the window with a sketchpad. "Biscuit portraits!" he announced, offering to draw people as pastries for one euro. By the time Mira caught wind and shut it down, he had already sold six, including one to a bewildered Canadian who thought he was buying a caricature.

Vesna turned into a one-woman marketing army. She whispered to tourists about "the secret family recipe" (Ophelia's grandmother would've choked at that lie), tied ribbons around take-away bags until the ribbon spool gave up, and convinced a man from Belgrade that he needed to buy biscuits "for the train ride, for his wife, and for the story."

Marija positioned herself at the back of the shop with her ledger, running silent calculations. When she murmured, "Raise butter biscuits to 2.70 tomorrow," Ophelia nearly fainted. "We're price gouging!" she protested.

"We're surviving," Marija replied.

By mid-afternoon, the bakery had turned into a pressure cooker. Flour dusted the counters like fresh snow. Jam streaked across aprons. The floor, freshly scrubbed that morning, looked like a battlefield of crumbs. The air thickened with butter and laughter and the scrape of chairs.

And Ophelia—tired, sweaty, terrified—realized she was *happy*. Deep-down, bone-deep happy, the kind that came from motion, from work, from doing the thing she thought she couldn't. But happiness doesn't prevent disaster.

At 3:00, the oven groaned. Aunt Unit had been running since five, and when Ophelia slid in another tray of plum jam biscuits, there was a cough, a sputter, and a small *pop*. The fan stuttered. The heat wavered. "No, no, no," Ophelia whispered, clutching the tray.

"Machine rebellion," Dino declared dramatically.

"Overheated," Mira corrected, already reaching for the breaker. "Turn it off. Let it breathe."

"But the line—" Ophelia gestured wildly at the customers snaking out the door.

"Scarcity is marketing," Marija said calmly. "You are sold out. They will return tomorrow. More customers, more money."

Vesna nodded firmly. "Leave them hungry. Desire is stronger than full stomachs."

The crowd groaned in disappointment when Ophelia announced the last tray was gone, but many promised to come back, muttering about tomorrow, about flavors, about how they'd heard from their cousin's friend's neighbor that these biscuits were "better than church."

By 3:30, the shop was quiet again. Chairs skewed. Crumbs everywhere. The till stuffed. Ophelia slumped against the counter, dizzy.

"I'm plumb tired but we survived," she said weakly.

"We thrived," Mira corrected.

"What a beautiful day," Vesna praised.

"I need wine," Dino announced.

Nika simply counted the till again and said, "Tomorrow will be worse."

Ophelia laughed until her sides hurt. She sank to the floor in the middle of the mess, flour in her hair, jam on her sleeve, the taste of butter still on her tongue. A cat wandered over to her and curled up next to her. She giggled, "What a day."

And even though exhaustion pressed heavy on her bones, she felt lighter than she had in months. The bakery had never looked so lived in.

The door opened ant it was Marija. "I'm here to help with today's paperwork."

Mira, who looked no less composed than she had at seven that morning, clapped her clipboard closed. "Assessment: chaos. Outcome: success. Improvements: many." She glanced at Ophelia. "Well, done Ophelia." Mira handed Marija the paperwork from the day's numbers.

Ophelia gave a shaky laugh. "Thank you.?"

"For day one," Mira said, "yes. The goal is to survive Tomorrow, we survive again."

Vesna plopped into a chair, fanning herself with an empty honey box. "Tomorrow I will bring wine at noon. It will be medicine, not indulgence."

"I vote for medicine now," Dino said, sweeping into the shop like he hadn't been gone for two suspicious hours. In his hands he carried a bottle of red wine and a loaf of crusty bread, both pilfered—or "borrowed with intention," as he called it—from his cousins' restaurant. "A toast," he declared, pulling glasses from nowhere like a magician.

Marija, still perched in her corner with her ledger, closed it softly. "Numbers are encouraging. Tomorrow, we adjust prices. Today, we drink." She accepted a glass as if it were an entry on a spreadsheet.

Nika, slouched against the doorframe, accepted hers with the indifference of youth, though her faint smile betrayed pride. "I didn't mess up the till," she said.

"You didn't mess up anything," Ophelia said, raising her own glass. "None of you did."

"Živjeli," Mira said, lifting her wine.

Ophelia followed and held up her wine, "Cheers."

Everyone repeated after her "Cheers."

Ophelia laughed until the laugh cracked into something wetter, and she blinked fast to keep the tears from spilling. She lifted her glass high. "To biscuits," she said.

"To biscuits!" they echoed, voices colliding, glasses clinking.

They ate the bread Dino had brought, dipped in Vesna's honey, drank the wine, and let the tension seep out like steam. The little shop that had rattled and heaved and nearly burst from the weight of its first day now glowed with the soft warmth of a job done. Not perfect. Not polished. But done.

At some point, Dino collapsed dramatically across two chairs, claiming creative exhaustion. Vesna began sketching plans for gift baskets "to capture the German market." Mira scribbled notes in a fresh column titled "Immediate Fixes." Marija recalculated tomorrow's change float. Nika simply sat, quietly satisfied. And Ophelia? She floated among them, pouring wine, laughing at Dino's antics, shaking her head at Mira's ruthless efficiency, marveling at Vesna's endless charm. She thought of Charles, then— how he would have teased her about "soft opening" turning into "biscuits gone wild." How he would have kissed her flour-dusted cheek and told her he'd never been prouder.

The ache came sharp, then softened. It sat with her, steady and unthreatening, like an old scar that twinges when it rains.

Later, when the glasses were empty and her friends drifted out into the night—Vesna with a basket of leftover biscuits for her neighbors, Mira muttering about bleach and extension cords, Dino reciting bad poetry to the moon, Marija guiding Nika home like a general leading a cadet—Ophelia stayed behind.

She cleaned quietly, wiping counters, sweeping crumbs, humming to herself. When the shoebox finally stood tidy again, she turned off the lights. Only the little lamp by the register remained, casting a golden glow on the counter.

She went to the door, unlocked it, and stepped out into the lane. The bay was ink-black, stars pricking through the sky. The sign above her head caught the faint light of the moon: **BISCUITS BY THE BAY.** The bee seemed to wink.

Ophelia leaned against the doorframe, tired to the marrow, and whispered into the quiet: "We did it. Day one." The mountains kept their secrets. The bay breathed. Somewhere in the dark, a gull shrieked like a heckler at a comedy club. And Ophelia, for the first time in a long, long time, felt not like a woman lost, but like a woman found. She locked the door, pressed her hand against the green paint, and walked into the night, leaving the shop to dream with her.

29

By the end of the first full week, Ophelia had acquired something she never asked for: a reputation. This was a reputation that whispered through cobblestones and rattled in espresso cups. She had become, without warning and without preparation, The Biscuit Woman.

It started innocently enough. A pair of children discovered that if they timed their morning walk to school just right, they could snag the warm air that rolled out of her shop when she opened Aunt Unit. They'd stand outside inhaling, eyes closed, sighing dramatically, then skip off yelling, *"Biskvit dama!"* The nickname spread the way nicknames always do—carelessly, but with staying power.

By Tuesday, fishermen were using it too, marching in before dawn, their boots dripping seawater across her freshly scrubbed floor. They'd grumble, "Biscuit Woman, two rosemary," as if she'd been born to serve them. Ophelia learned quickly not to argue—especially when one of them tried to pay her with a live crab. Mira intercepted, demanded euros, and threatened to cook the crab herself. The man returned the next day with exact change and an apology biscuit order twice as large.

Tourists caught wind next. They snapped photos of the green door, the honey jars gleaming in the window, and the chalkboard sign Vesna updated daily with terrible puns: *"Our biscuits rise to the occasion!"* or *"Flaky in the best way!"* Ophelia begged her to stop; Vesna doubled down. Soon hashtags sprouted like weeds: *#BiscuitLadyKotor,* *#NotACookie, #HeavenInDoughForm.*

The bakery, once a quiet experiment, now throbbed with life. Aunt Unit roared from dawn until dusk. Flour clung to every surface like ghostly fingerprints. The bell over the green door chimed so often that Ophelia swore she heard it in her dreams. And the people came. Not just once—*again.* That was the shocking part. Tourists returned the next morning before catching buses out of town. Fishermen swung by at odd hours, swearing the rosemary biscuits made their nets luckier. An elderly woman declared that the honey brush biscuits cured her arthritis (Mira muttered "placebo effect" until the woman gifted her wool socks). The chaos was relentless.

Mira, clipboard in hand, became both general and executioner. She drew up schedules with arrows and color coding, barking orders like "Rotate trays now!" and "You missed a wipe-down at the sink!" The scary part was—she was always right.

Vesna turned into an unstoppable marketing machine. She tied ribbons around bags, charmed tourists into buying honey "for their cousins in Zurich," and once convinced a skeptical teenager that biscuits were "the new protein bar." He bought three.

Dino leaned into "customer experience." He told jokes, exaggerated stories about Ophelia's "secret Southern family recipe" (just butter and stubbornness), and once offered a dramatic monologue comparing biscuits to eternal love. Mira nearly banned him from the premises, but the customers laughed—and bought more.

Marija adjusted prices daily. She hovered near the register like a hawk, scribbling in her ledger. If butter prices shifted even a whisper at the market, she raised biscuit costs by ten cents without blinking. "Survival," she explained flatly.

And Nika, the teenager with the braid, treated the till like sacred ground. She memorized regulars, counted change with a soldier's precision, and glared at anyone who tried to pay in coins smaller than ten cents. Customers obeyed her without question.

Ophelia—flour up to her elbows, apron permanently stained,

hair perpetually escaping its knot—found herself in the eye of the storm. She rolled dough, cut circles, fed trays into Aunt Unit, and smiled until her face hurt. The rhythm became a strange kind of song: roll, cut, bake, serve, repeat.

At night, when the bakery was empty and she was alone sweeping crumbs into a dustpan, she'd catch herself talking to the ghost, "I hope you enjoyed watching the day. As much as I love your company, please don't ever scare me."

The door squeaked a bit from the wind, and she said to herself, "time to go home." She stopped herself and realized what she just said, "time to go home? Home. I'm home."

~

Sure enough, she couldn't walk through the square without being stopped. Old men lectured her on "proper Montenegrin flour." Women offered unsolicited advice about yeast, even though biscuits didn't use yeast. Tourists begged for recipes and selfies. Children shouted, "Biscuit Lady!" when she passed, as if she were some pastry superhero.

Even Petar, her reluctant coffee ally, began muttering things that almost sounded complimentary. "Biscuit Woman doubled my coffee sales," he grumbled one morning. When Ophelia tried to thank him for sending customers her way, he waved her off. "Do not make me sentimental. It ruins espresso."

Still, his gruff acceptance felt like a coronation.

And so, by the second week, Ophelia was no longer just Ophelia. She was the Biscuit Woman of Kotor. A landmark. A joke. A story whispered down lanes and across the bay. It should have overwhelmed her. And sometimes, at night, it did. But mostly—it steadied her. The grief she carried was still there, heavy and constant, but for the first time since Charles, something else filled her hands. Something warm, fragrant, and real.

It was into this whirlwind, this half-life of flour and fame and fatigue, that Luka stepped through the green door.

The bell over the green door rang in its usual cheerful way, but for some reason, the sound landed differently. Ophelia didn't notice right away. She was elbow-deep in dough, hair coming loose from its bun, apron smeared with what looked like jam but might have been battle scars. Aunt Unit hissed behind her, the fan laboring with a tray of rosemary biscuits, and Mira was in the corner tallying numbers like she was prosecuting a crime.

"Biscuit Woman," Mira sang, sweeping past with a bouquet of ribbons. "Your public awaits!"

Ophelia groaned. "Tell my public I'm on strike." But when she turned, wiping her floury hands on her apron, she saw him.

He didn't fit the usual categories. He wasn't dressed like a tourist—no camera, no sandals with socks, no hat advertising a cruise line. And he wasn't quite like the locals she'd grown used to either. His clothes were simple but not careless: a button-down rolled at the sleeves, jeans faded from real use, boots scuffed from travel. Dark hair curled slightly at the temples, like it couldn't quite be tamed. He had the build of someone who worked with his hands, though his posture was relaxed, almost reluctant.

But it was his eyes that stopped her—gray-blue, like the bay under clouds, sharp enough to notice everything, kind enough not to say it out loud. He scanned the bakery, the trays, the chalkboard sign with Vesna's pun of the day (*"You Batter Believe It!"*), and then his gaze landed on Ophelia. She felt it like a touch. Startling. Solid.

"Dobro jutro," he said, his voice low, smooth, carrying the cadence of home but softened by years away. Then, switching to English with barely an accent, "What do you recommend?"

Ophelia blinked, realizing she had been staring. "Uh—everything?" She winced. Great sales pitch.

A corner of his mouth lifted. "Ambitious."

Mira, without looking up from her ledger, muttered, "Try rosemary. It survives tourists."

"Thank you," he said, with a politeness that carried weight, as if he'd been raised to mean it. He leaned a forearm against the counter. "I'll take one rosemary. And—" his eyes flicked to the jam tray—"one of those. Plum?"

Ophelia nodded, fumbling for the tongs. Her hands, traitorous, decided to misbehave, dropping one biscuit back onto the tray with a clatter. She nearly swore. He chuckled, low and warm, and she thought: *Danger.*

She handed him the bag. "Here you go. Fresh. Still warm."

He accepted it like it mattered. He tore off a piece of the rosemary biscuit, tasted it slowly, and closed his eyes for a fraction of a second. When he opened them again, something had shifted—approval, maybe, or recognition. "This tastes like my grandmother's kitchen," he said softly. "But lighter. Less heavy."

Ophelia's throat tightened unexpectedly. Compliments came often now—tourists gushing, locals grudging—but none had struck her like this. Less heavy. She almost laughed at the irony.

"What brings you here?" Mira demanded, swooping in before Ophelia could answer. "You are not tourist. You are not my cousin's friend's cousin. Who are you?"

The man smiled faintly, as if used to interrogation. "Luka," he said simply. "My family has a home here. I've been away. I came to stay for a while."

"Home," Mira repeated, narrowing her eyes. "And yet you do not smell like fishing or bureaucracy. Suspicious."

"Leave him alone," Ophelia blurted, more sharply than she meant to. Mira raised an eyebrow, smirked, and floated away like she'd lit a fuse.

Luka took another bite of biscuit, unbothered. "You're not from here," he said—not accusing, just stating.

"No," Ophelia admitted, dusting flour from her hands. "I'm from Woodard, Alabama."

"Alabama," he echoed, rolling the syllables as if tasting them. His smile deepened, not mocking, just curious. "Farther than Podgorica."

"Just a little," she said, and despite herself, she smiled back.

For a moment, the shop fell away—the noise of customers, Mira's muttering, Dino somewhere in the corner reciting biscuit poetry to an amused tourist. It was just Luka at the counter, biscuit crumbs on his fingers, eyes like storm-touched sea, looking at her as if she wasn't just the Biscuit Woman but a person worth knowing. And Ophelia, flour on her cheek and grief still tethered to her bones, felt something dangerous flicker in her chest: a spark.

If Ophelia thought Luka's quiet smile and storm-colored eyes would vanish into the churn of biscuits, she underestimated two things: small-town gossip and her friends.

It began the next morning. Vesna burst through the green door at sunrise, arms loaded with jars of honey and mischief. "Tell me everything," she announced before Ophelia had even tied her apron.

"About what?" Ophelia asked, genuinely confused.

Vesna gasped, scandalized. "About *who?* Luka! Tall, dark, polite, smells faintly of sea wind. He came yesterday, yes? He looked at you like you were the only woman in Kotor. I nearly fainted into the honey jars."

Ophelia flushed so red she nearly matched the plum jam stains on her apron. "He bought biscuits. That's all."

"Bought biscuits, stared into your soul—it is a short distance between these things," Vesna declared, setting down her jars like trophies.

Mira entered just then, clipboard already open, eyebrow arched. "Who stared into whose soul?"

"Luka," Vesna sang. "Our Biscuit Lady has an admirer."

Mira gave Ophelia a long, assessing look that felt like being audited. "You don't have time for admirers," she said briskly. "The rosemary stock is low, the oven fan needs replacing, and we still haven't solved the sugar supply issue. Men are distractions."

"He's not a distraction," Ophelia protested. "He's just—" she fumbled, "a customer."

"A customer who chewed slowly," Vesna added, eyes sparkling.

"A customer who asked questions," Mira countered. "Suspicious."

Before Ophelia could defend herself further, Dino swept in, late as usual, waving a sketchpad like a flag. "I wrote a sonnet about him!" he declared. "Shall I recite?"

"No," Mira barked.

"Yes," Vesna cheered.

Ophelia buried her face in her hands. "Please don't."

But Dino launched into it, anyway, planting himself on a chair like a poet laureate:

O Luka, man of biscuit bite,
With eyes of storm and jaw of might,
You chewed with grace, you chewed with care,
And left our Biscuit Lady bare—

"ENOUGH," Ophelia yelped, pelting him with a dishtowel. Customers glanced up from their tables, amused. Dino bowed deeply.

Marija slipped in then, ledger tucked under her arm, cool as a shadow. "What's this nonsense?" she asked.

"Romance," Vesna sighed.

"Distraction," Mira snapped.

"Marketing opportunity," Dino announced. "Imagine the slogan: *Biscuits so good they bring men home.*"

Marija rolled her eyes but said nothing, which was somehow worse.

Ophelia slammed her flour-covered palms on the counter. "Listen to me! I am *not* interested. I came here to start over, not to—" she faltered, grief catching her throat, "not to do this again."

The room quieted, just for a heartbeat. The weight of Charles's absence sat heavy between them.

Vesna softened first, her teasing fading to tenderness. She reached across the counter, squeezing Ophelia's wrist. "No one says you must. But you are allowed."

Mira cleared her throat, uncomfortable, but didn't disagree. Dino muttered something about destiny but quieter than usual. Even Marija murmured, "Permission is not weakness."

Ophelia blinked hard, willing tears not to fall. She dusted her hands on her apron, trying for levity. "It was just biscuits," she said.

But that night, sweeping crumbs from the shoebox floor, she remembered the way Luka had said *lighter, less heavy*. The way his gaze had felt steady, like an anchor dropped quietly in a storm. And she hated herself for wondering if he might come back.

The day ended the way all the days had lately: with Ophelia sweeping up crumbs and humming to herself, exhausted but unwilling to leave the shoebox messy. The streets outside were thinning. The cruise ship crowd had dispersed, the square slipping into its twilight lull. Lanterns glowed in windows, and the bay mirrored the sky's indigo.

She locked the door, pressed her palm against the green paint—her ritual—and stepped into the lane. Her feet carried her without thought toward the water. It was becoming habit, this slow walk after closing, the air cool, the salt breeze working like balm.

Tonight, though, she wasn't alone.

Luka sat on the low stone wall by the bay, back to the mountains, sketchbook balanced on his knee. His boots scuffed the cobblestones as he drew with steady strokes, head bent, brow furrowed in concentration.

For a moment, Ophelia considered slipping away before he noticed. But the thought was absurd. This was Kotor; slipping away was impossible. She cleared her throat softly. "Working late?"

He looked up, surprised but not startled. A smile tugged one corner of his mouth. "So are you."

She lifted her biscuit-dusted hands in mock surrender. "Guilty. I sweep, therefore I am."

He chuckled, the sound low, like the rumble of a boat engine across water. He closed the sketchbook but didn't hide it, just rested it on his knee. "It's the only quiet time. The bay listens better at night."

Ophelia tilted her head. "Does it answer?"

"Sometimes," he said. "Mostly it reminds you you're small. That can be comforting."

She joined him on the wall before she could think better of it.

"So, you are an artist?" she asked pointing at his sketchbook.

"Oh, this I just do for fun. My family owns a large fishing company in Budva. It's very successful. They keep a house here. Well, they have several homes throughout Montenegro."

"You're bragging."

"I do not mean to. You asked, so I tell you."

"So you are a fisherman?"

"No."

"Then what are you?"

He laughed, "I am a man in search of a dream."

"Hmmm." Ophelia smiled at the thought. He smiled back at her, and she felt herself flush. They sat in easy silence for a while, the bay stretching dark and endless before them. Somewhere, a gull cried; somewhere else, a boat creaked against its moorings. Finally, Luka spoke. "I was gone a long time. Work, cities, noise. Coming back...it feels strange. Like I'm a tourist in my own town."

Ophelia studied his profile in the lamplight. Strong jaw, hair curling where it refused discipline, eyes shadowed but steady. "I know that feeling. Except I don't even have the claim of home. I'm the tourist who accidentally moved in."

He turned to her then, gaze searching, not unkind. "Not so accidental. You chose this."

She hesitated. "Maybe. Or maybe it chose me."

The silence between them shifted—no longer empty, but full, stretched taut like dough waiting to rise.

Luka broke it with a half-smile. "Your biscuits—lighter, less heavy. I meant that as a compliment. My grandmother's food could anchor a ship."

Ophelia laughed, startled by how good it felt. "Mine could anchor a Southern Baptist dinner. Heavy is kind of our thing."

"Then you carry a gift," he said simply. No flourish, no performance—just the truth as he saw it.

And Ophelia, who had been told she was strong, brave, even admirable in her grief, found herself undone not by grand praise but by this: a man who thought her biscuits were a gift. She glanced away, blinking at the water. "You don't even know me."

"Maybe not," Luka said. "But the bay listens. And I listen too."

That was too much—too soon. Her chest ached in the familiar way, the scar tissue tugging. She stood quickly, brushing at her apron. "I should—there's laundry, and an oven that may explode tomorrow if I don't—"

He didn't stop her, only nodded. "Good night, Ophelia."

Her name in his voice startled her, soft as it was.

She managed a small smile. "Good night, Luka."

As she walked back toward her apartment, her heart thudded too loud, her cheeks too warm. She told herself it was nothing—just conversation, just friendliness. But deep down, where grief and hope wrestled like stubborn siblings, she knew something had shifted. And that terrified her almost as much as it thrilled her.

30

By the time the third week rolled around, Luka had quietly done something no one else in Kotor had managed: he slipped into Ophelia's days like he belonged there.

At first, she thought it coincidence. He showed up two mornings in a row, ordering rosemary biscuits with a cup of thick Montenegrin coffee. The next day, he lingered longer, chatting with Marija about flour prices and listening to Vesna hold forth on the superiority of local honey. The day after that, he returned in the afternoon, leaning on the counter as if he had all the time in the world.

By the end of the week, it wasn't coincidence anymore. Luka was simply there. Not every hour, not in a suffocating way, but enough that Ophelia began bracing herself for the sound of the green door opening, and the way it made her pulse skip.

He didn't always eat, though when he did, he savored slowly, deliberately. Sometimes he ordered the plum jam biscuits, sometimes the honey-glazed, sometimes just a single rosemary. But more often than not, he came to talk. And that was dangerous.

Because when Luka talked, people listened. His voice wasn't loud, but it carried the steady authority of someone who didn't waste words. He had stories—about storms at sea, about working abroad, about the way his grandmother used to cook lamb until the whole street smelled of rosemary. He spoke with humor, but never for attention; his words landed like pebbles in a pond, rippling quietly outward.

Ophelia, elbow-deep in dough, pretended she wasn't listening. But she always was. Worse, the town noticed. And once the town noticed, there was no going back. The fishermen began teasing her—"Biscuit Woman, when is the wedding?"—while tourists snapped photos of Luka as if he were part of the shop's décor. Mira rolled her eyes every time he appeared, muttering "distraction" under her breath, while Vesna clasped her hands to her chest like a romance novel heroine.

One morning, as Luka leaned against the counter, sipping coffee and watching Ophelia wrestle a tray out of Aunt Unit, Vesna leaned over and whispered (loudly enough for half the shop to hear), "He looks at you like you're a fresh tray of biscuits. Hot. Golden. Irresistible."

Ophelia nearly dropped the tray on her foot.

Mira didn't even look up from her clipboard. "Flirtation leads to inconsistency. Inconsistency leads to chaos. Chaos leads to ruin."

"Chaos leads to love," Vesna corrected dramatically, draping a ribbon over her shoulders like a scarf.

"Chaos leads to indigestion," Mira shot back.

Dino, perched in the corner sketching caricatures of customers, looked up and sighed. "Oh, let them be! History will call it *The Great Biscuit Romance of Kotor*. I'll design the wedding invitations—flour dust embossed, obviously."

"I am not getting married," Ophelia snapped, cheeks flaming. "I am not even—this is not—even—"

"Denial," Marija said calmly from behind the till, counting change with the precision of a sniper. "Stage one. It will pass."

Ophelia glared at all of them, flour streaking her forehead like war paint. "He's just a customer."

But even as she said it, Luka looked up from his coffee, caught her eye, and smiled. Not wide. Not flashy. Just steady, warm, unshakable. And Ophelia's heart betrayed her by stuttering like Aunt Unit's fan.

The problem with Kotor wasn't that it was small. The problem was that it was small and nosy, a lethal combination when it came to matters of the heart. By the time Luka had appeared in the shop three times in one week, the town had made up its mind: Biscuit Lady had a suitor.

The whispers began innocently enough—two elderly women on the seawall, muttering to each other as they dipped their bread into honey: "He leans too close." "She blushes too fast." "Her biscuits have improved since he arrived."

Within twenty-four hours, children were chanting it in the streets. "Biscuit Lady has a boyfriend! Biscuit Lady has a boyfriend!" They followed Ophelia down the lane, skipping in circles like it was some kind of medieval nursery rhyme. She tried bribing them with jam biscuits to shut them up; it only fueled the fire.

By day three, the fishermen joined in. "Does Biscuit Woman bake wedding cakes?" one of them bellowed as she passed. "We'll need one for the Biscuit Wedding!" The whole group roared with laughter until Mira threatened to dock their coffee supply. And her friends? They were the worst offenders of all.

Vesna behaved as if Ophelia were a duchess being courted. Every time Luka walked through the green door, Vesna would clasp her hands, sigh, and whisper, "Here comes fate," in a stage whisper that carried across the room.

"Stop it," Ophelia hissed one afternoon as she tried to bag biscuits with hands that absolutely did not tremble.

"Darling," Vesna whispered back, "you can try to hide desire, but your apron does not lie."

"My apron is covered in flour!"

"Exactly." Vesna winked as though she'd just proven Euclid's theorems.

Mira, meanwhile, treated Luka's every visit as a declaration of war. "He takes up counter space," she muttered one morning, scribbling on her clipboard. "Counter space is revenue space."

"He's a paying customer," Ophelia said through gritted teeth.

"He lingers," Mira shot back. "Lingering reduces customer flow. Reduced customer flow reduces profit."

"You make it sound like he's a plague."

"He might be," Mira replied darkly. "A plague with good bone structure."

Then there was Dino, who had officially made it his mission to turn Luka into a muse. He doodled Luka's profile in the margins of order slips, described him in exaggerated prose to startled tourists, and once slipped a napkin onto Luka's plate with the words: *To my rival in love—Dino.*

"Rival?" Luka asked mildly, handing the napkin back.

"Yes," Dino said grandly. "But a gentlemanly one. We shall duel with biscuits at dawn."

Luka chuckled and went back to his coffee. Ophelia wanted the ground to open up and swallow her. Marija, of course, kept her commentary short, precise, and devastating. "Men are distractions. But sometimes they are useful. Do not let this one be expensive."

"Expensive?" Ophelia yelped.

"Love always is," Marija said, and rang up a customer without blinking.

But the town wasn't done. The gossip grew legs, then sprouted wings. Within a week, Vesna's cousin in Budva sent a message: *Heard Biscuit Lady is in love. True?* A German tourist returned with flowers "for you and your handsome partner." Petar, of all people, leaned over his espresso counter one morning and smirked. "Careful, Biscuit Woman. You'll ruin your brand if you marry too soon."

"I AM NOT MARRYING ANYONE," Ophelia shouted in the square, startling pigeons into flight.

Every head turned. Half-smiles spread like wildfire. Somewhere, a child sang, "Biscuit Wedding!"

She stomped back to the shoebox, cheeks blazing, apron askew. Luka, of course, was waiting at the counter with his quiet half-smile, sipping coffee as if none of this circus had anything to do with him. "You're enjoying this," she accused.

"Me?" He lifted his brows, all innocence. "I only came for biscuits."

"Liar," she muttered.

He shrugged, unbothered, and broke his rosemary biscuit in half. "Want some?"

And just like that, despite herself, Ophelia laughed. Loud, unrestrained, startling even to her own ears. Luka looked at her like the sound was a gift. Which, she realized with a terrifying jolt, was exactly why the town was winning: because maybe, just maybe, they weren't wrong.

Despite Mira's protests, Vesna's theatrics, and Dino's attempts to immortalize him in verse, Luka kept returning. But unlike the rest of Kotor, he didn't arrive with fanfare. He simply appeared, steady as tide, with a nod and a quiet "Dobro jutro." And somehow, those two words began to settle into Ophelia's mornings like sugar dissolving in tea.

The first time he helped her was by accident. The green door had been sticking for days, the top hinge squealing every time it opened. Ophelia added "fix hinge" to her never-ending list, fully intending to ignore it until the apocalypse. But one afternoon, as Luka stepped inside, the door groaned like an old man. He frowned, bent to inspect it, then disappeared without a word. Five minutes later, he returned with a small toolkit.

"What are you doing?" Ophelia asked, holding a tray of jam biscuits.

"Listening to the door complain," Luka said simply, crouching down. "No one likes to be ignored."

Before she could protest, he loosened a screw, adjusted the hinge, and oiled it with something he produced from his pocket. The door swung open smoothly, no sound at all.

"There," he said, standing. "Happy now."

Ophelia blinked. "You...fixed it."

Luka shrugged, as if it were nothing. "A door shouldn't make life harder."

She wanted to argue—wanted to insist that she didn't need rescuing, that she could manage on her own—but the truth was, she hadn't even noticed how much that door squeal had grated on her nerves. She opened it once, then twice, just to hear the silence. And for some reason, it made her throat ache.

The next time, it was biscuits. She had one left on a tray, a single rosemary circle that hadn't sold, and she hated wasting food. Luka, sitting at the counter with his sketchbook, looked up as she stared at it. Without a word, he broke his own biscuit in half and pushed the piece toward her. She rolled her eyes. "You realize I have unlimited access to these, right?"

He smiled. "Still, it tastes better when it's shared."

She shouldn't have taken it. She did anyway.

Then there were the conversations, scattered like crumbs through her days. Sometimes they were about nothing: the weather, the tourists, the stubborn seagull that had developed a taste for biscuits. Other times, though, they wandered deeper.

"My father wanted me to fish," Luka admitted once, watching the bay from the window. "But I wanted the city. Work, adventure, something different. Now I come back and...it feels smaller. But also larger, somehow."

Ophelia dusted her hands, leaning against the counter. "Like it grew in your absence?"

"Or maybe I did," he said.

She didn't know what to say to that. But the way he looked at her, steady and open, made her wonder if she'd grown too— without even realizing it. And sometimes, Luka asked about her. Not in the nosy, interrogating way others did, but with genuine curiosity. "Why biscuits?" he asked one evening, as she wiped down the counter.

Ophelia hesitated. "Because I could make them. Because they reminded me of home. Because I needed something to keep my hands busy while my heart...while my heart healed."

Luka nodded, no judgment, no pity. Just understanding. "Then they're not just biscuits."

"No," she whispered. "They're not."

It was in these quiet moments—doors fixed, biscuits shared, words exchanged—that Ophelia realized Luka wasn't just a customer anymore. He was becoming woven into the fabric of her days. Not loudly, not dramatically, but with a patience that both unsettled and soothed her. And that was more terrifying than any gossip.

It had been one of those days that felt longer than the calendar allowed. A cruise ship had dumped two hundred tourists into the square, Vesna had staged an impromptu ribbon demonstration in the middle of the bakery, and Dino had nearly set himself on fire while trying to flambé a "romantic biscuit presentation." By closing time, Ophelia's apron was more flour than fabric, her hair a wild halo, and her feet two aching blocks.

She locked the green door with a sigh, leaning her forehead against it for a second before turning into the quiet of the square. The air was cooler now, carrying the faint brine of the bay. Most shops had shuttered, the chatter of the day replaced with the low murmur of evening conversations and the clink of cutlery from nearby cafés.

And there, leaning against the seawall as if he had been waiting all along, was Luka. She almost laughed—part nerves, part disbelief. "Do you have some kind of radar?"

He smiled, slow and unhurried. "Just good timing."

He walked with her as she headed toward the bay, the cobblestones uneven beneath their steps. For a while, they didn't speak, letting the sounds of the evening fill the space: gulls calling, water lapping, a stray accordion playing somewhere in the distance. It wasn't uncomfortable silence; it was...steady.

When they reached the seawall, Ophelia leaned against the stone, breathing in the salt air. Luka stood beside her, hands in his pockets, gaze fixed on the dark stretch of water where the mountains fell into the sea. "My grandfather used to take me out there," he said quietly, nodding toward the bay. "Old wooden boat. No motor—just oars. Said the sea only listened if you worked for it."

Ophelia smiled faintly. "Sounds exhausting."

"It was," Luka admitted. "But peaceful. Out there, the world felt...bigger. And smaller, at the same time."

They stood in silence again, the air between them charged but gentle. Ophelia felt the weight of Charles's absence press against her, sharp and familiar. Yet next to it, something else flickered—tentative, fragile, but alive. Luka turned then, his gaze steady on her. Not demanding. Not assuming. Just...asking. "Would you like to come with me?" he said. His voice was low, careful, as if he knew the weight of the question. "On the water. Tomorrow, maybe. Just the bay. Just the boat."

Ophelia's heart stuttered. Her first instinct was to retreat—to wrap herself in excuses about ovens and dough and the hundred reasons she wasn't ready. But beneath the panic, beneath the ache, was something undeniable: a longing she hadn't allowed herself to feel in a very long time. She swallowed hard, forcing a shaky laugh. "You don't even know if I get seasick."

"Then we'll find out together," Luka said, his smile quiet but sure.

And for the first time in months, maybe years, Ophelia didn't feel like the widow everyone pitied, or the Biscuit Woman everyone teased. She just felt like herself—messy, nervous, alive—standing by the bay with a man who looked at her as if the world had space for second chances. She didn't answer right away. But she didn't say no, either. And that, in itself, was something.

31

phelia woke with the distinct feeling she was about to make a very bad decision. It wasn't just the usual biscuit-stress kind of decision—whether to experiment with lemon zest or if Aunt Unit would explode before lunch. No, this was bigger. She lay in bed staring at the ceiling of her tiny apartment, the fan clattering above, whispering to herself: "It's just a boat ride. People go on boat rides all the time. Normal. Casual. Not a big deal." But the problem was, nothing in Kotor was casual. And certainly not when Luka was involved.

By the time she reached the bakery, Vesna was already waiting outside, practically vibrating with glee. "Well?" she demanded, before Ophelia even turned the key in the green door. "Are you going? Have you chosen your outfit? Do you want my lipstick? No, wait—lipstick is too much. A scarf. Yes. Romantic scarves flutter in sea breezes."

Ophelia groaned. "It's not a date. It's...an outing."

"An outing!" Vesna clapped her hands. "How Victorian. Will you promenade with parasols as well?"

Inside, Mira was at the counter with her ledger, her eyebrow arched in lethal disapproval. "You're not going."

"I haven't even decided yet," Ophelia muttered.

"You're not going," Mira repeated flatly. "The oven fan is due to break again, the sugar delivery is late, and we have orders for forty rosemary biscuits by tomorrow. The shop will not run itself while you go gallivanting across the bay with a man who—" she lowered her voice dramatically, "—smiles too much."

"He doesn't smile too much," Ophelia protested.

"Suspicious," Mira countered.

Just then, Dino sauntered in, hair wild, clutching his notebook like scripture. "I have written you a sea shanty for the occasion."

"There is no occasion," Ophelia snapped.

Dino ignored her, climbing onto a chair. "It goes: *Oh, the Biscuit Lady sails away, with Luka by her side—*"

Vesna clapped along. Mira slammed her ledger shut with such force the bell over the door jingled.

Marija entered then, calm as ever, depositing a bag of coins on the counter. "If you go, at least negotiate a dowry of olive oil. It lasts longer than romance."

Ophelia dropped her face into her flour-covered hands. "You're all insane."

But the madness didn't stop with her friends. By mid-morning, the square had become a betting ground. Children ran past shouting, "She's going! She's going!" Fishermen exchanged wagers over whether Ophelia would faint the moment the boat rocked. Even Petar, espresso pessimist of the century, leaned over his counter and muttered, "Wear shoes you can swim in."

By noon, Ophelia was ready to lock herself in the storeroom forever. But when the bell over the green door rang and Luka stepped inside, everything—the gossip, the teasing, the shanties—went quiet inside her.

He didn't ask in front of anyone. He didn't mention the town or the whispers. He just looked at her, steady as always, and said, "The bay is calm tonight. Still good for rowing."

And somehow, despite every bone in her body screaming that this was reckless, dangerous, too soon—she found herself nodding. Ophelia almost didn't go. She spent the late afternoon pacing her tiny apartment, muttering to herself like a woman possessed. "It's just a boat. People step onto boats every day. This is not Titanic. This is not romance. This is maritime transportation." She changed her outfit four times, each one worse than the last, before finally giving up and throwing on her usual flour-dusted dress. *If he wants glamour, he can row to Venice,* she thought grimly.

But when the clock struck six and the bells in the square tolled, she found herself walking toward the bay anyway, pulled by something she couldn't explain. Her heart thudded so loudly she was sure the entire town could hear it. And of course, the entire town *was* there.

Children perched on the seawall, kicking their legs, and whispering. Fishermen lounged nearby, pretending to mend nets but really waiting for a show. Vesna was front and center, waving a scarf like she was launching a ship. Mira stood stiffly in the back with her arms crossed, glowering as though she might arrest Luka herself. Dino carried his notebook, already sketching "The Great Departure," and Marija simply held up a jar of honey as though wagering it in some secret bet.

"Oh, for heaven's sake," Ophelia muttered, trying to push through them unnoticed.

"Ophelia!" Vesna cried, swooping toward her. "You look divine!"

"I look like I lost a fight with a flour sack," Ophelia hissed.

"Flour sack chic!" Vesna insisted. "Very avant-garde."

Mira's voice sliced through the crowd. "Don't drown."

Ophelia glared. "Thank you for the support."

Then she saw him.

Luka stood by a powerboat. He looked entirely unbothered by the circus gathering behind her, as if this moment belonged only to them. When their eyes met, Ophelia's panic softened, just slightly. "You came," he said simply.

"Against my better judgment," she muttered, stepping closer. I was expecting a wooden boat and oars.

"I'm taking us a bit farther out, I don't think I could manage rowing all that way."

He held out a hand as she hesitated at the edge of the boat. His palm was warm, steady, calloused. "Trust me," he said.

Ophelia stared at that hand. Every instinct screamed at her to retreat—to keep safe, keep small, keep away. But something deeper, quieter, urged her forward. Slowly, she placed her hand in his. The moment her foot touched the seat of the boat shifted, rocking gently. She gasped, gripping his arm. Luka's smile was soft, reassuring. "See? Not so bad."

"Not so bad?" she squeaked. "We're about to die."

Behind them, Dino shouted, "Farewell, Biscuit Lady! Write us from the afterlife!"

"Shut up!" Ophelia snapped, but Luka just chuckled, guiding her to sit next to him. With a practiced motion, he turned on the engine, and they were off. The town cheered as if they'd just won a sporting event. Vesna waved her scarf like a flag. Mira muttered something about *poor business decisions*, and Marija collected her honey bet.

But soon, the voices faded. The shopfronts shrank, the square blurred, and the water stretched out around them like a sheet of glass. Only the sound of the motor and the lap of the bay remained. Ophelia clutched the side of the boat, trying to steady her racing heart. Luka guided them easily, through the bay, as if he'd been born to it. She risked a glance at him—his handsome build, hair catching the last streaks of sun, profile calm against the rising mountains. For the first time all day, she exhaled.

The land behind them grew smaller. The sea ahead widened. And slowly, impossibly, the panic in her chest gave way to something else: wonder. The boat sliced through the water, and she couldn't stop smiling, with the breeze in her hair, and the expansive views. For a long time, Ophelia sat in silence, hands gripping the edge of the boat until she would occasionally wave at another passing boat. The square had long since disappeared behind them; the voices of her meddling friends were swallowed by distance.

Ahead, the bay stretched out like glass, its surface turning molten with the last gold of the setting sun. The limestone cliffs glowed pink and orange, shadows pooling in their creases. Gulls drifted overhead, lazy and unhurried.

And then, like a mirage, it appeared: a small island, rising from the water as though placed there by careful hands. White stone walls, a squat church with a pale blue dome, a bell tower standing against the sky. It was so improbable, so precise, that Ophelia blinked twice, convinced her brain was playing tricks. "What is that?" she whispered.

Luka followed her gaze, his expression softening into something almost reverent. He slowed the boat down, "Our Lady of the Rocks."

Ophelia frowned. "That sounds...made up. Like a tourist gimmick. Is it even real?"

Luka chuckled, dipping the oars again. "Oh, it's real. More real than most things here. Want to hear the story?"

Ophelia side-eyed him. "This isn't some ploy to distract me from imminent death by drowning, is it?"

"Maybe," Luka said, smiling. "But it's worth hearing."

He cut the engine and turned to face her. His voice carried across the water.

"Five hundred years ago, two sailors were returning from a dangerous voyage. They were exhausted, beaten by storms, sure they'd die before they reached home. But when they made it back to this bay, they found something caught in the rocks: an icon of the Virgin Mary, painted on wood. They believed it was a miracle, a sign of protection. So, in gratitude, they promised to build a church right there—on the sea itself."

Ophelia squinted at the little island. "But there wasn't an island."

"Exactly," Luka said, eyes gleaming. "So, they made one. Stone by stone. Every time sailors returned safely, they brought rocks and dropped them into the bay. Over generations, the pile grew until it became an islet strong enough to hold a church. They called it Our Lady of the Rocks. Even today, every year, we take our boats out and throw more stones into the sea to keep the island alive."

Ophelia stared, struck silent. The idea seemed impossible, almost absurd: building land where there was none, faith and persistence outlasting centuries.

"They built hope," Luka continued softly, "from nothing but gratitude and stones."

The words lodged in her chest, aching in a way that wasn't entirely painful. She thought of Charles, of the marriage that lasted one night, of the empty bed, the pitying stares, the way grief had sunk its anchor deep. She had come here running, hiding, clinging to biscuits as a lifeline. And here was this impossible island, proof that even from wreckage, people had built something solid—something lasting. "That's..." Her throat felt tight. "That's ridiculous. And beautiful."

Luka glanced at her; his eyes steady. "Most good things are."

He turned the engine back on, "I'll take you there."

The boat reached a little dock. Luka stood first, tying the rope, then offered his hand to her again. This time, she didn't hesitate. She stepped onto the island, the stones cool beneath her feet, the church looming small but impossibly steadfast.

She let out a shaky laugh. "So, you bring all the women here, huh? Works every time?"

Luka smiled, slow and unreadable. "Only you."

Her heart flipped, traitorous and wild. She looked away quickly, pretending to admire the curve of the dome, the way the last light of the sun caught on the bell tower. But her cheeks burned hot, and for once, she didn't mind if he noticed.

The islet was so small Ophelia could walk its length in less than a minute, but it felt endless in its stillness. The stones beneath her feet were worn smooth by centuries of hands and tides, every corner etched with the stubborn persistence of sailors who refused to surrender to the sea. The white walls of the church gleamed against the fading sky, its little blue dome catching the last blush of sunset like a jewel.

Luka gave her space, letting her wander while he leaned against the seawall, content to watch. She trailed her hand along the cool limestone, peered into the narrow windows, listened to the lap of the bay against the rocks. For the first time in months, she wasn't weighed down entirely by the ache in her chest.

Something lighter pressed in, almost giddy, like the air just before a laugh. "Do they still add rocks?" she asked, circling back to him.

He nodded. "Every July. The whole town rows out—boats filled with stones. We call it *Fašinada.* At sunset, we drop the rocks into the sea, keeping the island alive."

Ophelia shook her head in disbelief. "So, the people literally keep hope afloat. That's...either the most poetic thing I've ever heard or the dumbest."

"Both can be true," Luka said, his mouth curving.

She laughed, and it startled her—how freely it came, how it echoed against the stone and didn't sound strange in her ears. Luka's smile deepened, not because she laughed at his joke, she realized, but because she laughed at all. They stood there a while longer, the silence between them no longer heavy but full, like rising dough. Finally, Luka untied the rope and gestured to the boat. "Shall we?"

Ophelia hesitated, then nodded. He held her hand as she stepped in, steadying her balance, and for the briefest moment she let herself notice how solid he felt, how warm.

The boat ride back was amazing. He showed her all along the coast. Until now she had never realized how many homes were scattered about the bay. Kotor twinkled in the distance, lanterns flickering in windows, the square just a cluster of lights. As they slowly approached the shoreline of Old Town, the water lapped gently and he successfully docked and tied up the boat.

He sat back down inside the boat with her and for a long time, neither of them spoke. Ophelia stared at the reflection of the stars beginning to prick the bay's surface and realized, with a jolt, that she hadn't thought of Charles in hours. Not with guilt. Not with pain. Not at all.

The realization hit her like a wave—terrifying and thrilling at once. It didn't mean she had forgotten him, didn't mean the grief was gone. But for the first time, the grief wasn't the only thing inside her. There was space now—unfamiliar, tender, dangerous space—for something else.

Luka didn't push. "You don't have to decide everything to-night," he said. "Just keep saying yes. One small thing at a time."

"Decide what? Exactly." She teased.

"About me." He touched her hand gently and she accepted it. He let go for just a moment as he stepped on to the dock first, offering her his hand again. And though her heart hammered in her chest, Ophelia found herself smiling as she took it. One small yes.

32

Ophelia had barely set foot back on the cobblestones when she knew she was doomed. The bay was still whispering behind her, the memory of his boat's motor still steady in her ears, when the trap was sprung. Out of the shadows of the square emerged her so-called friends, circling like wolves who'd caught the scent of prey. Vesna was first, of course—fluttering toward her with a dramatic gasp that could have revived the dead.

"There she is!" Vesna cried, hands clasped to her chest. "The heroine of the Biscuit Ballad! The Lady of the Boat!"

Ophelia groaned. "Oh, for the love of—"

"You're glowing," Vesna declared, squinting at her like a jeweler inspecting a diamond. "Absolutely radiant. Look at her, Mira! She's glowing!"

Mira, arms already crossed, raised an unimpressed eyebrow. "You do have glow."

Dino swooped in next, wielding a sketchbook as though it were a sacred text. "Behold!" he cried, flipping the page around to reveal a dramatic charcoal drawing: Ophelia, standing on a boat, hair flying like a goddess, Luka standing behind her like Titanic position of Leo and what's her name."

Ophelia gawked. "That didn't happen!"

"It happened in spirit," Dino insisted, kissing the page. "Art transcends truth."

Marija appeared behind them, calm as ever, carrying a sack of flour. "Did you ask

about his family? Do they own olive groves? Vineyards? A goat at least?"

Ophelia blinked at her. "No, Marija, I didn't interrogate him about his livestock holdings."

"Missed opportunity," Marija said flatly, shifting the flour to her other hip.

They herded her into the shop, still half-closed, and pushed her onto a stool as though she were a prisoner of war. Vesna lit candles from the counter and arranged them around Ophelia like she was about to confess under oath. Mira pulled out her ledger, ready to document every lapse in judgment. Dino leaned forward with his pencil poised, eager to immortalize every detail in verse.

"Well?" Vesna demanded, eyes wide, leaning so close Ophelia could see the smear of lipstick on her teeth. "Tell us everything. The proposal? The serenade? Did he kiss your hand? Your lips?"

"None of that happened," Ophelia snapped, cheeks burning.

"Did you fall into water?" Mira asked, hopeful.

"No!"

"Did the moonlight catch your hair like spun gold?" Dino pressed.

"It was cloudy!"

"Ah, mysterious!" Dino scribbled furiously, muttering about metaphors for fog and destiny.

Vesna gasped, clutching her scarf. "Did he whisper eternal devotion?"

Ophelia slammed her palms on the counter. "We took me to an island! That's it! He told me a story about sailors throwing rocks in the water, and then we rowed back. That's all."

They all froze.

Then Vesna practically collapsed into a chair, fanning herself. "He took you to *Our Lady of the Rocks?*"

"Yes," Ophelia admitted, instantly regretting it.

Vesna shrieked so loudly the candles flickered. "That's sacred! That's destiny! You don't take a woman there unless you mean something!"

Mira narrowed her eyes. "Or unless he's trying to establish control of her emotions."

"Or steel biscuit recipes," Marija added dryly.

Ophelia buried her face in her hands. "You people are unhinged."

But beneath her exasperation, warmth bloomed. Because yes, Luka had taken her to Our Lady of the Rocks. Yes, he had told her the story like it mattered. And yes, it had stirred something inside her she wasn't ready to name. She peeked through her fingers at her friends, who were still arguing over what the boat ride *meant*, and thought: *God help me, but maybe they're right.*

By morning, Kotor had done what Kotor did best: taken a small, private truth and fed it a five-course meal until it waddled through town in a beaded gown. Ophelia woke to the sound of bells and the ping-ping-ping of her phone exploding with messages. Tilda: **DID YOU GO ON A BOAT, YOU MENACE?** Vesna: **Do not wear black today; grief is canceled.** Dino: **Drafting the libretto. Tenors secured.** Marija: **Bring exact change.** (Which, somehow, was about the boat.)

She dragged herself down to the shop through a gauntlet of knowing looks. Two aunties on the corner lifted their coffee cups like judges awarding points. A child zoomed past on a scooter, singing, "Biscuit Lady kissed the Boatman!" with the absolute conviction of a witness to history.

"I did not kiss anybody," Ophelia hissed to no one.

"Not yet," the child sang back, cruelly omniscient.

At the green door, someone had chalked a tiny heart next to the bee on the sign. Vesna feigned shock when Ophelia wiped it off. "Art vandal," she muttered, tucking a sprig of rosemary behind the bell like a blessing.

Inside, the morning rush bent into new shapes. Tourists asked for "the romance biscuits," lowering their voices as if ordering contraband. A British woman leaned over the counter and whispered, "Which flavor did he have when he fell in love?" Ophelia stared at her, horrified. "He ate rosemary," she said. "And he did not fall in love. He chewed."

"Chewed passionately," Vesna added from the honey corner.

Petar upped the ante across the lane by scrawling **BISCOTTO AMORE LATTE** on his chalkboard—wrong language, wrong pastry, irresistible marketing. When Ophelia marched over to protest, he shrugged. "Customers cry when I erase it. Tears are bad for milk foam."

Back in the bakery, Mira tried to pretend none of it existed by out-professionalizing the rumor mill. "We are not selling romance," she said, stacking take-away boxes with militant precision. "We sell starch." But even she wasn't immune: midway through the rush, a teenage boy asked, dead earnest, "Do you think love improves gluten?" and Mira—Mira!—blinked once and said, "Possibly," then added ten cents to his order for asking a stupid question.

Nika, goddess of the till, used the gossip to enforce efficiency. Anyone who asked about Luka paid exact change. Anyone who asked twice got their small bills returned as a shrapnel of coins. "Next," she said, with the gravitas of a border guard. In less than an hour, the queue learned: buy biscuits, tip generously, keep your theories to yourselves.

Marija maintained her own counter-propaganda by tapping numbers into the ledger like a metronome. "Hysteria is profitable," she murmured without looking up. "We're raising plum jam five cents. Today only."

Dino, meanwhile, had become the unauthorized town crier. He circulated with a tray as if deputized, delivering biscuits to tables with snippets of myth. "Yes, the boat glided under a double rainbow." (It had been cloudy.) "Yes, a dolphin escorted them like a priest He sold four aprons on the strength of one murmured, "When he looked at her, the oven sighed."

"Dino," Ophelia warned between trays, "if you invent one more celestial phenomenon, I will bake you into a commemorative loaf."

"Limited edition," he breathed, delighted.

By midmorning the rumor had acquired chapters. According

to the lace-stall aunties, Luka had rowed one-handed while playing a mandolin. According to the fishermen, he'd cut the oars and guided the boat with sheer masculine will. According to the schoolchildren, he'd proposed under the bell tower using a ring woven from rosemary and seaweed, which was both untrue and unhygienic.

Even Branko, the sign painter, came in for a biscuit and said, with a twinkle, "I can do a tiny boat on the sign. Discreet. For narrative coherence."

"No," Ophelia, Mira, and Marija chorused. Vesna quietly later commissioned him to practice on a scrap board. "For private use," she said, and wouldn't elaborate.

The worst was the pair of travel bloggers who drifted in around eleven, eyes luminous with the predatory light of people who monetize sunsets. "We heard," one whispered, as though intelligence agents lurked in the honey jars, "that there's a love story rising with the dough." They wanted to film Ophelia piping jam and then do an over-the-shoulder shot "as you gaze wistfully toward the bay."

Ophelia, who had never gazed wistfully in her life, tried to say no. Vesna, who understood the internet as a weapon, said yes. Mira said, "Absolutely not." Marija said, "How many followers?" and when told, recalculated, and permitted a tightly scripted fifteen seconds of wistfulness for two dozen paid pre-orders. Ophelia stared at the camera like it might bite until Luka—I am not thinking about him—flashed unhelpfully through her mind and she accidentally, briefly, looked almost soft. The bloggers sighed. "Authentic," they whispered, as if they'd trapped a rare butterfly.

By noon, even the practical processes had been infected. A woman asked, "Can I book the islet for a biscuit-themed vow renewal?" A man wanted "two lovers' bags"—one rosemary, one honey—"tied together with ribbon so their destinies don't drift." Nika deadpanned, "We do not bind destinies," and handed him two separate bags with separate receipts. He swooned anyway.

Petar sent over a tray of espressos without comment; Ophelia sent back a paper boat folded from a receipt. Someone snapped a photo at the exact second, she placed it on the saucer, and by afternoon, strangers were walking in asking for "the paper-boat coffee collab."

Through all of it, Ophelia kept moving, rolling, cutting, brushing honey, sliding trays, smiling until her cheeks ached. Beneath the ridiculousness, something steadier beat: she had gone on a boat. She had let the water hold her up. She had listened to a legend about a church built from gratitude. Her hands knew it even if her mouth denied it—her biscuits came out impossibly light, layers distinct as pages, as if air had decided to stay.

Between rushes she leaned against the counter, breathless. Mira slid a glass of water toward her without looking. "You are becoming content," she said, not approving, not disapproving— simply noticing.

"I am becoming tired," Ophelia said.

"Same thing," Mira muttered, but her mouth curved the tiniest degree.

Near closing, two things happened that nearly undid her. First, a woman about her mother's age lingered at the counter after paying. "My husband died last winter," she said simply. "Today I laughed. Your biscuits did that." She squeezed Ophelia's hand and left before kindness could become unbearable. Ophelia stared at the flour dust on her skin and had to look at the ceiling for a full minute.

Second, a small boy appeared holding a coin and a mangled paper boat. "For the lady of the rocks," he said solemnly, placing both on the counter. "So, she doesn't sink." His mother hissed apologies: Ophelia pressed a biscuit into his hand anyway and told him to keep the coin. Nika didn't even charge her for it. She just nodded, ledger-keeper of the unrecordable.

By the time the bell chimed for the last time, the bakery was a mess. Ophelia joyfully swept away the crumbs. Vesna collected ribbons, already humming a new marketing scheme. Mira double-checked the safety switches with practiced superstition. Marija counted the till and said, "Tomorrow we add a 'Fašinada' sampler." Dino left a sketch on the counter: Ophelia laughing in a boat, the bay a single line.

And Luka? He did not appear. Which was somehow both mercy and ache. The gossip ricocheted without the subject present, and Ophelia—who was not thinking about him, absolutely not—found herself listening for footsteps anyway.

She locked the door, pressed her palm to the green paint—ritual—and leaned her forehead against the wood. Through it all—the noise, the exaggerations, the hearts chalked by pranksters—she held one small, private truth in the quiet center of herself like a warm biscuit cupped in both hands: on the water, she had felt less heavy.

Outside, the bay breathed. Somewhere a radio played a love song older than the bell tower. Ophelia straightened, rolled her shoulders, and wrote tomorrow's specials on the chalkboard in her neat hand:

Classic Butter
Rosemary & Sea Salt
Honey Brush
Plum Jam
Fašinada Sampler (stone by stone)

She added, after a beat—because the town would write it for her if she didn't—No dolphin escort provided.

She stepped into the evening. The sign clicked softly in the breeze; the tiny bee cast its microscopic shadow. As she made for the seawall, Ophelia felt the day's absurdity loosen. The rumor would run until it ran out of breath. Tomorrow it would be something else. But beneath it, under everything loud, was the quiet that had started on the boat. She carried it with her, small and stubborn.

And when she finally lay in bed that night, the town's chorus faded to hum. A single sentence rose, clear as a bell, unasked and undeniable: *I want to see him again.*

The next morning, the square was quieter—at least by Kotor standards. The gossip hadn't stopped; it had simply settled into the cobblestones like morning dew. Ophelia walked to the bakery feeling like her footsteps were being measured, weighed, evaluated for romantic significance. But the shouting, the singing children, the scarf-waving—those had dimmed. What remained was a steady hum, the way a river murmurs after the floodwaters pull back.

Inside the shop, the ovens exhaled their steady breath, warm and constant. The scent of butter, honey, and flour wrapped around her shoulders like a shawl. It should have felt ordinary. Instead, it felt like a reprieve. She began to bake.

At first, her movements were mechanical: flour, salt, butter, rub, crumble. Water, stir, fold. Rolling pin pressing, cutting shapes, trays sliding in. But then she noticed—her hands were moving differently. There was a lightness in the way she folded the dough, as if her wrists remembered something she hadn't given them permission to feel. The dough lifted, stretched, folded back without resistance. Layers puffed up in the oven higher than usual, as though the biscuits themselves had learned to breathe deeper.

Mira noticed first. She came to check the trays and frowned, suspicious. "These are...fluffier," she said, poking a biscuit like a detective prodding a suspect.

Ophelia shrugged, avoiding her gaze. "Maybe the flour is in a good mood."

Mira said, still frowning. "It's *you. You* are the reason."

Ophelia flushed, busying herself with brushing honey on the tops of another batch. "Don't be ridiculous."

But it wasn't ridiculous. She could feel it. Something had shifted.

The night before, after the chaos of the shop, after the cruel scooter-children and Dino's operatic embellishments, she had lain in bed waiting for the grief to crash back in. Waiting for the familiar ache to reclaim its territory, to remind her she wasn't allowed to feel anything but loss. But the grief hadn't surged the same way. It was there—oh, it was always there, an anchor heavy in her chest—but it had loosened, just enough for a sliver of something else to slip through. Hope. It scared her senseless.

She pressed her palms against the cool counter, flour sticking to her skin, and let the thoughts rise unbidden. On the boat, she hadn't thought of Charles. Not once. Hours had passed, and she'd laughed, and she'd marveled at a church built out of stones and faith, and she hadn't thought of her dead husband at all.

The guilt followed, swift and sharp. How could she? How could she sit there while Luka told her stories and not picture Charles beside her, the husband she had for one single night before everything shattered? She should have carried him onto that boat like a torch, kept his memory blazing bright. Instead, she'd left him on the shore without realizing it.

Her throat tightened. She grabbed the rolling pin, pressing harder into the dough, trying to crush the guilt into flatness. But then another thought rose, stubborn as dough beneath her hands: maybe she deserved one night of forgetting. One evening where she wasn't The Widow, wasn't The Pity, wasn't the Biscuit Lady held together by butter and nerves. Maybe she deserved one small yes.

She sank onto the stool by the window, staring out at the square. A gull wheeled overhead, squawking at nothing. Across the way, Petar scrawled another nonsense drink on his chalkboard: **SEA SALT SOULMATE ESPRESSO.** She almost laughed. Almost.

Vesna swept in like a storm, as always, dropping off a basket of lavender. "He hasn't left yet, you know," she said casually, far too casually. "Luka. His family's still in town. He's around."

Ophelia's stomach swooped. "I don't care."

"You care," Vesna said, planting her fists on her hips. "But you're scared. Good. Scared means it matters."

Ophelia didn't answer. She couldn't. Instead, she busied herself with another tray, sliding it into the oven with unnecessary force.

All day, customers came and went, the rumor still humming, but she moved through it differently. She didn't fight the gossip, didn't deny or confirm. She just...baked. Her biscuits rose higher, flaked prettier, melted sweeter. And she realized, with dawning horror and wonder, that the change wasn't in the ingredients. It was in her.

When the bell over the door rang that evening, and Luka's shadow fell across the counter, she nearly dropped the tray in her hands. He didn't stride in with fanfare. He didn't carry roses or mandolins. He just stood there, calm as a shoreline, and said, "Smells good."

Her throat caught. She wanted to snap at him, to tell him to leave, to make a joke about fattening him up. But all she managed was: "It's just biscuits."

"Never just biscuits," he said quietly.

And just like that, her heart betrayed her again, thudding loud enough she was sure Mira could hear it from the back.

The shop had emptied for the evening, the last crumbs swept, the counters wiped, the hum of the oven settling into silence. Outside, the square had quieted, too, its earlier din of gossip softening into the clink of wine glasses and the hush of footsteps heading home. Luka lingered by the counter, tall and steady, while Ophelia fussed unnecessarily with the cooling racks. She rearranged biscuits that didn't need rearranging, wiped a spotless tray, adjusted the honey jar three times. Anything to avoid looking directly at him. "You work too late," he said finally, voice low and even.

She snorted. "Says the man who rows women into legends after dark."

The corner of his mouth tilted. "That's not a job. That was one evening."

"One evening the whole town has turned into an opera," she muttered.

"And you?" His gaze was direct but gentle. "What did you turn it into?"

The question lodged in her chest. She wanted to deflect, to crack a joke about seasickness or biscuit marketing. But the words tangled, heavy and fragile at once. She pressed her palms flat on the counter, grounding herself in the cool stone.

"I don't know," she admitted. "Something I shouldn't want, probably."

Luka didn't push. He just leaned back against the counter opposite her, arms folded, as if willing to stand in silence forever if that's what she needed.

The quiet stretched between them, not heavy, not awkward—just full. Outside, the bell tower marked the hour, its chime rolling across the bay. Ophelia finally looked up, and found him watching her—not with expectation, not with pressure, but with the same steady calm he'd carried on the water.

"You don't have to decide everything now," he said softly. "Just...keep saying yes. One small yes at a time." Her throat tightened. One small yes. That's what the island had been. That's what this was. Luka straightened, adjusted the sleeve of his shirt. "I'll let you close up," he said, and turned toward the door. He didn't ask to see her again. He didn't need to.

The bell jingled as the door swung shut behind him. Ophelia stood frozen in the quiet, the smell of biscuits and honey thick in the air, her heart thudding in her ribs like an impatient drum. She whispered into the emptiness, the words tasting strange but true on her tongue: "I want to see him again."

The confession hung there, private, and undeniable. For once, no Vesna, no Mira, no Dino, no Marija to twist it into theater. Just her, alone in the shoebox, admitting what the biscuits had already known. She turned off the lights, locked the green door, and stepped into the cool night. The bay stretched dark and endless, holding secrets like it always had. And for the first time since Charles had died, she let herself imagine a tomorrow that wasn't only grief. A tomorrow with yes.

33

Ophelia had just finished sweeping flour from the counter when she heard the knock at the green door. Too early for customers, too late for bread delivery. Suspicious. She wiped her hands on her apron, muttering, "If it's another blogger wanting me to 'smolder into the camera,' I swear I'll shove a biscuit up their—" She swung the door open and nearly swallowed her own tongue.

Luka. Standing there in the dawn haze, hair tousled, shirt rolled at the sleeves, looking infuriatingly awake. The square was still quiet, the sky barely blushing pink, and here he was— like the morning had been waiting for him. "Good morning," he said simply.

Ophelia blinked. "It's not. It's practically night. People are still drooling on their pillows."

He tilted his head, unfazed. "Come with me. Let's climb the fortress."

She stared. "The fortress? The one with a billion stone steps straight into the clouds? That fortress?"

He nodded, as though he'd suggested a stroll to Petar's café. "San Giovanni. Best view in Kotor. The sun's about to rise."

Ophelia barked out a laugh. "You want me to climb medieval stairs at dawn? Luka, I make biscuits, I don't audition for gladiator school."

Behind Luka, Vesna's voice spoke, "Did I hear fortress?!"

Vesna and Mira had just arrived to help open the bakery.

Ophelia cursed. "No, you didn't—"

Vesna shrieked like a seagull finding a french fry. "She's going! She's climbing the steps of destiny with him!"

Mira squinted down at Ophelia. "Take water. And shoes. Not sandals. You'll regret sandals."

Ophelia pressed her palms over her face. "Oh my god. Luka, do you see what you've done?"

He chuckled, a quiet sound, maddeningly serene. "I only asked if you'd like to climb."

"And now the entire town thinks I'm starring in a medieval soap opera," she snapped.

"They already think that" Luka said.

She lowered her hands, glaring. His calmness made her want to throw flour in his face. Or kiss him. Possibly both.

"No," she said firmly. "Absolutely not. I don't climb. I wheeze. I trip. I bruise my shins on furniture."

Luka's eyes softened, just enough. "One step at a time," he said, echoing the words from the boat. "That's all it is."

Damn him.

Ophelia hesitated, the square watching from behind its shutters, the smell of dawn mingling with rosemary and sea salt. The fortress loomed above them, its walls catching the first streaks of sunlight like a challenge. Her heart thudded. "Oh, for heaven's sake," she muttered, throwing off her apron. "If I die, bury me with biscuits."

"You go," Mira encouraged Ophelia with a hard slap on her butt. "We take care of biscuits."

Vesna screamed with glee. Somewhere, a child began chanting, "Biscuit Lady! Biscuit Lady!"

Luka only smiled, offering his hand like he had at the boat. "You won't die," he said.

Ophelia snatched her shawl, scowled for form's sake, and put her hand in his. The first step was fine. The second step was tolerable. By the tenth, Ophelia was convinced she had accidentally signed up for medieval torture. "These stairs were built by sadists," she wheezed, dragging herself upward. The stones were uneven, slick from centuries of feet, and cruelly steep. "Tiny, goat-kneed, mountain-dwelling sadists."

Beside her, Luka ascended with maddening calm. His stride was steady, his breathing barely elevated, like he'd been born on these stones. Which, given his roots, he might as well have been.

"They were built for defense," he said mildly. "The harder it is to climb, the safer the town."

"Well, congratulations," Ophelia panted, clinging to the wall like a drunken spider. "Kotor is very safe from me."

Behind them, the fortress bells tolled, and voices drifted up from the square. Vesna, of course, had organized a cheering squad. A gaggle of neighbors waved scarves and sang some improvised ballad about biscuits and bravery. Someone had even produced a tambourine. "Don't look back," Luka advised, glancing over his shoulder with amusement. "They'll only get louder if you encourage them."

Ophelia groaned. "I hate this town."

"You love this town," Luka corrected gently.

She shot him a glare, then tripped on a jutting stone. Luka caught her elbow before she could faceplant, steadying her with a hand that was far too warm, far too solid. "Careful," he murmured.

Ophelia yanked her arm free, scowling to cover the fact that her stomach had just done a humiliating flip. "Don't be nice to me. It makes this worse."

They climbed in silence for a while—or rather, Luka climbed, and Ophelia gasped like a fish on land. By the time they reached the first landing, her thighs were on fire, her lungs shrieking betrayal. She collapsed onto a low wall, fanning herself with the edge of her shawl. "This is hell," she announced. "Actual hell. I'm being punished for every time I didn't recycle properly."

Luka leaned against the wall opposite, entirely too composed, not a bead of sweat on him. "You're doing fine."

"Fine? I sound like a donkey giving birth."

He chuckled, and the sound was annoyingly attractive. "A determined donkey," he amended.

Ophelia threw a pebble at him. He caught it easily, turning it in his fingers before setting it on the wall beside him. "Every stone has been carried up here," he said, almost to himself. "One by one. By hands, by backs, over centuries. A fortress built from persistence."

She rolled her eyes, though part of her couldn't help but be moved. "Persistence is overrated. Elevators exist."

"Not here," Luka said simply.

She groaned and pushed herself upright, glaring at the endless steps snaking higher. "If I die, I'm haunting you."

"I'll look forward to the company," he said, maddeningly calm, and gestured upward. And so, they climbed again. Her shawl slipped. Her hair frizzed. She swore creatively in both English and the handful of Montenegrin phrases she'd picked up (which earned Luka a startled laugh when she mangled one beyond recognition). But for every stumble, every curse, he was there—steady, patient, offering a hand without insisting, slowing his stride without making her feel small.

By the time they reached the second landing, she was trembling with exertion. But something else was rising too: beneath the misery, beneath the sweat, a tiny spark of exhilaration. She was doing it. Step by stubborn step, she was climbing. And though she'd never admit it out loud, she kind of wanted to keep going.

By the third landing, something unexpected had happened: Ophelia stopped swearing. Not because her legs didn't hurt—they burned like she'd been set on fire from the knees down. Not because her lungs weren't still screaming—they were conducting a mutiny. But because, when she finally paused and looked back, her breath caught in an entirely different way.

The town lay below them, a mosaic of red-tiled roofs and narrow streets curling like ribbons through the stone. The bay shimmered, silver-blue, the mountains rising like sentinels all around. From up here, even Petar's café looked picturesque, the chalkboard scribbles just tiny smudges in the square. "Holy biscuits," she whispered.

Luka smiled; his hand braced casually against the wall. "Not bad, hm?"

"Not bad?!" She staggered to the edge, gripping the ancient stone. "This is—this is ridiculous. This is—" She waved her arms helplessly, words failing in the face of such beauty. "This is a postcard that swallowed another postcard and gave birth to the perfect baby postcard."

Luka's laugh rumbled low, warm, startling in its rarity. "That's one way to put it."

Ophelia leaned against the wall, still gasping, still aching, but now with a strange sort of giddiness curling through her. For the first time since Charles's death, the heaviness that had clung to her chest felt...less absolute. Like it had thinned, making room for air, for light, for color. They climbed on, slower now, not because Luka needed to but because Ophelia wanted to. She stopped every dozen steps to turn, to look, to point at something below. "That's my bakery!" she cried at one point, as if she'd just spotted a lost child. "Look at it! It's so tiny!"

Luka's eyes softened as he watched her. "It suits you," he said.

She squinted at him suspiciously. "Are you mocking me?"

"Never," he said, and though the corner of his mouth quirked, she believed him.

Halfway up, they ducked under an arch where vines crept over the stones. The air was cooler, scented faintly of rosemary and wildflowers. Ophelia pressed her palm to the wall, the stone warm from centuries of sun, and marveled aloud: "People actually built this. By hand. All of it."

Luka nodded. "They carried stones up from the bay. Day after day. Generation after generation. It wasn't quick, but it lasted."

Ophelia let that sink in. A fortress built on persistence. On patience. On time. It felt like a lesson she wasn't ready to admit she needed. By the fourth landing, something stranger still happened: she laughed. A real laugh, sharp and startled, when her shoe nearly slipped, and Luka caught her elbow again. "You're enjoying this," she accused, breathless.

He shrugged, utterly unrepentant. "I like seeing you fight."

"Fight? I'm flailing like a drunk tourist."

"You're still climbing," he countered, and that shut her up faster than any witty retort.

The higher they climbed, the quieter it became. The town's voices drifted away, the sea breeze whispered through the stones, and the only sound left was the rhythm of their footsteps, the scrape of sandals, the occasional gasp or chuckle. And in that quiet, Ophelia realized something terrifying: she was happy. Not distracted, not numb, not bracing for grief to pull her under again. Just...happy. The realization lodged in her throat, equal parts wonder, and fear.

At last, the final stretch of stone gave way to open sky. Ophelia stumbled onto the fortress summit with a strangled noise that was part gasp, part victory cry, part dying moose. She collapsed against the ancient wall, chest heaving, hair plastered damp against her forehead. "I did it," she croaked. "I'm alive."

Luka laughed softly and offered her his water bottle. She gulped half of it in one go, wiped her mouth with the back of her hand, and finally—finally—looked up.And the world punched her in the chest.

The bay of Kotor stretched below in a perfect horseshoe of blue, framed by mountains that looked like sleeping giants. The town, her town now, curled along the shore, its red roofs blazing against the morning light. The sky had opened in shades of pink and gold, clouds drifting like brushstrokes on a masterpiece. The bell tower below glinted, the sea caught fire with dawn, and for one dizzying moment, Ophelia felt like she was standing at the edge of forever. "Oh," she whispered. "Oh, wow."

Luka stood beside her, his arms folded on the stone wall, his profile carved against the sunrise. "I come here whenever I need to remember," he said quietly.

"Remember what?"

"That I belong," he answered, his voice carrying the weight of years. "When I was younger, I wanted to leave Kotor. Everyone did. It felt too small, too slow, too...old. I thought freedom was somewhere else. And maybe it was, for a while. But when I came back, I realized this place is in me. The walls, the bay, the stones we walk on every day. Home isn't what you escape—it's what pulls you back."

Ophelia swallowed hard; her throat thick. She wanted to tell him she understood. That Alabama had never been home, not really, that she'd tried to build one with Charles, but it had been ripped away before it began. And yet here—this impossibly beautiful, stubborn little town—was pulling her in, stone by stone, step by step. "I don't know if I have a home anymore," she admitted, her voice trembling.

Luka turned, not pitying, just steady. "Maybe you're building one."

The words settled into her like warm bread, impossible to ignore. Maybe she was. With biscuits and laughter and flour-dusted friends who wouldn't let her wallow. With mornings that smelled like rosemary and honey. With climbs that nearly killed her but rewarded her with skies like this. Her chest tightened with something she hadn't dared to feel in so long: possibility. The silence between them stretched, but it wasn't empty. It was full of wind and light and unspoken things. Luka didn't press, didn't crowd her. He just stood there, shoulder close enough to brush, letting her have the view, the moment, the choice. Ophelia's lips parted before she even thought the words through. Soft, almost to herself, but loud enough for him to hear: "Maybe this is home too."

Luka's eyes flicked to her, and for once, that calm mask cracked. A spark lit there, warm, and unguarded, and he smiled—not triumphant, not smug, just deeply, simply glad. They stood together on the fortress wall, the town below, the bay glittering, the sky opening wide. And for the first time in years, Ophelia didn't feel like she was falling apart. She felt like she was standing on solid ground. Or maybe—finally—she was standing at the beginning of something new.

34

The view from the top of the fortress had been enough to make Ophelia forget her aching legs for a while. But the moment Luka suggested they start heading down, her body reminded her in no uncertain terms that it was made of mortal flesh and biscuit batter.

"Downhill will be easier," Luka said in that maddeningly calm voice as they began.

"Easier?" Ophelia gasped, wobbling on the first slick stone step. "This is a death slide! They're practically vertical. You could ski down this."

"You'll be fine," he replied, steady as ever, walking as though gravity was his personal ally.

Ophelia, meanwhile, looked like she was auditioning for a slapstick comedy routine—one hand glued to the wall, knees bent, muttering threats at the stones. "If I break an ankle, I expect full compensation. Monetary and emotional."

Luka chuckled, catching her elbow as she nearly skidded on a loose pebble. "I'll carry you if I have to."

"Oh, don't tempt me," she muttered. "I'll fake a sprain right now."

The higher levels were quiet, just the sound of their footsteps echoing. But as they descended, the town began to reappear beneath them—closer, louder, more alive with every step. Ophelia kept stopping to catch her breath, though she claimed it was to "admire the architectural genius of these sadistic stairs." Luka patiently waited each time, his hands loose at his sides, his gaze occasionally lifting to the bay as if he'd never tire of it.

They reached the halfway point, where the steps widened slightly into a flat terrace. Ophelia plopped herself down with a groan that could have toppled seagulls' mid-flight. "That's it. I live here now. Bring me biscuits, tell my bakery it's orphaned, and please instruct Vesna to plant rosemary at my grave."

Luka sat beside her, unhurried. "You did well."

She gave him a withering look. "I survived. That's not the same as doing well."

He leaned back against the wall, his eyes on the shimmering bay. "You fought it. You kept going. That's well."

Something in his tone made her chest tighten. She looked away quickly, pretending to study the rooftops below. "You're exhausting, you know that? Calm, unflappable, philosophical. It's very annoying."

He smiled faintly. "And yet you're here."

Her stomach swooped in that ridiculous, traitorous way it had begun to do whenever he spoke like that. "Purely because gravity insists, I can't stay up there forever," she muttered, pushing herself to her feet.

The last stretch down was worse than the climb, if only because every muscle in her thighs had gone on strike. She groaned with each step, clinging to Luka's arm more than once when the stones tilted beneath her shoes. At one point, she stumbled so spectacularly she fell directly into him, her forehead thunking against his shoulder.

"Graceful as ever," she muttered, peeling herself off him.

"I've seen worse," he said calmly.

"From me?" she shot back.

He didn't answer, just gave her that infuriating almost-smile that said he liked watching her fight with herself more than anything.

By the time the final set of steps came into view, Ophelia nearly wept with relief. The town square lay at the bottom, its narrow streets waking with morning bustle. She could already hear the clink of cups at Petar's café, Vesna's shrill voice hawking rosemary, and—oh no—Dino's booming baritone warming up like a trumpet announcing doom. She groaned, clutching the wall. "They're waiting, aren't they? Like vultures."

Luka glanced down and nodded. "Half the town."

"Perfect. Just what every sweaty, half-dead, biscuit-covered widow dreams of—an audience."

He offered his hand, steady as always. "One more step," he said.

And because she couldn't not, Ophelia took it. The second Ophelia's sandal touched the square, the trap snapped shut. A roar of voices rose like a tidal wave—cheers, whistles, shouts of congratulations. Vesna was at the front, waving a lavender scarf so violently it looked like she was trying to lasso the sun. Dino had somehow acquired a mandolin and was strumming furiously, half-singing, half-yodeling: "She said yes at dawn! Yes, at dawn! The Biscuit Lady's heart is gone!"

"WHAT?!" Ophelia screeched, but her voice was drowned out by the crowd.

Mira stood with her notebook open, tapping her pen against the page. "Did he get down on one knee? I need exact phrasing for the record."

"There was no knee!" Ophelia shouted. "There was no record! There was no proposal!"

A child barreled through the crowd, tugging on her skirt with wide eyes. "Where's the ring, Biscuit Lady? Can we see it?"

Ophelia nearly choked on her own indignation. "There is no ring!"

The crowd ignored her. Vesna flung an arm around her shoulder. "Don't be shy, darling! The whole bay saw the glow! Sunrise proposals are destiny!"

"It wasn't a proposal!" Ophelia snapped, but the more she denied, the more convinced they became. By the time Dino reached his third fabricated verse—something about Luka swearing eternal love on a biscuit crumb—Ophelia was ready to dissolve into the cobblestones.

Luka, of course, stood calm as the mountains, arms folded, a faint smile tugging at his lips. Not denying. Not confirming. Just letting the madness swirl like it always did.

Ophelia spun on him, finger jabbing. "Say something!"

He tilted his head, unbothered. "What would you like me to say?"

"Oh, I don't know, maybe THE TRUTH?!"

Before he could answer, a new voice cut through the chaos—louder, sharper, and jarringly familiar.

"Ophelia!"

The square froze. Even Dino's mandolin went mute. Ophelia's blood ran cold. She turned slowly, like a woman in a horror film. And there they were: her family.

Her mother in pearls and church heels entirely unsuited for cobblestones, fanning herself dramatically. Her father in a golf shirt, dragging two oversized suitcases that bumped against the stones like irritated cattle. And—oh God help her—Tilda, arm's wide open. Ophelia's jaw unhinged. "What... what are you *doing here?*"

Tilda ran up to her and hugged her hard, "Girl! You got engaged? Where's the ring! I want to see." She excitedly grabbed her hand and stated, "Wait I'm confused. Do men do not give rings here?"

Her mother pressed a hand to her chest, teary-eyed. "We came to save you, baby."

"Save me? From what?"

"From this madness!" her father bellowed, glaring around at the townsfolk like they were cult members. "We've heard the stories. A widow, alone, in a foreign land, being taken advantage of by some—some *sailor boy!*"

Luka's brow arched, amused, though he said nothing. "Oh my," Ophelia muttered, burying her face in her hands.

Her mother sniffed. "Do you have any idea what people are saying back home? That you ran off, that you're... that you're..." She flailed her hand at the crowd. "...playing bakery in some village while you're supposed to be grieving like a proper widow!"

The gasp that went up from the square could've rattled the bay. Vesna clutched her scarf. Mira snapped her ledger shut like a judge slamming a gavel.

Ophelia's head snapped up, fury burning. "Excuse me? *Playing bakery?* Now you need to quit being ugly."

Her mother hurried forward, grabbing her hands. "Sweetheart, come home. We'll take care of you. You can't just... just bury yourself here, with biscuits and gossip and—and..." Her gaze flicked to Luka, who remained maddeningly steady. "...whatever *that* is."

Ophelia's stomach twisted. Humiliation, rage, confusion—all tangled in a knot. Around her, Kotor buzzed like a hive, the gossipers practically vibrating with glee at this new drama. She yanked her hands free and stepped back. "You don't get to swoop in here and tell me what I should be doing. You don't know what this is. You don't know what I'm building here."

Her father puffed up. "Ophelia, you belong with family."

And that—that word—hit her like a slap. Because hadn't she been building family here, too? In flour and laughter and chaos? In Luka's steady presence, in Vesna's dramatics, in Marija's ledger and Dino's songs? This town, as maddening as it was, had wrapped itself around her heart. Ophelia's chest heaved, caught between two worlds. And all she could think was: *God help me, what if I don't want to go back?*

By the time Ophelia managed to herd her family out of the square and into the bakery with Luka following inside, the rumor had already mutated. The crowd followed like a parade, whispering and buzzing, fueled by Dino's mandolin and Vesna's shrieks. Mira muttered about "unverified sources," while children darted around chanting, *"She said yes! She said yes!"* Ophelia slammed the door shut on the lot of them, locking it against the press of eager faces at the glass. She turned to her family, chest heaving. "Do you see what you've done?!"

Tilda squealed, "Oh my God! Ophelia your bakery is amazing! I love it."

Her mother corrected Tilda with a hiss, "Do *not* take the good Lord's name in vain Tilda!"

Tilda quieted in fear, "Yes ma'am."

Ophelia's mother smoothed her pearls, glaring around the flour-dusted bakery as though it were a dungeon. "What *you've* done, Ophelia. It is very clear that you have lost your mind. You've been here months, months, and now people are saying you became engaged to a foreigner at sunrise on a mountaintop—"

"Fortress!" someone shouted through the door. "It was a fortress!"

Ophelia screamed into her apron. Luka leaned against the counter, calm as stone, arms crossed. The faintest smile tugged at his mouth, even this chaos couldn't shake him.

"Well, we are here because you are coming home with us."

"No, I'm not."

"If it's about this bakery, if that's what you want, just come home and we can work it out." She took an envelope out of her purse and handed it to her. "Look I even brought you this check from Charles' parents. The house sold and they want you to keep the money for it. You see? You have the money to start a *real bakery* at home."

Something inside Ophelia snapped. "A real one?" she barked, voice trembling with rage. "You mean the one where everyone show's up and buys out of pity. The bakery that is labeled, the widow's bakery in the town that pitied me in church pews? The one where people whispered every time, I walked into the grocery store? The one where I couldn't breathe without choking on someone else's sadness?"

The bakery went still. Her mother blinked, flustered. "We just want you safe—"

"I *am* safe!" Ophelia cut in, chest rising and falling. "I'm not broken porcelain you need to glue together. I'm building something here. I'm working, laughing, *living.* And for the first time since Charles died, I'm not just surviving—I'm alive."

Her words rang in the silence. Her father shifted uncomfortably, staring at the floor. Then, like a lightning bolt, the door banged open—Vesna had picked the lock, naturally. She stormed in with a bundle of rosemary. "Wedding bouquets!" she announced grandly. "Special price for the Biscuit Bride!"

"THERE IS NO WEDDING!" Ophelia howled.

Too late. Tourists had caught wind of the rumor, and within minutes, her bakery was swarmed with wide-eyed travelers demanding "engagement biscuits." Mira, ever practical, started scribbling down orders on parchment scraps. Nika shoved a tip jar onto the counter with *'Future Wedding Fund'* scrawled in sharpie. Dino climbed onto a stool to debut his fourth verse about "a fortress kiss sealed in bliss."

Ophelia's family stood in stunned horror as the bakery transformed into a carnival. Her mother clutched her pearls so hard Ophelia worried they'd snap. Her father tried to shout down the crowd but was drowned out by Dino's mandolin. Tilda muttered, "This is insane," on a loop, like it might exorcise the madness.

And in the middle of it all, Luka—steady, unflappable Luka—moved behind the counter, calmly helping Mira pass out trays. As though it were the most natural thing in the world to serve biscuits while rumors of a sunrise proposal raged like wildfire.

Ophelia's heart twisted. Half in fury, half in awe. Because while her family tried to drag her back into grief, Luka was there, shoulder to shoulder, not asking her to explain, not demanding she choose—just being there. Her eyes burned. She shoved another tray onto the counter, muttering under her breath: "If one more person asks for a wedding cake sample, I'm throwing them off the fortress myself."

The bakery finally emptied as night fell, the last tourist clutching an "engagement biscuit" in a paper bag like it was relic from a saint. Mira counted the day's absurd takings with brisk efficiency, muttering about "unethical rumors" even as she tucked notes into her ledger. Vesna fluttered out into the square with her unsold rosemary, promising to "bless the union at dawn." Dino's mandolin trailed off down the street, his voice echoing about "love sealed in flour."

Ophelia stood in the wreckage, hair frizzed, apron smeared, every bone in her body buzzing. Her family sat stiffly at a corner table, untouched cups of tea cooling before them. The silence between them was heavier than the day's chaos.

After her parents had left for an afternoon nap and explored the town a bit they arrived back to the bakery and patiently waited at the corner table. Her family sat stiffly with untouched cups of tea cooling before them. The silence between them was heavier than the day's chaos. Her mother finally broke it, voice soft but stern. "Ophelia, this isn't you. This... circus. This isn't what Charles would've wanted."

Ophelia flinched at his name. "Don't you dare," she whispered. "Don't you dare use him to drag me back."

Her father shifted, defensive. "We only want you home. With people who love you."

Ophelia's throat tightened. "Home? You think Alabama is home for me? It's a graveyard. Every corner, every street, every face—reminds me of what I lost. Here..." She gestured wildly at the bakery, at the flour-dusted counters, at the crooked green door. "Here... here I feel. I feel."

Tilda smiled and encouraged her, "go ahead Phee, tell them how you feel."

Ophelia's mother waited and finally muttered, "You're deluding yourself. Playing baker in some postcard town with strangers isn't a life."

"They're not strangers," Ophelia shot back. "They're family. Maybe louder and nosier and more unhinged than I ever expected, but they're mine."

Her words hung in the air. Her mother's face pinched. Her

father sighed, heavy and resigned. Tilda gave Ophelia an encouraging hug and through it all, Luka stood by the counter, arms crossed, silent. Watching. Not interfering. When her family finally left—storming out in a flurry of pearls, golf shirts, and dragged suitcases—Ophelia sagged against the counter, trembling with exhaustion. The bakery was quiet now, save for the faint hum of the oven cooling.

She turned to Luka, eyes wide and wild. "Do you realize half this town thinks we're engaged? That my family thinks I've lost my mind? That my life is—" She waved her arms at the flour-streaked chaos. "—this?!"

He tilted his head, calm as the bay at dawn. "Yes."

She blinked, thrown. "Yes? That's all you've got? Yes?"

His lips curved in that infuriating, gentle almost-smile. "They're just a little ahead of the story."

Her breath caught. Her heart—traitorous, foolish, alive—stumbled in her chest. She stared at him, words gone, the weight of his meaning pressing against her like the dawn sun breaking over the fortress. Ahead of the story. Not wrong. Just early. Ophelia swallowed hard, her throat tight. For the first time since Charles's death, the future didn't feel like a void. It felt like a door. And terrifyingly, wonderfully, she wanted to open it.

35

The trouble began, as trouble always seemed to, with Vesna. At dawn, Ophelia awoke to the sound of her mother screeching in the courtyard outside the guest house, pearls rattling as she waved her fan like a general on campaign. "Ophelia! Come out here right this instant before these foreigners snatch you up for good!"

Tilda, who had spent the night with Ophelia looked outside, and with a scratchy voice murmured, "Your parents have lost their damn minds."

Ophelia buried her head under her pillow. "Please let me suffocate in peace," she groaned.

Too late. Vesna, never one to pass up a stage, strutted into the square with a basket of rosemary under her arm. "Foreigner?" she shouted, indignant, loud enough to wake half the town. "We are not foreigners, we are *family!* She belongs to us now!"

"Now who the hell is that?" Tilda groaned.

"That's Vesna." Ophelia groaned back under her pillow. She started kicking the bed and Tilda joined her.

"I'm too jet-lagged for this. I am worn slap out." Tilda pulled the covers over her head.

Within minutes, a crowd had gathered. Dino clutched his mandolin like a sword, Mira stormed outside with her ledger as though it were a weapon of law. Across from them stood Ophelia's parents, their suitcases lined up like barricades. Her father puffed out his chest, his Alabama drawl rolling heavy over the stones. "Now listen here,

y'all—we came across an ocean to fetch our girl home, and we ain't leaving without her."

"Fetch her like she is dog?" Vesna gasped, scandalized. "Shame on you! She is Biscuit Queen of Kotor! She feed us! She save us with flour!"

"She's my *daughter*," her mother shrieked, clutching her pearls so hard one popped free and bounced dramatically down the cobblestones.

Mira, deadpan, scribbled something in her ledger. "Correction: she is our economic asset. Tourism has risen five percent since her biscuits appeared. Removing her would constitute theft."

Dino struck a chord on his mandolin. "A crime against love! Against destiny!"

Ophelia shoved open her door "I'm about to fly of the handle, would you all just HUSH UP!"

No one did.

Soon it became a cacophony: Southern idioms clashing with Montenegrin exclamations, like dueling banjos with subtitles.

"You can't make a silk purse out of a sow's ear!" her dad bellowed.

"She is not ear of pig!" Vesna screamed back.

"You don't know her like we do." barked Ophelia's Father.

"Better than you," Mira said icily, clicking her pen.

Someone from the crowd shouted, "Kiss him again on the fortress!" which only fueled the fire.

Ophelia stood in the middle; arms outstretched like a traffic cop trying to stop two stampedes at once. "I swear, I will bake arsenic into the next batch of biscuits if y'all don't calm down!"

That, at least, bought her three seconds of silence. Long enough for Nika to snicker, "You'd still sell out before noon."

The locals erupted again. Ophelia slapped her forehead. This was her life now: Alabama versus Montenegro, family versus family, biscuits versus... biscuits. And she was somehow supposed to pick a side.

"Everybody go home! The bakery will be closed today. I need

a day off!" Ophelia yelled and returned to the her bedroom to find Tilda still snoring. Ophelia laid back down in bed next to her and Tilda stirred, "How did it go?"

"Oh, just dandy." Ophelia sighed and pulled the sheets back up over her head. A KNOCK at the door made her jump. "What now!" It was Luka. "Oh, good morning."

"May I come in?" He asked her. Ophelia looked back at Tilda sleeping.

Tilda muttered, "Don't mind me."

Ophelia stepped out with Luka, "Hi. Sorry about all this Alabama drama."

"Family is here because they love you. That is all. Go back to your bakery."

She pouted, "No. Everyone will show up and it will just be loud and messy."

"Life is loud and messy. Don't worry, Vesna scared your parents away by pretending to be the town crazy lady anyways, they will be gone all day."

"Are you sure?"

He leaned in and kissed her the sweetest kiss she could ever have imagined. "I'm sure."

Later that day she found herself unlocking the bakery and announcing it open to the neighbors. Her mother wandered in, pearls rattling, and declared as if nothing had happened, "Step aside, sugar, I'm going to show these people what real food tastes like."

"Are you serious?" Ophelia asked.

Without hesitation she walked behind the corner and moments later was elbow-deep in flour, muttering about "cornmeal ratios" and "cast iron traditions."

"Mother," Ophelia groaned, already exhausted, "this is my bakery."

"Your *temporary* bakery," her mother corrected, fanning herself with the church bulletin she'd inexplicably packed for Montenegro. "You can't possibly survive out here on—just biscuits. You are gonna have to start cooking corn- bread, pies, oh my honey, we've got to expand your menu?"

"What do you mean we?" Ophelia snapped, hands on her hips.

At that moment, three cats slinked in through the open door as if on cue. They hopped onto the counter with the dignity of kings, tails curling, and sniffed at her mother's cornbread batter.

"Oh, thank God, reinforcements have arrived."

Her mother wrinkled her nose. "You're letting strays in your kitchen?"

"They're not strays," Ophelia said fiercely, scratching one of that cat's chins as he purred like an idling tractor. "They're residents. They belong here more than either of us."

One of the cat's strutted across the counter, flicking his tail against the cornbread pan before sitting squarely in front of it, as if daring anyone to touch it.

"See?" Ophelia grinned, pointing. "Even the cats don't want cornbread in their territory."

Before her mother could retort, Vesna stormed in, wielding a wooden spoon like a weapon. "I told you to leave her be!" she demanded, then spotted the cats. Her eyes went wide. "Ah! The holy judges have arrived!"

The townsfolk poured in behind her, cheering as if the cats really were impartial referees. Mira flipped open her ledger with a sharp snap. "Documenting feline presence. Their decision will be binding."

Ophelia kissed the top of the cat's head. "That's right, babies. Tell her biscuits forever."

The cats, delighted by the attention, purred louder. One cat rolled onto his back in the flour pile, creating a ghostly cat-shaped print, which Nika immediately photographed and whispered, "Tourists will pay good money for holy cat-biscuit merch."

Her mother, undeterred, pointed at a cat still guarding the oven. "That one clearly favors cornbread. Look at him!"

Ophelia gasped, scandalized. "He would never betray me."

The cats meowed loudly in unison, as if seconding her declaration. Vesna nearly wept with pride, flinging her rosemary in the air. "The Biscuit Lady commands even the cats! Destiny!"

Her father leaned in on the doorframe, shaking his head, but even he cracked a grin watching his eldest cradle Butter like an infant while Biscuit kneaded dough on the counter. "Well," he drawled, "least the cats love her."

"Hi Daddy."

"Hey baby. I came to apologize. I see you and your Momma made up."

"Not quite." Her mother stated.

The cats meowed in chorus. Ophelia grinned. This was her life now: biscuits, chaos, cats everywhere—and she wouldn't trade it for the world.

Tilda burst in like a tornado, with her hair frazzled. "What'd I miss. I am so sorry. I couldn't get out of bed. I looked at the time and ran here as fast as I could. Why are there so many damn cats? Oh, good gracious, I'm so tired."

Mira walked straight over to her, "Oh dear. You come with me, we go get coffee and I do your hair."

"What?" Tilda touched her hair and felt it was a mess. "My hair?"

"Yes dear."

Ophelia bit her lip watching Mira escort her out softly, "You married?" Mira asked her.

"No? Why?" Tilda replied.

"It's okay, I find you good husband. Fisherman."

"Uh.... Okay."

The door closed behind them.

Ophelia served customers and her mother continued baking.

After about an hour of her father sitting and eating, he looked at his watch and Luka stepped in surprised to see her family there. Her father stood straight up and like a bull stared him down, "Just the man I wanted to see."

"Oh?" Luke calmly replied.

"Son, we've got to talk."

Ophelia froze halfway through refilling the sugar jar. "Oh no. Oh no, no, no. Dad—"

Her father held up a hand. "Hush, Ophelia. This is man-to-man."

"Oh God," she muttered, grabbing a cat and hugging him like emotional armor.

"Don't say the good Lord's name in vain darlin." Her mom corrected her.

Her father squared his shoulders. "Now, Luka, I don't know what kind of... Montenegrean—"

"Montenegrin," Luka corrected politely.

"—Montenegrin shenanigans you're pulling with my daughter but let me tell you something. You break her heart, and I'll tan your hide six ways from Sunday."

Ophelia groaned. Butter purred, completely unfazed. Luka nodded solemnly. "I understand. In Montenegro we say, 'If you harm someone's daughter, you answer to the mountain.'"

Her father blinked. "The mountain?"

"Yes." Luka shrugged. "It does not forgive."

One of the cat's meowed loudly, rolling in more flour as though to emphasize the point. Her father narrowed his eyes. "Well... back home, we got the Lord and a twelve-gauge shotgun. Same difference."

"Not much difference," Luka agreed calmly.

Her father wasn't finished. "You might think you can charm her with your... your mountains and your accent and your fortress hikes, but I raised that girl on grits and gospel. She's Southern stock, tough as hickory, and she deserves a man who under-stands that."

Luka tilted his head, utterly unbothered. "I think I understand. She is strong, stubborn, soft when she thinks no one is looking. Yes?"

Ophelia's heart did a very stupid somersault in her chest. Her father squinted, clearly unsettled. He reached for his last weapon: fishing. "You ever fish?"

Luka's face finally broke into a grin. "Of course. Sea bass, mackerel, sometimes squid."

Her father blinked. "Squid? Lord, I've never fished for anything that had tentacles."

Luka chuckled. "You should try. It is... how do you say... humbling."

The cats meowed as if agreeing, rubbing against Luka's legs. And just like that, the tension cracked. Her father leaned back, sighed, and muttered, "Well, hell. Least you're not a vegetarian."

Luka's grin widened. "Never."

Ophelia, face buried in her hands, peeked through her fingers at the absurd scene: her Southern dad and her Montenegrin almost-love, bonding over fishing while cats acted like referees. Her father jabbed a finger at Luka. "Fine. But if you ever hurt her, remember—I got kin in law enforcement."

Luka inclined his head. "And I have the mountain."

The two men shook hands, the cat still sprawled between them. Ophelia had intended to hide in her bakery until sunrise, but fate—had other plans.

36

"Dinner!" Vesna had declared, hauling her by the elbow. "We eat, we drink, we make peace."

Which was how Ophelia found herself at a long outdoor table, her two warring families—Alabama kin and Montenegrin locals—lined up shoulder to shoulder like rival armies at a ceasefire banquet.

At first, it was stiff. Her mother perched primly at the far end, pearls catching the lantern light, lips pressed tighter than her corseted posture. Vesna sat across from her, arms folded, glaring like she could set pearls on fire.

Mira polished her glasses and muttered about "damage reports." Dino tuned his mandolin ominously. Luka, of course, sat calmly beside Ophelia, sipping his rakija as if nothing could faze him. Tilda found herself surrounded by three very single men that Mira had stirred up for her. She played with her tightly braided hair and happily flirted while drinking her wine.

Her father jabbed a fork into a plate of grilled squid. "Lord Almighty. This thing looks like it crawled outta the Devil's tackle box."

The table tittered. Luka leaned in, smooth as silk. "You eat it with lemon. Tastes better than it looks."

Her father chewed thoughtfully, then muttered, "Not bad."

Ophelia nearly choked on her wine. That cracked the dam. Soon, stories flew like arrows—her father talking about bass fishing trips, Vesna countering with tales of storm-season octopus hauls. Nika boasted that the bakery cats had their own Instagram page with more followers than her.

Then came the food war. Her mother insisted on cornbread—she'd smuggled a pan into the café, heaven help them—while Vesna slammed down a tray of steaming biscuits.

"Cornbread is king," her mother declared.

"Biscuits are God," Vesna shot back.

Dino leapt onto his chair, strumming:

Cornbread rises tall, but biscuits melt the heart,

Both make you hungry, but only one is art!

The entire café roared with laughter. Even Mira smirked, scribbling in her ledger: *Outcome—stalemate. Both acceptable with honey.*

Ophelia sat back, dizzy with relief. For the first time since her family arrived, the air wasn't thick with tug-of-war. It was messy, loud, ridiculous—but there was warmth, too. A strange, impossible harmony.

Later, after too much rakija loosened tongues and laughter blurred the edges of stubbornness, Ophelia found herself walking home with Luka. The streets were quiet now, moonlight silvering the cobblestones. The cats padded along behind them like silent guardians.

She shoved her hands into her apron, still reeling. "That was... chaos."

"Your chaos," Luka said, voice soft.

She glanced at him, heart thudding. "You're not scared off?"

He shook his head, that steady half-smile playing on his lips. "No. They are just... loud. In Montenegro, family is loud too. Different words, same love."

Her throat tightened. She looked away, at the shadow of the fortress towering above. "I don't know how to make them all happy. My family, the town, you..."

He stopped, turning to face her fully. "You don't need to make everyone happy," Luka said simply. "You only need to decide what makes *you* happy."

Ophelia's breath caught. For the first time since Charles's death, she felt the future not as a weight—but as a possibility.

The morning her family left Kotor, the entire town turned up to watch. Of course, they did. Privacy didn't exist here; if you sneezed on one side of the square, someone on the other side shouted, "Bless you!" before you'd even found a tissue.

Ophelia stood in the square, apron still tied around her waist, as her family's luggage piled up like a barricade in front of the taxi. Her mother, pearls gleaming, dabbed dramatically at her eyes with a lace handkerchief that looked like it had survived the Civil War.

"Oh, my poor baby," she wailed. "Alone in this foreign land, surrounded by strangers—"

"Family," Vesna interrupted from her bakery window, arms crossed. "We are family. Which means you now are family."

Mira went over and hugged her mother who was stunned, "We take good care of your girl. We are all now family."

Her mother sniffed. She walked over and gave Ophelia hugs. A cat came up and brushed by her mother's leg and she let out a scream breaking their embrace. "Sweet baby Jesus!"

Tilda corrected her, "Now don't you be taken the Lord's name in vain."

They both burst into laughter. The taxi driver leaned on his horn, unimpressed by the Southern drama unfolding in front of him. "If we don't go soon, traffic," he muttered.

Her father gave her a loving hug and Ophelia looked between them—her mother with her pearls and handkerchief, her father stubborn as a mule. Tilda broke them up and gave her a huge hug. "I'll be back next year."

"Can't wait." Ophelia told her.

She squeezed her mother's hands one last time, gentle but firm. "I love you. But this is my home now. And I've got people looking out for me. Loud, nosy people."

Vesna beamed. Dino strummed a triumphant chord. Even Mira gave the faintest nod.

Her mother sniffled louder. "Well, don't say I didn't warn you when you run out of cornbread."

Her father cleared his throat. "You take care of yourself, baby girl. And if that Luka fellow gives you any trouble, you let me know. "I've got a few army buddies I can call up that owe me a favor."

Ophelia laughed, leaning in to kiss his cheek. "I'll keep that in mind."

Then he whispered in her ear, "and you take that check and invest into your bakery. I think you truly have something special here. I'm very proud of you."

He hugged her tightly.

The taxi driver honked again, longer this time. The luggage was shoved in, Tilda sat into her seat, and Ophelia's parents waved through the open windows. As the taxi rolled away, the townsfolk broke into applause—because of course they did. Someone shouted, "Come back soon!" and Vesna hurled a sprig of rosemary after the departing car like a protective charm.

Ophelia stood in the middle of it all, her heart full. It was bittersweet, yes—but as the square quieted again, she realized something she hadn't in a long time. She felt... settled. Rooted. Not torn in two anymore. Butter rubbed against her ankle. A nearby cat stretched out enjoying the sunshine, "Yeah," she whispered, smiling down at them. "We're gonna be just fine."

By dusk, the square had quieted. The Cruise ship horns had

faded, tourists had trickled off toward dinner, and the air smelled faintly of salt and grilled fish. For the first time in weeks, Ophelia's bakery was hers again—no mother waving wooden spoons, no father muttering about varmints, just her and the familiar hum of silence.

She tied her apron back on, more out of habit than need, and started cleaning. The clatter of trays, the scrape of the broom over the flour-dusted tiles, the squeak of the rag against the counter—it was all comforting in its ordinariness. Work had always been her way of breathing through the noise.

Still, the space felt different. Quieter, yes, but not empty. The cats had made sure of that. One leapt onto the counter as though to supervise, curling himself into a fluffy croissant atop the cooling rack. Another pawed at the broom like he wanted a turn, while another lurked under a chair, golden eyes glowing in the lanternlight, the eternal shadow in her kitchen. "You three," Ophelia said, shaking her head fondly. One purred loudly, stretching so that flour dusted from his fur onto the counter. Ophelia laughed. "Well, guess that's one way to season the biscuits."

She wiped down the tables, her thoughts drifting where they always did when the noise stopped—back to Charles. She saw him clearly sometimes, leaning against the kitchen doorway back in Alabama, grinning as she tested new recipes. He'd had a way of making her feel seen without words, just by standing there with his coffee mug, nodding along as if her biscuits held the secrets of the universe.

"Don't you go thinking I've forgotten you," she whispered, sliding a stray photograph from under the register. His smile in the picture was soft, easy. The sight of it didn't knock the air out of her anymore—it pressed against her like a quilt: heavy but warming.

For a long time, she sat there with the photo propped against the sugar jar, the cats weaving around her ankles, the smell of flour and rosemary lingering in the air. She thought about Alabama—Sunday mornings in church pews, funeral casseroles lined up like battalions, her mother's unrelenting voice telling her who she should be. Then she thought about Kotor—the square buzzing with laughter, Vesna's fierce loyalty, Mira's deadpan quips, Dino's absurd mandolin ballads. Both lives were hers, but only one felt like home now.

The broom clattered as Biscuit knocked it over, startling her out of her thoughts. Butter yawned from the counter, stretching luxuriously. Midnight padded forward and butted his head against her shin until she bent to scratch behind his ears. "All right," she murmured. "I get it. Enough moping. Time to move forward."

She stood, brushing flour from her apron, and for the first time since Charles's death, she didn't feel crushed by the idea of tomorrow. She felt curious. Almost eager. The cats meowed, circling her feet like they agreed. And in that quiet moment, surrounded by her ridiculous feline coworkers and the hum of her bakery, Ophelia realized: she wasn't alone anymore. Not really.

The bell over the bakery door jingled, startling Ophelia so hard she almost dropped the rag she'd been wringing out. Midnight darted under a chair, Butter twitched an ear but refused to move, and Biscuit pranced toward the sound like he was welcoming royalty.

Luka stepped inside, his shoulders filling the doorway, his shirt sleeves rolled to his elbows, and in his hand, a bottle of red wine that caught the lanternlight. His smile was soft, the kind that didn't try too hard, just waited for her to notice.

"Still working?" he asked.

Ophelia set the rag down, tucking a strand of hair behind her ear. "Always. Bakery doesn't clean itself."

Luka glanced at the cats now circling his legs like adoring subjects. "You have helpers," he said, amusement tugging at his mouth.

"Helpers?" Ophelia laughed, lifting Butter off the counter. "These three cause more trouble than they fix. Biscuit tried to climb into the flour sack yesterday. Looked like a ghost haunting my kitchen."

Luka chuckled and held up the wine. "Then maybe you deserve a break. Drink with me?"

She hesitated only a heartbeat before nodding. "All right. But I'm not responsible for what happens if you drink me under the table."

He moved easily through the bakery, fetching two mismatched mugs from the shelf. Ophelia almost stopped him—old habits of Southern hostessing—but she found she liked watching him do it, as if he belonged there, in her space, without asking permission.

They sat at one of the small tables near the window. Outside, the square was quiet, lanterns swaying gently, casting golden shadows across the cobblestones. Inside, the bakery smelled of butter and flour, the kind of perfume that lingered in her hair and skin no matter how often she scrubbed.

Luka poured the wine. "To biscuits," he said, raising his mug.

Ophelia clinked hers against his, grinning. "To cornbread being banished from this square forever."

"Ah," Luka said, smirking. "Your mother will curse me from Alabama."

"She already does." Ophelia laughed, the sound easing something tight inside her chest.

They drank, and the warmth of it spread between them, easy as breathing. For a while, they sat in companionable silence, the cats sprawled like lazy chaperones around their feet. Finally, Luka tilted his head toward her. "You are quieter tonight."

She traced her finger around the rim of her mug. "It's the first time in weeks the bakery's been mine. No one fussing, no one hollering, no one trying to tell me biscuits are a mistake."

"And how does it feel?"

Ophelia thought about it. About Charles, about Alabama, about her family driving away that morning. "Good," she admitted softly. "Strange. But good. Like I can breathe again."

He nodded; his eyes steady on her. "You built this place. It is yours. No one can take that from you."

Something in her chest shifted at his words—something old and aching, loosening just a little. Butter leapt onto her lap, purring like a tractor engine. Luka reached across the table, scratching the cat behind the ears until Butter practically melted. Their hands brushed—just barely—but enough to send a little spark racing up her arm. "You are Biscuit Queen," Luka teased, lips curving.

Ophelia rolled her eyes. "Don't you start. Vesna's already planning a crown. Probably made of dough."

"I would wear one," Luka said, utterly serious.

She snorted into her wine. "You're ridiculous."

"Maybe," he said, shrugging. "But it makes you laugh."

And it did. For the first time that day, she laughed without any weight pressing it down.

They refilled their mugs, talked about fishing and mountains, her father's endless warnings, and how cats somehow ruled the square without ever paying rent. And through it all, Ophelia realized something startling: she wasn't thinking about how much she missed Alabama, or how afraid she was of staying in Kotor forever. She was simply here—with Luka, with her bakery, with her cats—and it felt like enough. More than enough.

By the time the wine bottle lay empty between them, the bakery had fallen into a hush so deep it felt sacred. The cats were sprawled across the counters like sentries who'd given up their watch, bellies exposed in unrepentant sleep. The lanterns flickered, casting butter-colored light across the flour-speckled tables.

Ophelia leaned back in her chair, her cheeks warm from the wine and laughter. She hadn't realized how much she'd needed this: the quiet, the gentleness, Luka sitting across from her like it was the most natural thing in the world.

Eventually, she stood, brushing flour from her apron. "Well," she said, her voice soft but certain, "time to close up."

Luka rose with her. He waited as she blew out the lanterns one by one, the bakery growing dim until only the glow from the square spilled in through the window. She slid the key into the lock, turned it with a click, and for a moment, she just stood there with her hand on the doorframe, staring out into the night.

When she turned, Luka was there. He held out his hand. Her

chest tightened, and she gave him hers without hesitation. His hand was warm, steady. Together, they stepped into the moonlit square.

The cobblestones gleamed silver under the lanterns. The bay shimmered, black and endless, as though the stars had spilled themselves into the water. The cats padded silently behind them like guardians, their tails high, their eyes glowing like coins.

They walked without speaking, their footsteps echoing off the stone. The square was nearly empty—nearly. From a balcony above, someone leaned out, squinting down at them. A voice rang through the quiet:

"KISS ALREADY!"

Ophelia stopped dead, whirling toward the shadowed balcony. "Lord have mercy! Can't folks mind their own dang business for five blessed minutes?"

The square erupted in muffled chuckles. A few locals had clearly gathered in the shadows, pretending to be busy with late-night chores, but really watching. Vesna's voice floated faintly from somewhere near her doorway: "Do not make us wait all night!"

Ophelia's cheeks flamed. "These people," she muttered, "are nosier than Baptists at a picnic."

Luka laughed low in his chest. He turned toward her, his thumb brushing across the back of her hand. His smile was soft, unhurried. "Maybe they are right."

Before she could roll her eyes or deliver another Southern comeback, he pulled her gently into him. One hand cupped her cheek, the other steady at her waist. His lips found hers, warm and certain, tasting of red wine and promise. The square seemed to exhale all at once. Cheers erupted, clapping, a whistle or two. Someone shouted, "Finally!" and Ophelia broke away just long enough to holler back, "Y'all need to mind your manners!"

Then Luka kissed her again, and this time she forgot all about the peanut gallery. Her grief, her doubts, her stubborn fears—they were still there, but softer now, woven into something bigger. She didn't need to leave them behind. She could carry them and still step into joy. She could still love Charles, and love this man, and love this town, and love herself, all at once.

When at last they broke apart, the cats twined around their ankles, purring like approval. Luka laced his fingers with hers, and together they kept walking, through the square, toward whatever was waiting.

For the first time in a long time, Ophelia wasn't afraid of tomorrow. She was ready for it. And if someone shouted again for another kiss—well, maybe she wouldn't yell back this time.

THE END

ABOUT THE AUTHOR

 Kacie Foos lives in Chattanooga, Tennessee with her husband Mike, daughter Frankie, their three dogs Winter, Loki, and Love and a white rabbit named Easter. She grew up in the Pacific Northwest in a magical little city called Spokane, Washington. At an early age she took an interest in acting, which blossomed into a career in Hollywood. She graduated from AMDA LA, but also studied film at UCLA, Shakespeare at RADA in London, and even lived in Paris, France studying French literature. While living in Hollywood, she developed a passion for writing for theater and the screen. This blossomed into a dream of writing novels. *The Park House* was her first successful release, and *Kiss Me in Kotor* is her second of many more stories to come. To learn more, visit www.kaciefoos.com.